Five Minutes Late

Rich Amooi

FIVE MINUTES LATE
By
Rich Amooi

Also by Rich Amooi

Dog Day Wedding – A Romantic Comedy
Visit http://www.richamooi.com/dogdaywedding

To be notified of new releases,
sign up for Rich's newsletter.
http://www.richamooi.com/newsletter

I dedicate this book to my wife, my love, my kiss monster, Silvi, who makes me laugh and smile every day. You're the one who encouraged me to write. You're the one who told me I could expand my short story about Cedric and Ellie into my debut novel.

Thank you for your support and your love. You're the best thing that ever happened to me. I love you so much I want to scream.

Ahhhhhhhhh!

There.

I feel better.

Chapter One

"For the last time, I'm not possessed by demons," said Cedric Johnson.

"Could have fooled me," said Tony. "I need to perform a circumcision on you."

"Okay, number one, you know it's an exorcism, so quit trying to steer the conversation back to body parts and sex. Number two, it was just a dream about death. Everybody has them."

"Not me."

Cedric loved him like a brother, but Tony Garcia's imagination didn't have an off switch.

"I'm going to wear garlic around my neck."

Cedric rolled his eyes. "Great, now I'm a vampire." He pressed the speaker button on his cell phone, set it on the kitchen counter, and prepared his morning coffee. "And why are you calling? I'm going to see you in fifteen minutes."

"I'm having a light bulb moment."

"Of course you are."

Tony was his best friend and general manager of Cedric's company, Papa George's Heirloom Garlic. He liked to brainstorm on expanding the company, and although he was the smartest guy Cedric knew, some of his ideas were out there.

"How's this?" Tony continued, "We could sell garlic necklaces at the midnight showing of *Twilight* at theaters across the country."

"And why would that appeal to teenagers?"

"You're right, you're right."

Cedric added sugar to his coffee and took a sip as he waited for Tony to continue. He knew he wouldn't have to wait long.

"Okay, got it," said Tony. "Perfect for teenagers. Condoms. Garlic-scented condoms."

"I'm hanging up now."

"Wait, I need to tell you—"

"Tell me when you get here."

Cedric disconnected and reached down to scratch Tofu between the ears. The West Highland Terrier dropped to the floor and rolled over on his back, his short white legs shooting to the ceiling in an obvious effort to give Cedric more area to work on.

Smart dog.

Ten minutes later, the doorbell rang, followed by a Phil Collins drum solo on the door.

Tofu went nuts—as usual—sprinting toward the door. "Arf. Arf, arf, arf."

"Tofu, it's Tony. You should be used to him by now. Relax." Cedric opened the door to Tony, who sported his usual jeans and rocker T-shirt: Maroon 5 plastered across his broad chest. Cedric gave him the why-the-hell-do-you-do-that look.

Tony shrugged and tucked some of his long black hair behind one ear. "I can't help it if I like to hear the little guy bark." He ran his hand along the length of Tofu's back, stopping at his butt to scratch it. Tofu leaned into the scratch and moaned as his body shook from the power of Tony's hand. "Dude, he's having an orgasm."

"That's disgusting."

"And that's why you don't have a woman in your life. You think orgasms are disgusting."

"No. I think *dog* orgasms are disgusting. And the reason I don't have a woman in my life is I choose not to."

"Pansy-ass."

"Scumbag."

"Dickweed."

"Numbnuts."

The exchange may have sounded immature coming from a couple of guys in their thirties, but Cedric enjoyed the occasional silly verbal sparring with Tony. Plus, life was too short to be serious all the time.

Cedric held up his index finger. "Hang on, I'm not ready."

"What a surprise."

Cedric ran to the family room, put on his shoes, grabbed his coffee cup from the kitchen counter, and returned to the front door, where Tony was still petting Tofu.

Cedric grabbed Tofu and tucked him under his arm. "Come on …" He closed the door behind them.

Tony slapped Cedric's arm with the back of his hand. "I almost called you at two in the morning. You won't believe the news."

"Get in first."

They piled into Cedric's SUV and took off on their weekly trek to the farm in Gilroy. He loved the early-morning drive from San Jose, and never got tired of watching the sun come up over the mountains to the east as they passed through Morgan Hill on Highway 101.

"I hope your news has to do with our numbers and not with the latest woman you've fallen for."

As the general manager, Tony handled the marketing as well as Internet sales of the products on their website.

Tony did a drum roll on the dashboard. "We tripled our normal monthly sales."

"No way."

"… in two days."

Cedric gritted his teeth. "Very funny." He glanced over to Tony who had a dead-serious look on his face.

Tony had built the company website from the ground up and maintained it. It included an online store, recipes with garlic, company history, and a secure payment system. His degree in Web Programming and Graphic Design at San Jose State came in handy.

But what Tony just told him was insane.

"A hundred and twenty thousand?" said Cedric.

"Yup."

"In two days?"

"Yup again."

"What caused the spike?"

"The fresh heirloom garlic. There was also a huge jump in the fresh peeled. The shallots kicked ass too."

Initially, Cedric only sold fresh garlic, like his grandfather. Tony had convinced him a few years back to expand their online presence by offering roasted garlic, sun-dried tomatoes, fresh ginger and shallots, and many other specialty items. Tony's instincts paid off as regular garlic customers began adding other items to their online shopping carts before checking out. The business doubled within a year and has steadily grown ever since.

Cedric glanced over to Tony and then got his eyes back on the road. "Where are the hits coming from?"

Tony laughed. "You wouldn't believe me if I told you."

"Try me."

"Martha Stewart."

Cedric's mouth dropped open as he turned to Tony in disbelief.

"Hey!" Tony grabbed the steering wheel and straightened the car after Cedric had veered off into the other lane. "You trying to kill us?"

"It's your fault! You got me excited!"

"If you expect me to believe you had an explosive erection that hit the steering wheel, knocking us into—"

"Focus! Back to Martha Stewart. How the hell did that happen?"

"Remember when I sent samples of our garlic to some of the top restaurants in California?"

Cedric nodded. "We got like ten contracts from that."

"Twelve."

"Okay, how does Martha Stewart fit into the equation?"

"So! I had the brilliant idea of also sending our garlic to Rachael Ray, Mario Batali, José Andrés, Bobby Flay, The Barefoot Contessa, Wolfgang Puck, and Martha Stewart. Not exactly in that order."

"You're a genius!"

"Tell me something I don't know. Anyway, Martha was talking on her television show yesterday about the quality of garlic available in the United States, that most of it comes from China, yadda yadda yadda. Get this … then she said 'if you want to kick up your recipes a notch, you can always use Papa George's Heirloom Garlic.'"

"Holy crap."

"Holy crap is correct. I went into our client database and saw her name right there, Martha Fucking Stewart. She purchased garlic from us four times over the last year. She's got a million people who like her on Facebook. We hit the jackpot."

"We're going to run out of garlic."

"That's a good problem to have."

Cedric chuckled. "Have you told your dad yet?"

"Yeah, I called him on the way to your house."

Tony's father, Antonio, managed everything on the garlic farm: the workers, soil preparation, planting, mulching, harvesting, cleaning, grating, packaging—everything. The farm was a well-oiled machine that produced some of the finest garlic in the country, year after year.

"Speaking of my dad … you know we don't have to do these weekly meetings with him anymore. If you need to talk with him, just pick up the phone. It's a lot easier."

Cedric knew that. Their weekly jaunt to Gilroy wasn't about the business—hell, they probably only talked about garlic five percent of the time. For Cedric, it was about being with good people. The Garcias were the closest thing he had to family.

"You know how much your family means to me," said Cedric.

"I know. You spoil my parents."

"Anyone else in my position would do the same."

Cedric appointed Tony's parents, Antonio and Ana, co-proprietors of the company and moved them to live on the farm, free of charge.

"No way," said Tony.

Cedric felt as if someone had grabbed his heart and squeezed it. "We take care of each other. That's what families do."

"Well, Mamá says you need to come over more often and eat more."

Tony's mother, Ana, was always cooking something. Chilaquiles was a typical breakfast in their home—corn tortillas, scrambled eggs, cheese, and green chili. It was Cedric's favorite Mexican dish.

"She's trying to fatten me up."

Tony laughed and rubbed his belly. "I know the feeling."

Thirty-five minutes after leaving San Jose, Cedric exited Highway 101 and drove through Gilroy, along one of the rural county roads toward the farm.

"What the hell?" muttered Cedric. He slammed on the brakes and pulled off to the shoulder. Tony grabbed Tofu before he fell off his lap, as the car slid on the gravel, coming to a stop slightly sideways.

"I'm pretty sure I shit my pants." Tony looked down at Tofu. "What about you?" He lifted Tofu's tail and looked underneath. "All clean."

Cedric didn't say a word. He just stared at the farm across the street, Papa George's old property.

"You see dead people? Do I need to drive a stake through your heart?"

Cedric kept his eyes on the property and didn't respond.

Papa George started the garlic revolution in that house. It had history, not only in the garlic industry, in Cedric's family as well. His grandfather sold the property back in the fifties and bought a much larger property—where they've been ever since. Cedric drove by the place every week, but it seemed different today.

Cedric cocked his head to the side and continued to study the farm. "Something's not right."

Tony squinted. "The driveway is chained off."

"And the farm equipment is gone."

"You think the Abbotts sold the place and moved?"

"I'd be surprised. Mr. Abbott swore he'd sell it to me if they ever decided to move. I'm not sure what's going on, but I'm going to find out."

Cedric made a promise to his mom on her deathbed he'd acquire the land when it became available, to build a garlic museum there and keep the family history alive.

"Maybe my dad has heard something," said Tony.

A few minutes later, Cedric drove under the wrought iron arches of his farm and down the long driveway lined with palm trees on both sides—queen palms his grandfather planted over fifty years ago. The classic white farmhouse with the wraparound porch, complete with rockers, always brought back wonderful memories of Cedric and his grandfather rocking and talking after dinner, as they watched the sunset.

Cedric spotted Tony's dad in the field inspecting the garlic. "He never stops working."

"Never."

Antonio climbed the tractor and drove to the main house to meet them. Cedric pulled in behind Antonio's old Chevy pickup and opened his door. Tofu leaped from the car and sprinted toward the chickens, sending them skittering off in different directions. Cedric laughed as he approached Antonio.

"Buenos días, Cedric," said Antonio, smiling as he hugged Cedric

"Buenos días, Antonio." Cedric smiled back, admiring the silver-haired man with tanned, wrinkled skin weathered by four decades of hard work under the hot Gilroy sun.

Antonio turned to Tony. "Buenos días, hijo." He kissed his son on the cheek.

"Good morning."

Antonio shook his finger at Tony. "You're losing your Spanish."

"No, señor."

Cedric put his hand on Antonio's shoulder. "Do you know what's going on with Papa George's old property? It looks like the Abbotts are gone."

Antonio shrugged. "I saw him and his wife a couple of weeks ago at the Farmers' Association meeting and they didn't mention anything."

"It almost looks as though they cleared the land to sell it."

"Let me text him and see."

Cedric laughed and eyed Antonio's phone.

"What? You think I'm too old to text?"

"I didn't say that."

"You don't think I'm hip, that's it. Well, I'll have you know that I was thinking of getting an Xbox."

Cedric blinked a couple of times. "Really?"

Laughter erupted from Antonio. "No. Not really."

They laughed and headed inside for the meeting—more like a great meal, with a side of chitchat. It was held in the kitchen, at the large solid oak farmhouse dining table that seated ten. They would discuss the latest news in the world of garlic, farming, the weather, this year's crop, and any issues with the equipment, but it wouldn't last long. Sooner or later—usually sooner—Ana would change topics to Cedric's nonexistent love life.

Cedric entered the kitchen with Tony and Antonio and smiled as he stared at the back of Ana's head, her black hair up in a bun.

She placed a bowl in the sink, wiped her hands on her rose-print apron, and turned around. "Buenos días, hijo."

Cedric loved it when she called him son. "Buenos días," he said, kissing her on the cheek. He was sure the lines he saw around her eyes weren't from aging, but from all of the smiles she shared with him over the years.

Tony kissed his mom. "Hola, mamá."

"Hola, hijo." She spooned chilaquiles onto the plates and gestured to the chairs. "Sit down and eat."

The men obeyed orders, grabbed the forks, and put them to work.

Ana sat and turned to Cedric. "Have you found yourself a good woman yet?

Right on cue.

"It's been exactly one week since the last time you asked me that." He took a bite of food and moaned.

"And what's your answer this week?"

"Yes." Three heads turned in his direction. The chewing stopped as Ana, Antonio, and Tony waited for Cedric to continue. "And I'm in love."

Tony pointed his fork at Cedric. "Bullshit. I would have heard about it."

"You don't have to believe me if you don't want to."

"Okay, what's her name then?"

Cedric grinned. "Martha Stewart."

Laughter filled the kitchen as the eating continued.

"Well, if that's the case, I'm in love with her too," said Tony.

"Me too!" said Antonio, promptly smacked on the arm by Ana.

Ana wiped her mouth and tapped her fingers on the table. "I'm still waiting for a real answer."

Cedric finished chewing and set his fork down. "No, I don't have a good woman. But if it makes you feel better, I don't have a bad woman either."

"You're going to meet someone soon, I know it." Ana rubbed Cedric's arm. "She'll show up when you least expect it, you need to be open to it."

"I think I'll just place an advertisement on a billboard. Wanted: Woman who cooks as well as Ana Garcia and is just as pretty."

Antonio let out a hearty laugh. "Impossible!"

Ana kissed Cedric on the forehead. "Gracias, hijo."

There was a noise at the front door.

Tony pointed. "That must be her, Cedric, your new love."

"Right," said Cedric.

Ana laughed as she got up and walked to the door. A few seconds later, Tofu sprinted into the kitchen and screeched to a halt in front of the cupboard below the sink.

"Arf! Arf, arf, arf."

Ana opened the cupboard and pulled out a plastic container filled with rawhide treats.

"Someone is spoiled," said Cedric.

Antonio's phone beeped and he grabbed it from the table as Cedric watched with anticipation, hoping it was from Mr. Abbott.

Antonio read the text. "You were right."

Cedric's eyes opened wide. "About the property?"

"The Abbotts lost the property after five years of unpaid taxes. They moved to Oregon just last week."

Cedric sat up in his chair and leaned forward. "Please tell me I have a chance to buy the place."

Antonio scrolled down on his phone. "He says the Tax Collector is going to sell it at auction, so yes, it looks like you have a chance."

"Good." Cedric flopped back in his chair and smiled. "That's what I wanted to hear."

Antonio smiled. "You'll have a lot of competition for that land."

"True. But all I need is a chance."

"How much do you think it'll go for?" asked Tony.

Cedric shrugged. "Hard to say, I'm guessing two to three million. I'll pay whatever they want. My promise to my mom is the most important thing in the world to me."

Ana smiled. "This is wonderful."

Cedric nodded. It was more than wonderful.

He couldn't help but wonder how much better it would be with a woman in his life.

On second thought, he needed to scratch that thought from his brain.

The last thing he wanted was his success marred by another tragedy.

Chapter Two

Ellie Fontaine beamed with satisfaction as she helped the eighty-year old man download his first audiobook—just one of the many things she enjoyed doing as a librarian at the Willow Glen Library. She loved helping people and felt she played a part in making the world a smarter place.

The old man put in his earbuds and kissed Ellie's hand. "Thank you, dear."

Ellie smiled again. "My pleasure." She watched him walk away, wishing the man was fifty years younger. They sure don't make men like that anymore.

"My, my, my," said Julio Cruz, Ellie's coworker.

Ellie rolled her eyes at him. "Don't say it."

Julio ignored her. "A bottle of wine for you, a bottle of Viagra and a pacemaker for him, and you'll be ready for a nice little chitty chitty bang bang."

Ellie held up her hand. "Stop. You know I'm visual."

"Is Julio torturing you again?" asked Peggy, smiling and setting down a stack of pamphlets and manuscripts on the service desk counter. Peggy Fleming was the Library Branch Manager and one of the most positive people Ellie knew.

Ellie gestured to Julio. "He's suggesting I get drunk and make it with an eighty-year old man on Viagra."

Peggy smiled. "Sounds like a lovely evening."

Julio stuck out his tongue and displayed his I-told-you-so smile.

Ellie sorted through the pamphlets. "Call me picky, but I prefer a man born after the Jimmy Carter Administration."

Peggy laughed. "By the way, we need to talk. I have some news from the hiring committee."

Ellie clasped her hands together and let out a deep breath. "Okay."

She was finally going to find out if she got the promotion.

"Just give me a minute. There seems to be a life-threatening situation at the vending machine."

Julio looked toward the machine. "Out of Coke again?"

Peggy shrugged and smiled as she went to help.

Julio turned to Ellie and grabbed her hands. "*You* are going to get the job!"

Ellie hoped so. When Peggy announced her retirement a few months back, she encouraged Ellie to apply for her position and said she would do everything in her power to make sure she got the job. Ellie loved being a librarian, but felt she could contribute even more as Branch Manager.

She looked over toward Peggy. "She would have said something, don't you think?"

"Not in front of me. She knows I would have screamed and she probably didn't want me scaring everyone in the building." Julio hugged Ellie. "You're going to get it and you deserve it."

Ellie smiled. "Sure you don't wanna get married?"

"You know Hugo wouldn't like that. Besides … you're going to find your own man. Maybe tonight's your night."

"We shall see."

Ellie could always hope. Tonight was the first of three dates lined up this week from the dating website.

Peggy returned from the vending machine. "Crisis averted, just a stuck dollar bill. Okay, let's talk."

Julio squeezed Ellie's hand and mouthed "good luck" to her. She followed Peggy back to the staff office.

Good news. Good news. Good news.

When the door closed behind them, Peggy turned around. "Okay, here's the latest. You and the other final candidate, Margaret Rossewood, both have the same amount of experience as librarians and your references are practically carbon copies. We've been at a standstill in the hiring process. Since the vote is deadlocked and neither side is willing to budge, the board has agreed to settle it in an unorthodox way."

"Mud wrestling?"

Peggy laughed. "Keep up that sense of humor, you're going to need it."

"Oh God, what is it?"

"The person who raises the most money for the fundraiser will be the next Branch Manager."

Pickles!

Ellie hated asking people for money, even if it was for a good cause.

And this was *definitely* a good cause.

"I have to beg for money," Ellie muttered.

Peggy nodded. "If you want the job."

The library had a recent break-in and the thieves targeted the children's area, stealing one of the largest and most valuable collections of picture books in the state and vandalizing hundreds of other books. Eight computers were stolen as well. The fundraiser was to replace the books and computers and repair the damage. Ellie was heartbroken after the crime occurred. Still …

"Can I sell a kidney instead?"

Peggy laughed. "Good one."

"I'm not joking."

Peggy threw her palms in the air. "That's what they came up with and I couldn't think of a better way to handle it." She squeezed Ellie's arm. "You can do it, Ellie. Nobody works harder than you and I've always pictured you in my position."

Ellie had been picturing herself in the position too. One thing was for sure, she was going to have to step out of her comfort zone if she wanted a shot at it now.

She left the staff office and found Julio on a stepladder, pinning up artwork from Willow Glen Elementary School on the wall. She stood there, deep in thought.

Julio glanced down at her. "You need to turn that frown upside down."

Ellie forced a smile, shrugged, and told Julio about her conversation with Peggy.

Julio climbed down and put his arm around her. "Then I guess we need to get you some money!"

"Maybe we can just shake that tree and money will rain down over us."

Julio stared through the window at the giant oak tree in the courtyard and his eyes lit up. "Money doesn't grow on trees. It grows *underneath* them."

"This would not be the first time you've lost me."

"I just read a story about a library in the Midwest that ran a brick fundraising campaign. They sold bricks that circled the base of a tree at their library, and people who donated had their name and message engraved on the bricks. A hundred dollars for a brick, and get this, they raised over ten thousand dollars!"

"Seriously?"

Julio nodded. "They even found a local contractor to donate the bricks and the labor to install them."

Ellie stared at the oak tree in the courtyard and smiled. "That's a wonderful idea."

"I'm surprised you haven't hugged me yet." He tapped his toes. "I'm waiting."

Ellie lunged forward and hugged Julio. "Thank you. I'll need to get approval, but I don't think that'll be a problem. This is good. Great, actually."

She finished up her workday and stopped by Nothing Bundt Cakes to pick up a treat for her grandpa Frank. He loved the cinnamon swirl cake with the frosted petals on top, and she never got tired of surprising him with one.

***

Grandpa Frank swung open the door and smiled. He wore his usual outfit—a plaid shirt with khaki pants and a cardigan sweater. Ellie loved his solid white head of hair; it was elegant.

"My princess," he said. "What a surprise to—" His gaze dropped to the bag she was holding down by her side. "What do you have there?"

Ellie smiled as they walked to the kitchen. "You know exactly what I have. That's why you're drooling."

They both laughed as Ellie pulled a plate from the cupboard. She took the cake from the plastic container, placed it on the plate, and grabbed a fork from the drawer.

"You're not going to have some?"

"I have a date."

"I can save half for you, just in case you don't make it to the main course like the other dates."

"Maybe tonight will be different. I have a new dating system in place."

They sat at the kitchen table and Grandpa Frank didn't waste time, diving into his favorite treat. The pastry was disappearing right before her eyes. He nodded as he chewed. "The best." Finally coming up for air, he asked, "A man you met online?"

Ellie nodded. "He's an accountant."

"An admirable career. And what's this new system you're talking about?"

"It's more like a filter. I put together a list of what I want in a man. Non-negotiable things."

"Really." He didn't look convinced.

She pulled a piece of paper from her purse and handed it to him.

Grandpa Frank nearly choked on the pastry as he read the title at the top. "The Perfect Man?"

Ellie nodded. "I know there's no such thing." She stared at the paper for a moment. "Maybe I should rename it. Anyway, I make sure they have most of these traits before we meet, then the rest I find out in person."

"Wow." He cleared his throat and pushed the empty plate away. "That's … quite a list."

"You always told me I deserved the best."

"You do, but according to this list, the best does not have back hair."

Ellie blinked.

Pickles!

Grandpa Frank had back hair.

"And what's this … unibrow?" he continued. "Sounds like these are bad too …"

Double pickles!

He had one of those as well.

Ellie grabbed the list from Grandpa Frank's hand and placed it back in her purse. "Okay, okay, maybe I need to remove one or two items."

Grandpa Frank shrugged. "Things were so simple in my days. Your grandmother and I met at a malt shop in Anaheim. Have I told you this story?"

Ellie loved the sparkle in his blue eyes when he talked about his marriage. "Tell me again."

"She served malts at the counter and *I* drank them." He chuckled. "There was something special about her. I knew it the first time I'd laid eyes on her. Just one look and that was it. That summer I spent just about every single dime I had on malts, and I think I gained a few pounds too! But I felt comfortable with her and we chatted for hours about everything and nothing. I didn't know what I was looking for, and I certainly didn't have a list. It just felt right."

"That's so sweet, Grandpa."

"And holy cow she could kiss like nobody's business."

"Grandpa …"

They both laughed.

"It will happen when the time is right, sweetie. And maybe with someone you least expect." Ellie nodded. "How are things at the library?"

"God!" she groaned startling Grandpa Frank. "I can't believe I didn't tell you. They narrowed down the candidates to me and another woman, Margaret Rossewood."

"That's great!"

"Well, yes and no. They're stuck now. Half the board wants me, and the other half wants Margaret. I've met her and she's an amazing person, smart too."

"Can't be smarter than you. Impossible."

Ellie smiled. "Thanks. It's not an IQ competition, though. They decided the job is going to go to the person who raises the most money for the fundraiser."

Grandpa Frank scratched his chin and thought about it. "I guess there are worse ways to decide, like drawing a name from a hat. At least this way you can work as hard as you want for the job."

"True. Julio came up with an idea to sell bricks that will go around the base of the oak tree in our courtyard. Donors will have their names engraved on the bricks. One hundred dollars for a brick."

"What a wonderful idea."

"Yeah, but I still need to ask people to donate, and you know how I feel about money. It brings out the worst in people."

"And the *best* in people. Hang on, I'll give you a good example."

He left the kitchen and returned a minute later with his checkbook and a pen. "I'd like fifteen bricks please."

Ellie put her hand to her mouth. That was fifteen hundred dollars. "No, no, no."

"Why? Not enough?"

She laughed as her eyes began to tear up. "No, that's not what I meant. It's just …" She stood up and kissed Grandpa Frank on the cheek. "Thank you, you're the best."

He wrote the check and handed it to her. "You're welcome. And if you're up for a challenge, I have a way you can raise more money."

Ellie narrowed her eyes. "What are you talking about?"

Grandpa Frank laughed. "How many dates do you have coming up with men from this dating website?"

Ellie had no idea where he was going with this. "Three. Why?"

"Perfect. I challenge you to get to a second date with one of them."

Ellie cocked her head to the side. "What do my dates have to do with the fundraiser?"

"It's simple. If you make it to a second date with the same man, I'll buy another five bricks for the cause."

Ellie's mouth hung open. That was an extra five hundred dollars.

"What?" asked Grandpa Frank.

"You're serious?"

"You bet! I want you to be happy, Ellie, and you're never going to be if you don't give these guys a decent chance. It's hard to get to know someone over just one date."

"You haven't met some of these guys. It's like they're from another planet."

Ellie was up for the challenge, though. Three possible second dates meant a potential fifteen hundred dollars closer to getting the promotion. Not to mention, the possibility of meeting a great guy in the process.

Still. Easier said than done.

An hour later, Ellie waited in front of the giant pine tree near the post office, where she agreed to meet her date, Richard. She checked her watch as he walked up.

Right on time. Good.

But her smile faded—along with her hopes for an extra five hundred dollar donation from Grandpa Frank—after he uttered three little words.

"Hi, I'm Dick."

Ellie blinked and tapped her fingers on the side of her leg. "What happened to Richard? Not too many people can say they have the same name as former President Nixon."

"His friends and family called him Dick."

Great. Ten seconds into her date and she already had a dilemma. Could she see herself introducing this guy to people in the future as Dick? Without laughing?

Ellie searched for another angle. "Richard is very masculine."

His left eye fluttered like a moth stuck in her front porch light. "I prefer Dick."

Pickles!

If the male-organ-name-change thing wasn't bad enough, the guy was wearing polyester pants a size or two too small, putting his marbles and Dick Junior on display for the world to see.

"My father's a Dick too," he continued.

The conversation reminded Ellie of a bachelorette party. She was tempted to ask him how long they were going to talk about dick.

"Traditions are sacred in my family, as you can tell," he said.

"I think traditions are lovely. Well, except my brother's. He thought it would be funny to give me a wedgie every year on my birthday."

"Boys will be boys."

"Actually … he still does it."

Dick blinked.

Great.

No sense of humor.

Strike one!

Ellie had recently implemented the Three-Strikes Law on her dates; she'd give the guy three chances to screw up or display a quality she didn't like. She didn't want to hurt people's feelings, but you had to draw the line somewhere. Her last relationship—with Vlad—turned into a nightmare. There were signs at the beginning, and she chose to ignore them. Never again.

Dick pointed to the other side of the street. "Let's cross." He grabbed Ellie's hand and pulled her sideways toward Rafael's Steakhouse. She had considered giving him another strike for his manhandling until she was hit by the aroma drifting over from Rafael's.

She inhaled deeply and smiled. "Something smells wonderful."

"Aqua Velva."

Clueless. And he wore the same aftershave as Grandpa Frank. Great. At least he had excellent taste in food. Rafael's had amazing tri-tip sandwiches and cheesecake.

Dick made a sharp turn to the right, passing right by the front door of Rafael's. Where the heck was he going? Ellie's eyes opened wide as they got closer to the building on the corner.

No, he wouldn't. Please. Please. God no.

Her heart rate sped up.

A first date was supposed to be romantic—well, in her opinion. Surely he wouldn't …

Dick reached for the handle, swung the door open, and waved Ellie through, like he was welcoming her to the White House.

Pickles!

She paused at the front door. "You're kidding, right?"

"Not at all, they have the best wings in the world."

Wings. Right.

Ellie knew any guy who came to this place was most likely a breast man.

"Welcome to Hooters," said the hostess. "Two?"

Dick nodded. "Yes, please."

The woman—or more accurate, scantily clad girl—grabbed two menus and gestured for them to follow. "Right this way."

As they followed the hostess, Ellie glanced around the restaurant at the countless monitors showing sporting events and the fine wood detail of the bar and ceiling.

"The wings are why I always come back," said Dick.

"Right." Ellie eyed the waitresses in their short shorts and low-cut blouses, with their cups that overfloweth. As the waitress took their drink orders, Ellie found her thoughts wandering just a tad.

I can fit half of the waitress's left boob in my purse.

This was going to be more difficult than she thought—she needed to focus.

Dick cleared his throat. "We'd like separate checks please."

The waitress looked over to Ellie. "Umm … Okay."

Dick turned to Ellie as well. "Naturally, I assumed you'd want to go Dutch. Equality for women … and all that."

"How noble of you," said the waitress, frowning at Ellie.

Ellie forced a smile at the waitress before she walked away.

Strike two!

Dick pulled out a receipt book and calculator. "Speaking of splitting things evenly, I need to do some quick calculations before we get to the courting."

"Courting?"

"Absolutely."

The things Ellie had to endure to find a man. Ever since her two best friends got married and moved away last year, she felt more pressure than ever to find someone to settle down with. With no parents in the picture, and a brother who lived in Wyoming, to say Ellie's social life took a big hit would be an understatement. The only people she'd been hanging out with recently were Julio and Grandpa Frank. They were great—wonderful, actually—but she wanted more.

Dick smiled and slid on his reading glasses. "Okie dokey, I put forty dollars' worth of gasoline in my car to come here this evening. Based on the eighty miles each way I'll drive, never exceeding the speed limit, calculating traffic and construction delays, and a car that gets exactly twenty-point-seven miles per gallon …" He punched in some numbers on his calculator. "I expect to use thirty-two dollars of said gasoline, which means *your* share would be sixteen dollars."

Ellie stared at him and waited for the laugh that never came.

He was serious.

Do it for the promotion. Do it for the promotion. Do it for the promotion.

Dick smacked himself on the forehead. "Almost forgot, I'm going to have to pay six dollars to cross back over the Golden Gate Bridge tonight to get home. Your half of six is three, plus the sixteen you owe me for the gas, for a grand total of—"

"Nineteen dollars. Let's just round it up to twenty. Do you accept cash?"

Dick slapped his thighs with the palms of his hands as his left eye fluttered. "You are *wonder*ful. I love your enthusiasm. And getting the money out of the way will make it less awkward later on when we, you know, say good night. Unless we end up saying good morning!" Dick winked and wrote her a receipt for the twenty dollars, asking for her signature at the bottom. "Press hard."

Strike three!

Five bricks—five hundred dollars—down the drain.

"Excuse me, Dick." Ellie handed him the pen and receipt. "I just need to freshen up a bit." She grabbed her purse and stood up to leave. "Be back in a jiffy."

"Of course, of course. Well, don't take too long. I want to tell you about some great investments with IRAs that will just knock your socks off."

"I can't wait." She forced another smile as her body shivered, anxious to escape. "Neither can my socks."

Ellie walked through the tables toward the lobby, knocking over a fake indoor plant in the process. She righted the plant, pushed the front door open, and tripped over the welcome mat, falling straight into the crotch of a teenage boy in a stinky soccer uniform. The boy smiled.

Ellie wiped her face. "Sorry."

She popped back up, brushed off her hands, and waited for a group of people walking by so they could shield her as she passed by the window in front of Dick. She took a quick glance through the window to see if Dick had a clue as to what was going on, but he was busy cleaning his calculator.

As Ellie walked to her car, she thought of the losers she'd gone out with recently. Men she'd found through online dating. They seemed fine on their profiles. But you learn so much more about a person when you meet them face-to-face and they show their true selves. Especially when they open their mouths.

On paper, Dick was a ten. In person, a big fat goose egg. Okay, maybe that was harsh. He was on time, so she had to give him credit for that.

Ellie laughed. "A night with Dick and hooters." She scooted behind several people at the intersection and waited with them for the light to change. It was just after six and the traffic was extra crazy today, for some reason. As she waited, she couldn't help but notice the broad shoulders and nice butt of the man in front of her. She leaned to the side to see what his face looked like. Very nice. Handsome. He had smooth olive skin and short black hair. Italian or Greek. Maybe Spanish. And possibly stupid.

What was he doing?

The man looked both ways, like he wanted to cross the street—even though the light was red.

Bad idea, considering the amount of traffic.

"Don't even think about it …" Ellie knew the intersection very well.

The man ignored her and proceeded to step off the curb.

"Hey, are you crazy?" She grabbed the man's arm and pulled him back as a UPS truck zipped by, the driver honking his horn.

Chapter Three

Cedric's heart slammed into his ribs. He watched as the UPS truck that almost took him out, disappeared down the street.

What an idiot.

He was running five minutes late to meet a real estate lawyer, obviously not paying attention. Cedric had a lot on his mind, but that didn't mean he had to jeopardize his own life and/or break the law. You can't solve problems when you're dead.

He spun around and saw a woman with dark, shoulder-length, wavy hair, and big brown eyes that matched the color of the UPS truck. His gaze dropped to her hand that still held on to his shirt.

No ring.

Yeah. Like he was going to do anything about that.

"Dude, that truck would have killed you," said a man next to her with a San Jose Sharks hat. "She saved your life!"

"Not necessarily," the woman said, letting go of Cedric's shirt and kindly trying to smooth out the wrinkles. "The most common injuries from the impact of a car are broken legs and hips. He could have easily recovered in six to eight months."

"He was a goner," said the man, walking away.

Ellie shook her head. "People exaggerate."

"I've done it a million times," Cedric said, grinning.

Ellie smiled and it felt like someone kicked Cedric in the gut. What a glorious smile—the kind that could easily melt the cheese on his favorite grilled eggplant sandwich. Cedric lost the ability to speak.

What was going on here? Maybe the woman had hypnotic powers. Yeah, that had to be it. In fact, maybe she worked with a gang of thieves. She hypnotizes people with her beauty and someone else swoops in and steals the person's money. Cedric casually dropped his hand down to his pocket, checking for his wallet.

"Are you okay?" asked the woman.

He stared at her lips that seemed to be saying, *kiss me.*

"What?" She covered her mouth with her hand. "Do I have something in my teeth?"

"Huh? No! It's just ... did you have braces as a child?"

Cedric wanted to punch himself in the face. That had to be the most idiotic question in the history of the world. He knew he was out of practice, but what a pathetic attempt at trying to engage in a conversation with the opposite sex. Maybe she wouldn't think anything of it.

"That's an odd question."

Damn.

"But, yes, I did," she continued. "Shouldn't be a surprise, though. Forty-five percent of children need braces on their teeth at some point."

"Is that so?"

This woman was a walking Wikipedia.

"Yes," she said. "Although seventy-five percent of people fear the dentist."

"I now have a fear of large brown trucks."

The woman laughed. "You'll be okay. Just watch where you're going."

"Good advice." Cedric stared at the woman who seemed to be radiating kindness. "How did you know the UPS truck was coming?"

"The company has ninety thousand trucks. It was very likely."

Cedric laughed. "You're funny."

"Thanks. I should get back to work."

"And beautiful."

"Thanks again. Take care."

The light turned green at the intersection and the woman gave Cedric another heart-stopping smile as she walked past him to cross the street.

"Wait," said Cedric.

The woman stopped, turned, and stepped back up onto the curb. "Yes?"

Cedric couldn't help notice her skirt doing a little cha cha cha with the breeze. If the world ever had a leg shortage, it could borrow some from her.

She narrowed her eyes at him.

Busted.

Cedric grimaced. "Sorry. Must be in shock from the near-death experience."

"Of course." The woman cocked her head to the side to analyze Cedric. "Anything else?"

Cedric was trying hard to get himself back out there, but that voice in his head returned—as it always did—and snapped him out of his female-induced coma.

Relationships equal pain.

He didn't answer and just stood there, waiting for her to get the hint.

It didn't take long before the woman's smile disappeared. Then so did she.

***

The next morning rolled around and Cedric slipped on a T-shirt and shorts, as Tofu lay completely sprawled out on his doggy bed.

"I'm an idiot. Did you know that?"

Tofu opened one eye to look at Cedric, and then closed it, returning back to his bliss.

"I met a woman. You should have seen her. Brunette, beautiful brown eyes, legs for days, kind, smelled nice … but when that moment came, you know, the chance to ask her out? I fell flat on my face. Splat."

Tofu popped up on to all fours and ran to the window.

Cedric laughed. "No, I didn't say cat, I said … never mind." He sat down on the reading chair next to the bed to put on his running shoes. "Time for a run, buddy."

Tofu showed his enthusiasm by banging the hell out of the geranium plant next to the window with his tail, knocking leaves and flowers to the floor.

"Control your tail or you're going to lose it."

Tofu jumped onto Cedric's lap and licked his chin. Cedric smiled and scratched Tofu between the ears.

"Okay, okay. You can keep the tail. But you need to do something about that doggy breath."

He turned up the volume on his iPod. "Beautiful Day" by U2 pumped into his ears as he ran down the sidewalk on Lincoln Avenue toward downtown. He enjoyed the peace and the fresh morning air as he passed the Starbucks, Hicklebee's Bookstore and La Villa, the Italian Delicatessen.

Cedric stopped at the bus stop in front of the Wells Fargo Bank and put his foot on the bench, retying a shoelace that had a mind of its own. A woman at the ATM turned around and seemed to be watching him, but he pretended not to notice her long legs, short skirt, and turquoise blouse with an illustration of what appeared to be something from Picasso. His eyes finally lifted to see her face and—

Holy hell in a wishing well.

His guardian angel. The woman who saved him from being plastered by the UPS truck. And judging by the look on her face, she was just as surprised as he was.

Cedric turned off his iPod and removed the earbuds. "We meet again."

"Yes." She slid some bills into her wallet and stepped away from the ATM. "Been hit by any large trucks lately?"

Cedric laughed. "No. I met a beautiful woman last night who taught me a valuable lesson."

The woman blushed. "I see. And what would that lesson be? Let me guess, wait for the light to change before crossing?"

Cedric nodded. "And also … don't forget to say thank you."

The woman nodded and smiled. "I'm Ellie, by the way."

"I'm Cedric. And seriously, thank you for last night. I was rude." He shrugged. "I guess my mind was somewhere else." Like on her legs. And her hair. Can't forget those lips either. "Or maybe I just have some unresolved issues."

Ellie laughed. "Who doesn't?"

"Good point."

There was something about this woman—besides her beauty—that Cedric liked. She had personality and he was pretty sure they had a connection. Otherwise, why would she still be talking to him? The thought of asking her out got his heart pounding. Maybe small talk first would calm his nerves before he asked her.

"You work around here?"

"Yeah, just around the corner at—"

Tofu yanked the leash from Cedric's hand and took off down the sidewalk. "Crap! Excuse me, gotta run. Nice seeing you!" he added as he sprinted down the street.

Great timing, Tofu. He must have seen a squirrel or a cat. Cedric wasn't holding onto the leash very well, obviously distracted by Ellie. He wanted to talk more with her, but if anything happened to Tofu, he'd be devastated.

"Arf. Arf, arf, arf."

"Tofu, stop!"

The dog finally stopped a hundred yards down the street by a row of bushes on the side of a building.

When he caught up to Tofu, Cedric gasped. "Holy crap."

Tofu was sniffing a man who lay on the ground. A dead man?

He moved toward the man to get a closer look. Most likely in his forties, the man was dressed in shorts, a T-shirt, and tennis shoes. He must have been on the way to the athletic club, Cedric thought, as he eyed the man's bag of tennis rackets.

Tofu sniffed the man's shoes and Cedric grabbed the man's wrist and checked for a pulse. He thought he felt something faint, but wasn't sure.

"Arf. Arf, arf, arf."

Tofu licked the man on the face and Cedric pulled him back.

"No, Tofu."

Cedric pressed 9-1-1 on his cell phone, then clamped it between his shoulder and cheek, tying Tofu to a post.

"9-1-1," answered the dispatcher. "What's your emergency?"

"I found a man on the ground, unconscious." Cedric's phone slipped from his hands and landed in between the man's legs. "Crap." Cedric reached in to grab his phone.

"Sir, are you there?"

"Yeah. I'm here."

"Sir, where are you?"

"Right next to—" Cedric stared at his phone that was in two pieces, the body of the phone still in his hand and the battery that fell in between the man's legs. His heart raced. He got down on his knees and looked into the man's mouth. There didn't appear to be anything blocking the airway, so he loosened the man's jacket, tilted his head back, pinched his nostrils shut, and blew air into his lungs.

He paused a moment and then blew air into his lungs again and heard the sound of a car approaching. Cedric felt as if somebody was watching him, and he tried to stay focused. He grabbed his cell phone battery from between the man's legs, counting the time in between compressions and looked behind himself, noticing a Chinese man sitting in an old Ford Escort station wagon. The man watched Cedric through the driver's side window.

Tofu barked and the man took off. He traveled about thirty feet, slammed on the brakes, put it in reverse, and drove backwards, ending up right back where he was a few seconds earlier.

Cedric watched the man throw a newspaper from the car window, landing perfectly in front of the door of one of the shops. He nervously looked over to Cedric again and then took off.

Cedric looked back down at the man on the ground who now had his eyes open. "You okay?"

The man coughed. "Never been better."

Cedric wiped his mouth.

"You didn't just …"

"What?"

"Mouth-to-mouth?"

"Of course. I thought you were dying."

The man wiped his mouth too. "God. People don't do that anymore. Hasn't anyone heard of chest compressions? And even *that* wasn't necessary. You're the fourth one this week."

"The fourth?"

"I'm a chronic fainter."

Cedric blinked.

"Orthostatic hypotension is what they call it," the man continued. "It may be linked to Lupus. Whatever the reason, I faint almost as much as I go to the bathroom. Hey, give me a hand, would ya?"

Cedric grabbed his hand and pulled him up to his feet. "You pass out every day?"

The man nodded and brushed off the rear of his pants, then the front. "And I've fainted in some odd places too. My class reunion, a 49er game, the confessional booth. Heck, I've even fainted while driving."

"No."

"Oh yeah. They took away my license after I drove into the Guadalupe River last year. When I came to, I was down stream near the town of Milpitas, wondering how the hell a duck got in my car. They sure poop a lot, don't they?"

The man's legs buckled and he hit the ground. Unconscious again.

"This can't be happening."

Cedric saw a light on in one of the buildings and pounded on the door. He stopped when he heard the sound of a siren.

A cop got out of the car and approached Cedric. "What's going on here?"

A second car pulled up and the other cop checked the man on the ground.

"I'm looking for help," said Cedric.

"That business doesn't open for two hours."

"I was out for a run and found that guy by the tree, unconscious. He's got Orthopedic Hyperness."

"Ortho what?" The cop noticed the cell phone in Cedric's hand. "How come you didn't just call 9-1-1?"

"I did. My phone fell apart and died."

"All by itself?" The cop studied Cedric for a few moments. "We got a call reporting a sexual assault in the area."

"I didn't see anything. And why are you looking at me that way?"

"You seem nervous."

"I thought the man was dying! If you don't believe me, I'm sure they were recording my 9-1-1 call.

"Uh huh. Can I see some ID please?"

"Shouldn't you be helping him?"

"We're going to get him help, but what I need from *you* right now is some form of identification."

Cedric reached for his pocket and handed the cop his license. Unbelievable.

The cop pointed toward the curb. "Please have a seat."

"Did I do something wrong?"

"Sit on the curb."

"It would be a pleasure."

Tofu obviously didn't like how Cedric was being treated. "Arf. Arf, arf, arf."

"Sir, control your animal."

"Tofu, no."

Tofu stopped barking. Cedric sat down on the curb as the man in the Ford Escort returned. The Chinese man waved the first cop over and then pointed at Cedric and at the man on the ground. The cop walked back over to Cedric.

"We have a witness who says he saw you fornicating with the guy by the bushes."

"What?"

"He says he saw you kiss him repeatedly and then reach between his legs and fondle him."

Cedric ran his fingers through his hair. This can't be happening. "I was trying to save his life," he said, louder than he had anticipated.

"Hey, there's no need to yell. Now, I'm not a medical expert, but I'm smart enough to know you can't save a man's life by jacking him off."

Over a thousand good cops in San Jose and Cedric got one with an attitude.

The unconscious man was awake again and talking to the other cop. Cedric jumped up.

"Ask him." Cedric pointed to the man. "He'll tell you. I didn't do anything wrong."

"Calm down, sir."

"It's true," the man said, approaching Cedric. "He was trying to help me. I passed out. I tend to do that often."

The cop looked over the guy from head to toe. "Have you been drinking?"

"No," said the man. "I have a medical condition. Please, nothing happened here, I promise you. Please let this kind man go."

The cop glanced over to his partner who was just getting off the phone.

"Dispatch confirmed he called 9-1-1, but was cut off."

The other cop just shrugged his shoulders. "Okay then." He turned toward the chronic fainter. "You should consider wearing a medical ID bracelet so people are aware of your condition."

"I can't," said the man. "I'm allergic to metals."

"They come in plastic. Get one."

"Yes, sir."

Cedric ran his fingers through his hair as the cops walked away. "I need a vacation."

"Sorry you had to go through that," said the man as he and Cedric watched the two police cars drive away. "But thanks, I appreciate you being so kind, helping a stranger."

"You're welcome." Cedric held out his hand. "I'm Cedric Johnson."

"Owen Fitzpatrick."

Cedric eyed the tennis bag. "You've got a lot of rackets there."

Owen laughed. "I guess you could say I'm a tennis enthusiast. Some people say I have a racket obsession and that wouldn't be far from the truth. You play?"

"Used to. I played on the varsity team in high school. After that, not so much. Don't even think I have a racket anymore."

Owen pulled a business card from his wallet and handed it to Cedric. "I could always use another playing partner. Give me a call if you ever want to hit the ball around. You can borrow one of my rackets."

Cedric shrugged. "I wouldn't want to stink up the court."

"Hey, don't let the rackets fool you, I'm not that good. If you change your mind … no pressure."

"Sounds good. I'm curious, have you ever passed out playing tennis?"

Owen laughed. "Surprisingly, no. And I hope I never do."

They said their goodbyes and Cedric turned to walk back home, since he now lacked the motivation to continue the run. Although, truthfully, he should get back anyway, since he had a long list of things to accomplish for the day

As he walked with Tofu, about a football field's length in front of him, he noticed a woman crossing the street, wearing a turquoise blouse, just like the one Ellie wore.

Was that her? It sure as hell seemed like it.

Funny, Cedric had the sudden urge to run again.

He flew down the sidewalk with Tofu matching his speed stride for stride, like a champion show dog. He arrived at the corner where he saw her standing and—

"Crap," he said, looking around.

She'd disappeared somewhere between the Starbucks and the library. Cedric let out a deep breath and looked in both directions again.

He had his opportunity and he blew it.

Chapter Four

Ellie recalled her date's profile as she waited in the lobby of the restaurant. Chuck "The Buck" was a recent transplant from Tyler, Texas, and a former bull rider and underwear model. He retired at the age of thirty-five and moved to the Bay Area just two months ago, looking to meet a California girl. He was honest and open in his online dating profile about what he wanted—just two things: to settle down and to have a family "pronto."

He'd decided the Bay Area was the perfect place to do just that, since it was home to his favorite company, Google, and because he'd read an article about the sexy, smart women of Silicon Valley in *American Cowboy*.

As she waited in the lobby for him to arrive, her phone vibrated in her purse. Maybe he was going to be late. She pulled her cell out and looked at the caller ID. It was her brother, Derek.

"Hey there. Anything important? I'm waiting for my date to arrive."

"You pissed away five hundred bucks from Grandpa Frank? That was guaranteed money in the bank."

Ellie switched the phone to the other ear and sighed. "I know, I know, but these guys are nothing like their dating profiles!"

"You're the pickiest woman in the world."

Ellie loved talking to her brother … even when he gave her crap. They'd been close ever since they were kids. Derek encouraged Ellie to move to Los Angeles to attend UCLA for her Library and Information Science degree. It wasn't until he moved to Wyoming that they didn't talk as much. Still, it just took a few minutes on the phone to make it seem like nothing had ever changed.

"Am not picky," Ellie lied.

"Obviously you don't want the promotion bad enough."

Not true. Ellie had been dreaming of being Branch Manager for years. "For your information, I still have two more dates this week. That's a potential thousand dollars. And I have to run, I see my date in the parking lot."

"Well don't let what happened to you in the past affect what's going on in your life now. Get Vlad out of your head and try to enjoy yourself. Love you."

"Love you too."

Ellie disconnected and watched as Chuck slid out of his Cadillac Escalade Hybrid, sporting a classic cow-brown suede vest with matching chocolate and pearl crocodile skin boots.

She tried not to judge him by what he was wearing—she didn't like materialistic men—and wanted to give him a chance since he seemed so nice during their email exchanges and phone calls. She loved his accent.

And he was gorgeous.

One thing that did not make any sense was why this guy would choose International House of Pancakes as the location for their first date. Sure, Ellie *loved* IHOP, but for a dinner date?

Ellie checked her watch. Right on time.

She watched through the window of the lobby as Chuck swaggered toward the front door like a runway model. Confidence. She liked that. Upon entering the restaurant, he smiled.

Ooh. Very nice smile.

Chuck took off his black beaver fur cowboy hat and held it behind his back. "Hello little lady." He ignored her outstretched hand and kissed her on the cheek.

Ellie smiled. "Hi."

Chuck grabbed her hand and spun her around as he checked out her body. "Well, butter my butt and call me a biscuit, you certainly are a looker, aren't ya? Even better in person."

"Thank you." She felt dizzy from the spin.

He seemed to be visually measuring Ellie, his eyes shooting back and forth from her left hip to the right. "And hot damn, you've got a body primed for pregnancy."

Ellie forced a smile, certain she didn't hear him correctly. Must have been his Texas accent. She tried to think of words that sounded like pregnancy. *Ecstasy. Leprosy ...*

"Excuse me, Ellie, I need to use the restroom before we sit, if you don't mind."

"Of course. I'll be right here waiting."

"Thank you very kindly."

Ellie loved his manners. She loved his backside even more.

"Nice butt, cowboy," said Ellie, watching each cheek move in those perfectly-fitted Wrangler jeans as he walked toward the bathroom. Left. Right. Left. Right.

"Amen, sister," said the hostess who was probably old enough to have a subscription to AARP Magazine.

Chuck returned a couple of minutes later.

"Okay," said the hostess, smiling. "Ready?"

"Yes, ma'am, thank you very kindly," answered Chuck as he and Ellie followed the hostess to their table.

They sat and immediately ordered their food and drinks. After chatting pleasantly about Texas, bull riding, cattle drives, boots, and of course, the weather, out of the blue, Chuck changed the subject to women and their reproductive parts. Ellie was ready to change the subject, but he kept firing away with the questions.

Chuck scratched the side of his face. "So, you're telling me that the uvula is not part of the vagina?"

"The uvula is that tiny dingle ball hanging in the back of your throat. You're thinking of the uterus. You thirsty?"

Chuck grabbed the glass of Coke. "My mouth is dry enough to spin cotton." He drank the entire glass and flagged down the waitress for a refill. When the second Coke came, he drained that one too. "Most women have enough tongue for ten rows of teeth, but you're a quiet little thing."

Ellie smiled. "Sorry. It just looked like you had something on your mind."

"Well shut my mouth, you're one smart cookie. If my mamma taught me anything, she taught me it's better to keep my mouth shut and look stupid than open it and prove it."

"Sounds like your mother was wise."

The waitress brought their appetizer and set it on the table. "Okay, here you go, crispy chicken strips and fries and two sides of mayo." She smiled and grabbed Chuck's coke glass. "Another refill?"

"Yes, ma'am. Thank you kindly."

Obviously, they were not on the same page when it came to eating healthy. And how the heck did he stay so skinny eating stuff like this? She had ordered the whole-wheat pancakes with blueberries. His profile said he was a health nut. His choices today showed otherwise and she just couldn't overlook that.

Strike one!

Ellie had difficulty keeping her eyes off the giant platter of cholesterol in front of her; it smelled so good. "Did your mother give you any other good advice?"

"Oh yeah. She also said to always drink upstream from the herd."

She laughed and grabbed her orange juice. A sense of humor was a good thing.

"But I've been beating around the bush, Ellie, and I just need to say somethin' right here, right now. So here goes it. I like what I see, Ellie. A lot. And bottom line is … I'm gonna come clean. I mentioned in my profile that I wanted a couple of babies, but that's hogwash."

Do it for the promotion. Do it for the promotion. Do it for the promotion.

"Ellie, I wanna have … a *boat load* of babies."

She nearly spit up her orange juice. "Excuse me?" She wiped her mouth.

"Babies." He skipped the fork this time, grabbing a chicken strip with his hand and taking a bite. "That's what I'm talkin' about. Six to eight babies … minimum. Ten preferably. What's the ratio of boys to girls in your family? I'd like all boys. I could have my own personal rodeo crew!"

Strike two!

She needed to amend her Three Strikes Law so she could give two strikes at the same time.

"And it would make me happier than a gopher in soft dirt if you'd make them babies with me, Ellie. Pass the mayo please."

Ellie's mouth opened, but nothing came out. She passed the mayonnaise to the gopher, who spooned some on his plate. He grabbed another chicken strip and a handful of fries, dipped them in the mayonnaise, and stuffed them in his mouth. The fries looked and smelled good, but Ellie had lost her appetite.

He smiled, closed his eyes, and chewed. "Just like mama's."

Chuck looked like he was going to cry. At least she now knew why he'd picked IHOP. The food there must remind him of his mom's. That's sweet.

But not sweet enough.

It looked like this cowboy was heading for strike three, within a matter of minutes. She felt it coming.

"Anyhoo, where was I? Oh yeah, I came here to the Bay Area since I heard there were a whole hell of a lot of intelligent women here, like yourself. I want our children to be smart, Ellie. There's nothing wrong with that, is there?"

"Chuck …" Ellie forgot how to form complete sentences.

"Please, call me Buck. And look … we all got pieces of crazy in us, some have bigger pieces than others." He pointed a mayo-covered fry at her. "I'm not saying I'm all that and a bag of pork skins, but I can provide for us, Ellie, I can tell you that. I made a killin' buying Google stock way back in the day so you won't have to worry about nothing but staying home and making babies and being happy. And if you know your way around a kitchen, hey, a couple of hot meals every day wouldn't be too shabby either. You know what I'm saying?"

Ten babies plus he wanted her to cook for him every day. Right. Maybe in her spare time, she could work on finding a cure for cancer too.

Strike three!

Time for this cowgirl to saddle up and get the heck out of Dodge. Another five hundred dollar donation from Grandpa Frank down the drain.

"That's an amazing offer, Chuck."

"Buck."

"Buck." She smiled, but instead of running this time, she decided to be honest. "Look, I think you're a kind man, but I just don't see myself having ten kids. Or even five or six. There's nothing wrong with you wanting that. In fact, I think it's wonderful you know what you want. But that's not what I want."

Buck nodded. "I understand."

"I'm going to go now, if you don't mind. Otherwise, it may feel awkward."

"Sure you don't want to eat?"

"No thank you. You're a good man and I wish you luck."

"Right back at you, Ellie."

As she walked down the street, she thought of her luck with men. Dick and Buck.

Then there was Cedric.

She chuckled as she replayed the scene from this morning over in her head: Cedric in his running shorts with those sexy legs, chasing after his dog. She wouldn't mind if she ran into him again and—

Bam.

Ellie ran into a cement wall. She was disoriented and looked up. The cement wall had a face just like the man she was thinking about.

Cedric.

Cedric looked down at the woman who just did a face plant into his chest.

Beautiful Ellie.

He grinned. "We keep running into each other. Literally."

She felt her nose. "Yeah. I trust you were able to catch up with your dog this morning?"

Cedric nodded. "He gave me a good workout."

Ellie smiled and Cedric felt a small thump in his chest.

That's it, he had to do it. No delaying, just ask her out. "I was wondering if—"

"Ellie," a police officer in uniform said, cutting off Cedric.

Great.

It was the cop from this morning.

"Oh God," Ellie muttered. "Vlad."

Cedric could see Ellie tense up, tapping her fingers on the side of her leg.

Vlad inspected Cedric from head to toe. "The fornicator. You get around, don't you?"

"What are you talking about?" asked Ellie.

"This guy was—"

"About to leave," said Cedric.

Vlad stuck his hand in front of Cedric's chest. "Not so fast. How do you two know each other?"

He didn't throw the question out casually; it was like Cedric was being interrogated. Cedric's gaze dropped to the badge on his chest. V. Cunnings.

"We don't know each other, actually," said Cedric. "We just—"

"Good. Now you can go."

What a dick.

Ellie held up her hand. "Wait a minute. You and I don't have anything to talk about."

"We need to talk about us," said Vlad.

Obviously this cop was Ellie's ex.

Ellie shook her finger in the air. "No. There is no 'us.' Please leave. I was talking with Cedric."

Vlad shifted his focus to Cedric and then back to Ellie. "How do you know his name if you don't know each other?" The guy needed a napkin to wipe the jealousy from his tone.

Ellie put her hands on her hips. "That's none of your—"

"Ellie, there you are!" Buck came running over. "I've given it some serious thought, and I would be okay with four kids. Maybe we could have a few extra goats and horses to make up the difference. Would that work for you?"

Ellie covered her face with her hands.

Vlad inspected Buck from head to toe. "Who's this cowboy?"

"Name's Chuck, but they call me Buck." He held out his hand, but Vlad left him hanging.

Vlad turned to Ellie. "How many guys are you seeing?"

"Look," said Cedric, feeling uncomfortable in the middle of an odd situation. "I'm just going to take off."

"Good idea," said Vlad.

Ellie held up her hand. "No. I'm the one who's leaving. I need to find a hole to crawl into."

She walked away and Buck threw his hands up. "Ellie, wait! What about the babies?" Buck shrugged and turned to Cedric and Vlad. "One of these days, I'll figure out women. In the meantime, you boys wanna grab a beer?"

"No," said Vlad and Cedric simultaneously, each walking away in separate directions.

Chapter Five

Cedric bolted awake, sweating. He looked around the bedroom, squinting, and disoriented. What the hell was that? Another messed-up dream about dying, that's what that was. The only bright spot was the appearance of Ellie in the dream.

Lovely Ellie.

The dream started as usual, no surprises. He sat on the examination table in the doctor's office, waiting. He studied the colorful poster on the wall showing the muscles and organs of the human body. Next to the poster was a life-size skeleton hanging from a floor stand.

He stared at himself in the mirror, thinking. "This is bullshit."

At the age of thirty-four, Cedric had felt good about almost everything in his life. His work. His health. His circle of close friends.

He stood and lifted his hospital gown, analyzing his naked body in the mirror. Still not an ounce of fat. Muscles in all the right places. He rubbed his washboard abs in a circular motion then released the gown, returning to the examination table. This didn't make any sense.

"I take care of myself. I shouldn't be here."

From the outside, Cedric was the absolute picture of outstanding health. The only problem was, you never knew what was going on underneath the hood. Maybe his "issues" were the result of the greasy burgers, junk food, soft drinks, and candy he devoured as a kid. Or maybe it was something in his genes, passed on to him from his—

Don't go there.

He surveyed the room for a distraction and grabbed the hands of the skeleton.

"I'll be honest with you, sweetie," Cedric said to the skeleton. "I was tempted to jump your bones earlier. But just between you and me..." he leaned closer "...I think you overdid it with the Weight Watchers, you know? You need to get a little more junk in your trunk."

The door swung open and the doctor raised an eyebrow, catching Cedric holding the hands of the skeleton. "Shall I leave you two alone?" she asked.

Holy crap.

The doctor was Ellie. Ellie was a doctor.

"It's fascinating," Cedric said, ignoring her comment and pretending to inspect the bones. "The bone structure of the human arm. The clavicle, the humerus, the—"

"Please stand up." Ellie grabbed a pair of latex gloves and slipped them on.

"Okay." Cedric dropped the hands of the skeleton, now very aware he was naked underneath the gown. What was she going to do?

He got a nice whiff of her perfume—something with roses—and he felt his heartbeat kick into second gear as she moved closer. She smelled nice.

Very nice.

Cedric blinked.

Something was happening down in the region of his family jewels, and he was pretty sure someone had accidentally clicked the auto-salute button.

He looked down and blinked.

Holy hell.

His hospital gown had turned into a Cirque du Soleil tent.

"Please lift the gown for me."

"Now?"

"Yes. Now."

Cedric, now fifty shades of pink, lifted the gown. "Sorry." He looked down at his unit, which was now approximately the size of a hammer. "Not sure what happened there."

"Uh huh." Her eyes opened wide as she grabbed his left testicle and smiled. "Turn your head and cough."

Cedric coughed, hoping to get the examination over as soon as possible.

"I'm surprised at the size of your..." she looked down at his package and then removed the gloves, tossing them in the trash. "...brain, Mr. Johnson."

"There's no need to be so formal."

"You can drop the gown now."

"Oh..." As the gown fell back down, it got stuck on his protruding member, which now looked more like a fleshy towel hook.

Doctor Ellie sat down at the computer station and logged in. She clicked a few buttons and turned the monitor in Cedric's direction. Zooming in, she used her pen to point to a dark spot on the right side of the image.

"You have a small tumor here on the right frontal lobe of your brain."

Talk about an erection killer.

"This would explain your constant headaches and difficulty thinking. It could also be the cause of your occasional mood swings."

Cedric felt the sudden urge to put his fist through a wall. "You've got to be joking."

"This is no joking matter. Especially since your testicles are going to shrivel up to the size of garbanzo beans."

"What the hell are you—"

"Odd, I'm craving hummus all of a sudden. With a nice green salad."

"You're serious?"

Ellie nodded. "But now for the bad news—"

"Bad news? What the hell was that you just gave me?"

"You're going to die."

"Whoa, whoa, whoa, wait a minute."

Ellie handed Cedric a stack of papers. "Please sign these papers quickly so the insurance company pays us."

Cedric stared at the papers in amazement. That's it? And all Ellie could think about was the insurance money? Did she not care about the feelings of her patients? No compassion? No sympathy?

Ellie checked her watch and then swiped the papers from Cedric's hands. "Darn, too late. You only have twenty seconds left to live. That's too bad, a real shame. Fantastic hair, by the way. If we had more time, I'd love to run my fingers through it."

"Can't you save my life again?"

"Sorry, love biscuit." She began to count down. "Five, four, three, two, one …"

Ellie ran from the room, the building shook, and the walls rumbled as a UPS truck came crashing into the examination room, taking out Cedric in the process.

Two hours after the dream, Cedric lay on the cream-colored leather couch in the office of his Psychologist friend, Michael Vela. His eyes scanned the enormous built-in bookshelf, filled with hundreds of books, patient files, miniature white Roman sculptures, and the head of Albert Einstein.

"Why do you always lie down?" asked Michael. "I told you people don't do that anymore."

"Maybe I just stopped by to take a nap."

"You want me to tuck you in?"

Cedric laughed.

Michael tapped his pen on the desk. "What's the latest on Papa George's property?"

"We're waiting to hear back from the Tax Collector about the auction."

"You must be excited."

"I am, but I'll feel more relaxed once I know for sure that I can actually bid on the property. I don't see why not, but I don't have confirmation yet."

"I'm sure everything will be fine."

Cedric nodded and closed his eyes, thinking of his latest dream again. Brains shouldn't be allowed to let you have dreams like that.

"You look preoccupied."

Cedric opened his eyes, sat up, and shrugged. "Tony says I'm possessed by demons."

"And you believe him?"

"Well, after what's been happening to me recently, I'm starting to wonder."

Michael closed his laptop, stood up, and walked around to the front of his desk, his butt leaning against the edge. "Technically, that would mean a ghost has merged with your consciousness and is controlling your mind, thoughts, and decision making ability. Does that sound about right?"

"Oh. Okay, maybe not."

"What's going on?"

"Well, where do I begin … I almost got killed by a UPS truck. I found a man on the ground I thought was dead, and I've had more than a few dreams about death. Everything is death related."

"They're just coincidences."

"I don't know about that.

"Do you die the same way in every dream?"

"No. It's like a death buffet, a variety of ways of dying to choose from. No dessert."

Michael laughed.

"At least I got a new doctor this time. The doctor in the dream before Ellie's was a giant A-hole."

"What was he like?"

Cedric pondered the question. "Okay … so if you went to a cloning factory and asked the lab technician to mix the cells of a male whore, a caveman, a donkey, and … a used-car salesman—with a dash of sun-dried rat feces—you'd be presented with an exact genetic copy of the doctor in my dreams."

"He sounds sweet."

"He also told me it would take major surgery to remove my head from my ass so I punched him. But since it was a dream, my fist went right through him and he laughed, pulled out a gun, and shot me in the balls."

Michael chuckled. "Maybe you *are* possessed by demons."

Cedric blinked.

"I'm kidding. Look, your girlfriend died and your mom died. These are huge events in your life and you just can't make them go away. The only thing you can do is change the way you feel about those events. Acceptance is key."

Yeah. Easier said than done.

The day Cedric's girlfriend died was supposed to have been memorable for another reason. Cedric was going to pop the question. He had the ring, the proposal plan, everything ready. A car that ran a red light changed that.

It's been very difficult to accept.

"And you need to get laid," Michael continued.

"You sound like Tony."

Cedric hadn't had a date since Cindy died two years ago. That also meant he hadn't had sex in two years and three days.

"Well, in this particular case, Tony's right. It's time. You need a woman in your life."

Cedric stood and walked over to the bookshelf. He reached for Albert Einstein's head and rubbed it. "What do you say, Einstein? You're a smart guy. Should I let another woman in or is she going to just die like the others and rip my heart into a thousand pieces?"

"Living your life in fear is no way to live."

Cedric nodded. "My heart believes you. But for some reason, my mind is not listening. My mom dying from cancer was bad enough, but then I got blindsided by Cindy's death."

Cindy was in San Francisco at the Macworld conference that day. During one of the breaks, she called Cedric and left a message saying she was enjoying the conference, she missed him, and was walking down the street to grab a quick lunch. Cedric calculated from the accident report she died about a minute after she'd left that voicemail message for him, hit and killed by a tourist who was driving while looking at a map.

"Did you hear me?"

"No."

"I asked you if you think of women in an intimate way."

"Of course. On the kitchen counter, the living room floor, in the shower. Wherever."

"That's good."

"That's not the issue, though. I've been tempted plenty of times. But a voice pops into my head that puts an end to everything before it begins. It tells me relationships equal pain. That's what happened when I was talking with Ellie."

"Who's that?"

"A woman I met. We had some type of connection, I'm almost positive. But then I shut her down."

Michael nodded. "This is more common than you think. You know, sometimes it helps to put your focus on others, instead of thinking of yourself so much. What have you been doing lately for fun?"

"Not much. But you know I enjoy my work."

"Yes and that's good, but you need things outside of work, you know that. You may want to consider doing some volunteering. Even pickup tennis again."

"Funny you mention it, tennis has been on my mind."

"Do it then. Look, we have to wrap this up, but what I can leave you with is this: focus on things that will enhance your life. Focus on the positive things you love. It wouldn't hurt picking up a book at the library, something on positivity maybe, or gratitude. Swing by and do yourself a favor. They may even need some volunteers over there for something. Kill two birds …"

Cedric hadn't been to the library in years. He had wonderful memories with his mom there. Great idea.

"Sounds like a plan." Cedric stood up and hugged him. "Thanks, man."

"You bet."

"What do I owe you?"

Michael laughed. "Another round of golf?"

"You got it. How many rounds do I owe you now?"

"Six." He grinned. "But who's counting?"

Chapter Six

Cedric couldn't remember the last time he'd set foot in the library, but he loved the feeling, surrounded by all of those books. He developed a love and appreciation for books at an early age and that helped him do well in school. He's read hundreds and hundreds of books and even has a room in his house dedicated to just books.

"Can I help you?" asked the impeccably dressed male clerk with a nametag that said Julio Cruz.

"Yeah, do you have any volunteer opportunities?"

"Yes, I think we do. You need to talk with Her Highness, Miss Peggy Fleming, the Branch Manager."

"Peggy—"

"Obviously she's not the Olympic ice skating champion Peggy Fleming, although she does kind of look like her. Anyway, she's in charge of the volunteer programs and pretty much everything else under this hot tin roof." Julio pointed to the woman at the desk with the giant globe. "That's her over there sitting with her back to us, wearing the lovely two-piece Jaclyn Smith ensemble."

"Great, thanks." Cedric wondered if he'd ever heard a man use the words "a lovely two-piece Jaclyn Smith ensemble."

He approached Peggy and cleared his throat.

Peggy swung around and popped out of her seat like a Jack-in-the-box. "Hello!"

Cedric was pretty sure she had enough energy to power all of the casinos in Las Vegas. Impressive, considering she must have been right around sixty or sixty-five years old. Her clothes and makeup were perfect, and she had a Jiffy Pop hairdo that defied gravity. She did look like *the* Peggy Fleming. Was she trying to make herself look like the woman on purpose or was it just a freaky coincidence? And how many Red Bulls had she had?

"Did you have a question?"

"I wanted to see if you had any volunteer opportunities."

"Absolutely! Please take a seat." She grabbed a file from the top drawer of her desk as Cedric sat down and contemplated her energy level.

She handed Cedric the list of jobs. "This is what we have at the moment. There are two great opportunities that involve children. How are you with reading?"

"The font's small, but I can read it just fine." He started in on the info on the paper.

"No, no, no. I mean, would you feel comfortable reading out loud? To children?"

"Oh." He loved the idea of reading to them. His mother used to read to him every night before he went to bed. It was one of those things he always looked forward to, and he's pretty sure that helped him shape him into who he is today. This volunteer opportunity sounded absolutely perfect. "Sounds great."

"Bless your heart." She pointed to something on the list. "Then I think you would be perfect for the STAR program. It stands for storytelling and reading, which is just what it sounds like. You would be reading books and telling stories to children. You wouldn't be trying to teach them to read. You'd be motivating them to want to learn to read. It would be wonderful to have a male role model since all of the readers are women."

"Do you have some sort of training or do you just throw me into the alligator tank?"

Peggy laughed. "The training process is simple. I'll even share techniques on how to make the stories come alive. You would need to commit to at least two hours per week for six months. A background check, fingerprinting, and TB test is required and provided by the library."

"Two hours doesn't seem like much."

"Each reading is thirty minutes, so it's not too much of a commitment."

"Count me in." Cedric was excited about the chance to be involved. "I'd love to be a part of it."

"Fantastic! I'm Peggy, by the way. Peggy Fleming."

"Cedric Johnson. Nice to meet you."

"Nice to meet you too!" She pointed to the paper again. "Just go to this website here and fill out the online application and we'll be in touch soon. Training for new volunteers is required, and we could start that next week, if you'd like."

"I don't think it'll be a problem. While I'm here, can you tell me if you have books on positivity or gratitude?

"Absolutely! We even have some on meditation and yoga. In fact, I'm part of a meditation group if you'd like to join us sometime."

"I'll keep that in mind," he said, wondering how difficult it was for Lady Red Bull to meditate. "And the books?"

"Oh, of course." She pointed to a row of books. "You can find them over there in our nonfiction section. I'll send someone over there to help you, if you'd like."

"That sounds great, thank you."

"Thank *you*. I'm here if you need anything else."

Cedric wandered over to nonfiction and browsed through books from Deepak Chopra, Eckhart Tolle, and the Dalai Lama. All of the Chicken Soup books were there. A bright green book caught his eye.

He leaned in to grab it and heard a female voice. "Probably not the best choice."

Cedric felt a chill run through his body. He had memorized that angelic voice; it was tattooed on his brain.

Ellie.

He turned around. "Why is that?"

Judging by the dazed look on her face, she was obviously surprised to see him too. "Oh … Cedric."

"In the flesh … Ellie."

They engaged in an impromptu staring contest, not a word spoken, but Cedric lost when he blinked after his eyes started to burn. "So …"

"So …"

"What would you recommend for me?"

Ellie squished her eyebrows together. "What would I recommend for you?"

"Yeah." He held up the book. "You said this was not a good choice."

"Oh! Right. There are much better options." She giggled. "Besides, you probably only picked it because of the color."

Cedric stood there a moment, in awe of the woman who knew him so well. "You are so wrong," he lied.

She smirked. "Is that right?"

"I picked it because of the font. Times New Roman is like an aphrodisiac to me." He pretended to loosen his collar. "Is it hot in here?"

"Did you follow me?"

"I was getting ready to ask you the same thing."

"Yeah, but, *I* was here first. Unless you think I anticipated you coming here, quickly applied for a job, was hired, and waited until you showed up."

Cedric laughed. "You … are very cool."

He saw Ellie blush, which made her even more beautiful. Her eyes had some type of a force field that sucked him in.

My name is Cedric and I will be your love slave. Take me, I'm yours.

"Let me know when you're back with me here. I can wait."

"Coffee," Cedric blurted out.

"Pardon me?"

"Coffee is good."

God. His attempt at asking her out was pathetic.

She had a certain look on her face. How would you describe it? Like someone who was at a museum looking at a painting and trying to figure out what the hell it was. Either that or she had a sudden bout of constipation.

"Was that a statement or a question?" she asked.

He knew he needed to ask her out quickly, before the voices returned. "Neither. Both."

Crap.

She stared at him and had to be thinking he was an idiot.

Obviously she must have felt the uncomfortable silence between his acts of stupidity, because she pulled a book from the shelf and handed it to him. "This is a great book. I highly recommend it."

Cedric analyzed the cover. "*Excuses Begone* by Wayne Dyer." Cedric turned the book over to see the back cover and then flipped through a few pages.

Ellie pointed to the book. "You don't have an excuse not to read it."

Cedric read the title again, closed the book, and grinned. "Clever."

She smiled. "I try."

"The font isn't the most exciting, but the book looks interesting. I'll check it out. Literally."

"Let me know if you need anything else." She turned to leave.

"Hey." Cedric took his eyes off her ass before she caught him, but holy hell, it was a work of art that belonged in the Guggenheim Museum.

She stopped and turned around, but didn't answer.

Cedric's heart raced and he forced a smile to try and hide his jitters. "Let me buy you a cup of coffee … to show my appreciation."

"So, now we're back to the coffee again, are we?"

Cedric nodded. "It's the least I can do."

"For finding you the book?"

"For saving my life."

"Uh huh …"

"We can go to the Starbucks on the corner."

"I just got here and I need to at least work for a couple of hours before I can take a break."

"Not a problem." He raised the book and smiled. "I have Wayne Dyer to keep me company. I'll just find a seat and you can let me know when you are ready."

***

Three hours later at Starbucks, Cedric and Ellie grabbed their drinks and chose a table near the window overlooking Lincoln Avenue. Cedric immediately noticed an older man eating a scone. "Crap."

Ellie sat up in her chair. "What?"

He mentally slapped himself in the head for being an idiot. "Sorry. I should have asked you if you wanted a snack or something to go with that coffee. Can I get you something? I don't mind getting back in line."

"No, no. Thanks. There's going to be some food at the library later. We're celebrating a co-worker's birthday today. Well, actually, it's the Branch Manager."

"Peggy Fleming?"

Ellie's eyes widened. "Yes. You know her?"

Cedric tried to keep a straight face. "Oh yeah, we go way back."

"Wow. Small world. How long have you known her?"

"Well, let's see … I met her, oh, when was it? Oh, that's right. About three and a half hours ago when I entered the library."

Ellie hit Cedric playfully on the arm. "You're bad."

"Thanks," he said, laughing. "Glad you noticed."

He enjoyed the smile on Ellie's face. She was playful and he liked that. They sat there for a few moments in silence, people-watching, exchanging smiles, sipping coffee, not saying much at all. But the silence didn't feel uncomfortable. It was like they were just hanging out together, passing time with a good cup of coffee, without a care in the world. It felt good.

No. It felt great.

Cedric took another sip of his coffee. "So."

"So."

"You're a librarian."

Ellie nodded. "For the last eight years."

"Very cool. What do you like about it?"

"Hmm. Well, for starters, no two days are alike. One moment I'm helping a child with a picture book, or a senior citizen with a hobby, and the next I'm showing someone tools for learning a new language. I like helping people find answers."

Cedric smiled again and nodded. "Did you always know you wanted to be a librarian?"

Ellie shrugged. "I was a total bookworm in middle school and high school. But I think it was when I became a library aide in my junior year of high school that I was pretty sure my career would have something to do with books. There was one point when I was reading a book a day."

"You must have a lot of information stored underneath that wild hair of yours."

Ellie blushed. "I know a few things."

"Who was the first person to walk on the moon?"

Ellie sighed. "Seriously? If you are going to try to stump me, you need to come at me with something better than a fifth-grade question."

"So, you don't know?"

"Neil Armstrong."

"Correct … and you're right, that was too easy. You must be good at Trivial Pursuit."

"They hired me as a consultant for their Book Lovers Edition."

Cedric blinked.

She smiled. "You don't believe me? Try me."

Cedric sat up and rubbed his hands together. "When was the civil war?"

"Which one?"

"Very good." Cedric laughed. "American."

"1861 to 1865."

"The Spanish?"

"1936 to 1939. Look, I appreciate the effort, but I can answer these questions with ninety-nine percent of my brain cells tied behind my back."

"Is that right?"

She nodded. "Got anything else more … stimulating?"

Cedric grinned. "Of course. Stimulation is my expertise."

Okay. He couldn't believe he said that. What was he thinking?

"Well then, give it to me."

Cedric smiled. "Scientific name for garlic?"

"Allium sutivum."

He made the sound of a buzzer. "Nice try, but that's incorrect."

"No it's not."

"It's allium *sa*tivum."

"Oh come on, close enough."

"Sorry."

"You got a thing for garlic?"

"I guess you could say that." Cedric took a sip of his coffee, feeling much more confident about things. "What's the world record for the longest kiss?"

Ellie hesitated and bit her lower lip. Why the hell did she have to do that? Now he was looking at her mouth again.

"Are you making up this question?"

Cedric chuckled. "It's a fact. I think I read it on the Chapstick website."

"And you don't think they said that to promote kissing and sell more Chapstick?"

Cedric shrugged. "I'd like to give them the benefit of the doubt."

Ellie smiled. "I admit I don't know this one, so I'm going to guess."

"I'm okay with that."

"Three hours?"

"Seriously? Three hours is nothing."

"Nothing? You've kissed someone for three hours?"

Cedric nodded. "Sally Farnsworth … eighth grade."

Ellie laughed. "We would have some seriously chapped lips after three hours of kissing."

"I'm not sure. Let's find out." Cedric pretended to get up and startled Ellie.

"Sit down. We are not going to kiss."

Cedric laughed. "Today."

"Today what?"

"We are not going to kiss *today.*"

Cedric was pretty sure he saw her trying to hold back a smile.

"Look," said Ellie. "Are you going to tell me the answer or not?"

"Fifty-eight hours."

"What? Impossible."

"No it's not."

"A fifty-eight hour kiss?"

"Yes."

Ellie was deep in thought. "God. How would you go to the bathroom?"

"Very carefully."

They both laughed and then her smile zapped him again. Good and strong. He tried to fight it, but for the moment couldn't. He'd been with Ellie for only ten minutes, but it seemed like they already knew each other. It felt so easy. So effortless. And her smile…

Wow.

Her smile was like a triple karate kick to the chest. And when she flashed those pearly-whites, she went from attractive to breathtakingly gorgeous in a fraction of a second.

He wondered what it would be like to touch her cheek, to kiss her, to hold her hand. He felt the urge. She crossed her legs and her summer dress slid up her thighs.

Is there a Nobel Prize for legs?

Cedric heard a door slamming and realized it was his mind, trying to get his attention.

Relationships equal pain.

This was not a date. Just coffee.

He sat up in his seat again, pretended to pick something off his shirt, and then looked over at Ellie. He pictured her head as a rotten apple, just to cool himself down. He was panicking and hoped Ellie wasn't paying too much attention. But who was he kidding? She was a woman and the species noticed everything.

"You're sweating. You okay?"

Of course she noticed.

Cedric wiped his forehead. "Yeah, I'm fine."

Ellie studied Cedric's body language—crossing one leg over the other, then switching back. The guy was obviously nervous about something. Still, she couldn't help but admire the polo shirt that stretched across his chest and showed off his broad shoulders and toned arms. He definitely took care of himself, but wasn't one of those guys who looked like he needed to show it off. His hair was black and wavy, long enough to show some style, but not too spiky and gelled to look like he tried so hard. His green eyes seemed nice, inviting, and down to earth.

Cedric had a lot of potential—much more potential than any of her handpicked dates from the website. She liked him so much, she totally forgot about her list. She hoped he didn't live with his mom, had a job, and was void of back hair.

She perked up in her seat, now curious about Cedric's back.

"Nice shirt." She reached over and grabbed the material on his sleeve, pretending to feel it.

"Thanks," said Cedric, looking suspicious.

"It feels like the same material as one of my dresses. Do you know what it's made of?"

Cedric raised an eyebrow. "Not sure. You want to check the tag? I guess that's better than me taking off my shirt in the middle of Starbucks and handing it to you."

"Starbucks may have a no-nudity policy, so I can just check the label."

"Good point."

She smiled, stood up, and walked behind him, proud of how easy that was. She grabbed the collar of his shirt and pulled it away from his neck. He smelled good, like soap and coffee. She had the sudden urge to plant her lips on his—certainly not for fifty-eight hours, though. A person's got to eat.

Ellie realized the charade was taking way too long and she stared down his back. Satisfied, she smiled, let go of the collar, inhaled his wonderful scent again, and returned to her seat.

"Fifty-fifty," said Ellie. "Polyester … and cotton."

"Good to know," he said.

"So, what do you do for a living?" asked Ellie, trying to change the subject again.

"I'm a farmer."

"Like a *farmer* farmer?"

Cedric laughed. "Yes. Red barn and all."

"You don't look like a farmer."

"Well, I admit that I don't do any of the labor."

"Don't tell me … garlic?"

Cedric nodded. "And cherries."

"Garlic and cherries. Now that's an odd combination."

"Initially, it was just garlic, had been that way for three generations in the family. But then the neighbor next door was selling his land, and it happened to come with fifteen hundred cherry trees."

"That's a fascinating field. What was your major in college?" She cradled her coffee as if it was keeping her hands warm.

"I didn't go to college. My grandfather owned the business and the farm in Gilroy, then I took it over."

"And your father?"

"He hasn't been in the picture for a while."

"Oh." Ellie tried to think of something else to say since it was obvious he wasn't going to elaborate on the subject. "I'm very close to my grandfather. Sounds like you are close to yours too."

"I was."

"Oh." No father. No grandfather. Better not ask about his mother. "Sorry."

Cedric gave a half-smile. "Thanks."

"Ever been married?"

Cedric shifted in his seat. "Almost, but …" He shrugged.

Not very positive.

"Well, at least you're getting yourself back out there and dating."

Cedric crossed one leg over the other again. "I don't date. I've just been focused on the business."

What did he mean he didn't date? What the heck were they doing in Starbucks? It wasn't considered a date?

"Of course, of course," she said, completely confused. "How come you don't date?"

"Anybody ever tell you that you ask a lot of questions?"

"Yes. I mean … no. Well, sometimes my mouth rambles. Especially when I'm nervous."

Cedric tilted his head to the side. "Why would you be nervous? We're just having coffee."

"Just having …" She shrugged. "It's just that—I don't know. Have you ever tried online dating?"

God, she couldn't believe she just asked that.

"I don't believe in online dating." Cedric stood up. "I'm so sorry. I … just remembered that I have to meet with a customer. God, I can't believe I forgot."

"Oh …"

"I'll walk you back to the library."

She slowly got up. "Okay."

They walked back to the library in silence as Ellie tried to figure out what had happened. They approached the front of the building and the electric door slid open.

Ellie forced a smile. "Thanks for the coffee."

"You're welcome. Well … I guess I'll see you around."

"Okay, see you around."

Whatever that meant.

Chapter Seven

Cedric walked away from what was perhaps the most beautiful woman in the world—and maybe the smartest too. At least his day couldn't get any worse.

Or so he thought.

Cedric watched in the distance as a motorcycle cop placed a ticket on his windshield.

He couldn't even begin to imagine what the ticket could have been for. There was no meter there, he was parked straight, and his registration was up to date.

The cop slid his helmet over his head, strapped the buckle under his chin, swung a leg over his motorcycle, and straddled the bike.

"What's the ticket for?" asked Cedric, approaching him.

"Why don't you read it?" He slipped on his leather gloves.

Nice guy. His voice sounded familiar. He looked down at the badge on his chest.

V. Cunnings. Cedric grabbed the ticket from the windshield and searched for the infraction.

"What?" He walked to the back of his car and saw for himself the broken taillight. "That wasn't broken when I got here, I'm sure of it." He glanced down to the ground at the plastic pieces from the taillight and pointed to them. "Someone just did this."

"Do you have a witness?"

"Of course I don't have a witness. I just walked up. You saw me."

"Well then …" He started the motorcycle. "I can't help you."

"Did you do this?"

Vlad got off of his bike and got in Cedric's face. "You better watch your accusations, if you know what's good for you. I have no problem taking you downtown and throwing you in a cell for a day or two."

Cedric opened his mouth and Vlad held up his index finger. "Don't fuck with me."

Vlad turned back to his bike, swung his leg over it, revved the engine a few times, and took off.

Cedric folded the ticket and tucked it in his pocket. "Unbelievable."

***

"What a jerk!" Ellie paced back and forth in front of her computer screen as Julio listened on the speakerphone.

"Who?" asked Julio.

"Cedric, the guy I had coffee with. Seriously, he deserves to be kicked in the balls."

"Ouch. Not the boys."

Ellie could not believe her eyes as she stared at Cedric's online dating profile. The online dating profile of the man who said he didn't date.

"He lied to me! He has an online dating profile and it says right here he was on the website within the last twenty-four hours. He's dating alright."

"Nothing wrong with that."

"Yeah, but he said he didn't believe in it. How could you not believe in online dating anyway? Online dating exists, so you have to believe in it. You can choose to not *participate* in it. But since it exists, you have to believe. That's like saying I don't believe in the stars or the moon. Well, you know what? Look up in the sky. Do you see what I see?"

"Oh, I love that song. So does Hugo." Julio sang, "Said the night wind to the little lamb …"

"He obviously believes in it because I can see his profile right here on my monitor."

"Do you see what *I* see?"

"I'm pissed."

"Sounds like someone needs another spa day. Me too, I'm way overdue. Do you want me to book it?"

"Oh God, what's wrong with me? I'm a decent person. I'm not unattractive."

"You're scorching hot, and believe me when I tell you, men notice."

"I don't have anything sagging yet. I have a good heart. I do a couple of walk-a-thons every year for a good cause. That's something, isn't it?"

"Definitely a spa day is needed. I'll book it. Day or evening?"

She continued to pace back and forth. "I must be a loser for him to lie to me like that."

"Evening, of course. It would be difficult to get away during the day."

"Are you listening to me?"

"Yes. You're a loser and that's why he lied to you."

She swung around and stared at the speakerphone. "Hey!"

"I'm kidding. I'll tell you what I think. You like him. A lot."

"What are you talking about?"

"Honey, it's as plain as day and it's sweet, but you know what? The giant woman with the mustache at the opera hasn't sung yet. You have nothing to worry about. You're smart and sexy and he'll be back. And when he comes back, just say no."

"No?"

"Trust me. No. That will make him want you even more."

"Maybe I don't want him to want me."

"Yes you do. What's Mr. Cedric's last name?"

"Johnson. Why?"

Julio didn't answer.

Ellie stared at the phone. "Are you there?"

"I remember him! He came into the library."

"Who?"

"Your lover, Mr. Cedric Johnson."

"He's not my lover. And what did you do, Google him?"

"Of course I did, and I must say, he is de-li-cious. And guess what else?"

"I don't want to know."

"Yes you do."

"Okay, yes I do … just tell me then."

"This Cedric of yours—"

"He's not mine."

"Can I finish?"

Ellie let out a loud breath. "Yes."

"Cedric is quite possibly the most generous person I almost know."

"I'm trying to hate him and you're not helping. What did he do?"

"He has a cherry farm in Gilroy."

"I already knew that. He also sells garlic."

"Yes, but back to the cherry farm. Did you know one hundred percent of the proceeds from the cherry sales go to a program he created called 'Cherries for Children?'"

"Okay. No, I didn't know that."

Great. The lying bastard was a kind man.

"Listen to this … every year, he picks a different organization to donate the proceeds to. Big Brothers, Big Sisters. Make-a-Wish Foundation. March of Dimes. Hey! Maybe you should start your own charity … March of Ellie. Then you can use the money to get your promotion."

"Not going to happen."

"And guess how much he donates."

Ellie let out another big breath. "Ten thousand."

"Not even close."

"One hundred and twenty-eight thousand dollars. And fifty cents."

"Half a million."

Ellie turned toward the phone. "Five hundred thousand dollars?"

"Does that not make him amazing?"

More than amazing. But Ellie didn't answer.

Julio spouted off some other things about Cedric he found online, and it got her thinking. Who was Cedric Johnson? Okay, so it looked like he had a generous side. That doesn't mean he couldn't have a bad side.

"Did you hear me?" asked Julio.

"What?"

"I said you have to agree the man has some admirable attributes."

"Okay, maybe. But obviously, he's not interested in me."

"Maybe he's the answer to your fundraising problems. You need money. He's got money. It's the perfect fit."

"Not going to happen."

Ellie had never had so many conflicted feelings in her entire life. She just didn't know what to think of Cedric. She liked him. She hated him. But Julio was right; he definitely had some positive qualities.

"He rubbed me the wrong way," she said.

"At least you got a little rubbing in."

Ellie chuckled. Cedric was odd at times. "He's got issues."

"Who doesn't?"

"Yeah, that's what I told him."

Everyone had issues. Ellie knew she wasn't perfect and some might say she was obsessed with the time, but she had her reasons. And what's wrong with being on time?

Nothing.

"You need to ask him for money. A lot of it."

"No! Vlad used money to get whatever he wanted and I hated that. And I'm not going to lead Cedric on. He may just donate because he thinks he can get somewhere with me."

"And if he donated, would he get somewhere with you?"

"No. Yes. I don't know. But I'd feel like a hooker if I did it."

"That could be your new job title! Branch Manager Hooker. It's got a nice ring to it."

Ellie laughed. "We need to hang out more often, Julio."

"I'll be the sister you never had."

"Thanks, I feel better. In fact, I'm going to call Cedric on the online dating thing. Let's see what he has to say."

Chapter Eight

Piccadilly Pete's had the best breakfast on the planet, and when Cedric found something he liked, he put it in a headlock, wrestled it to the ground, and never let go. That's why just about every Wednesday for the last five years, Cedric has eaten a tofu scramble at Pete's. Two hundred and thirty-nine tofu scrambles. Counting today … two hundred and forty.

Pete Vestal, the owner, strolled over toward Cedric and smiled. "Cedric," he said, slapping him on the back and glancing down at his plate. "Everything good today?"

Cedric wiped his mouth and smiled. "You're still batting a thousand."

"That's what I wanna hear. What happened to Tony today?"

"He's running late, I guess."

Pete laughed and slapped Cedric on the back again. "That's a switch!"

"Hey! I'm not late all the time."

"You're right. Ninety percent of the time is not all of the time."

Cedric laughed and pointed to the front door after it swung open.

Pete looked over toward Tony, walking in their direction. "Tell him the new waitress is off limits."

As Pete walked back to the kitchen, Tony slid into the booth across from Cedric. "Hey."

"Hey."

Tony raised the empty coffee cup and waved it in the air at the waitress. He grabbed a packet of sugar and held it in his hand. The waitress arrived with a pot of coffee and poured him a cup.

Tony checked her out from head to toe. "You're new."

She rolled her eyes. "You're obvious."

Tony studied her for a few more moments. "And a personality too. Damn, we're off to a good start."

"Pardon me?"

"You ever heard of those stories where a man meets a woman and knows at that very minute, without a shadow of a doubt, he's going to marry her one day?"

She eyed his bright yellow shirt and brown shorts and smiled. "Listen SpongeBob, Pete warned me about you. He said you try to pick up on anything with boobs. He also said you had a small package and always complain about a burning sensation when you pee." She burned a hole into both of Tony's eyes as Cedric laughed. "Now, will you be eating something today or just dreaming?"

Tony smiled. "You and me. Married. Mark my words."

"I'm going to mark them right now, if you'd just order …"

"Stack of pancakes, but I want them burnt."

The waitress raised an eyebrow and wrote the order. "Pancakes … well done."

"No. Not well done. *Burn* them."

"I don't get it."

"I mean, burn the pancakes … as in 'we should probably throw those away unless we can find some sucker who wants to eat them.' I'm that sucker."

She looked over to Cedric.

Cedric shrugged. "He thinks he got salmonella poisoning from undercooked pancakes. Just go with it."

"As you wish."

Tony smiled and watched the waitress walk away. "God." His eyes traveled from her head down to her feet again. "So nice …"

"I was told to tell you that she's off limits."

"What? Pete said that?"

Cedric nodded.

"I shouldn't be surprised considering the lies he told her. I don't have a burning sensation when I pee. It's more like a throbbing—"

"I'm eating."

Tony glanced over toward Pete who wagged his finger at him. "That's just not right. I've got a lot to offer her."

"Sure you do. And if you tell me how many inches, I'm going to switch tables."

Cedric watched Tony as he tore the sugar packet and added it to his coffee.

"No, this is different. There's something about her."

"*Any*way, obviously you got my message." Cedric was doing his best to change the subject.

Tony stirred his coffee. "Yeah. Tell me about Mr. Chronic Fainter."

"Tofu found him during my morning jog. I thought he was dead." Cedric stared at Tony, thought for a moment, and then decided to tell him. "I had another dream too."

"Oh God. Don't tell me."

"This one was different."

"Right. Were you going to die?"

"Yes, but—"

"It's the same thing. Jesus, I told you before, it's a sign."

"I don't believe in that."

"You're possessed by demons."

"That again."

"I'm serious, cock sprocket."

"Asswipe."

"Dipshit."

"Nutsack." Cedric was completely satisfied with his brotherly verbal exchange with Tony, ready to move on. "By the way, I haven't heard from the Tax Collector yet, but I did do some research online and found out the county has switched to an online auction for seized properties. *And* I saw Papa George's place on the list of upcoming auctions!"

"Very cool. Just make sure you have a backup."

"What do you mean?"

"I mean, you need to have a backup laptop and a backup wireless Internet source. I know how important this is to you. Imagine you're bidding back and forth with someone and your computer crashes or you lose your Internet. That would suck donkey dick."

"Crap, I didn't think of that."

"That's why you pay me the big bucks. I have a better idea. I'll be there with you with my laptop as the backup. I need the details ahead of time … day, time, website, item number, everything. Do you need to make a secure online payment?"

"No. They only take cash or cashier's check within a certain timeframe."

"Good. Hang on, here comes the bride."

The waitress returned, squared her shoulders, and stared Tony down. "The cook refuses to burn your pancakes. He doesn't want to jeopardize the integrity and reputation of this establishment by delivering an inferior product."

"An inferior—"

"Do you want them the way normal people eat them?"

Tony smiled. "First of all, what's your name?"

The waitress hesitated and then spoke. "Maria."

Tony stared at the waitress for the moment. "Of course."

She placed her hands on her hips and tilted her head slightly. "What?"

"You had to be Maria. Look at us. I'm Tony and you're Maria, and *we* are Tony and Maria. Like from *West Side Story.* That's romantic!"

Maria sighed. "Tony died a bloody death in *West Side Story.* You think that's romantic?"

"Yes! They shared something special before he was shot. I want to be like him; I want to die in your arms."

"Ignore him," said Cedric. "I do."

Maria studied Tony. "Are you going to stalk me?"

Tony slapped the table with the palm of his hand. "This woman is a firecracker. And I love the way that apron wraps around her waist. I wish I was that apron."

"You do realize that I can hear you?"

Tony laughed. "Oh man! See what you do to me?"

"Sorry." Cedric gestured to Tony. "He doesn't get out much. He'll be better once the sedatives kick in."

"You going to answer my question anytime soon?" asked Maria.

"Sorry," said Tony. "I was obviously distracted. What was the question again?"

"I asked you if you wanted your pancakes the way the other seven billion people in the world eat them."

Tony looked over toward the kitchen at the cook, who was staring back at him. "Fine. But if I die …"

Cedric watched Maria walked away. "You seriously think you're going to get somewhere with her? You fall in love every other week. What's different about this one?"

"My hard-on feels different than the ones in the past. That's the difference."

"Please don't elaborate."

"What's the problem?"

"You've known that woman less than five minutes and she already hates you. She's not putting in your order now. She's probably online searching where to buy pepper spray."

Tony nodded. "Maybe so, but at least I'm trying. That's more than I can say for you."

Cedric took a sip of his coffee and stared out the window. "Let's not talk about it."

"I think we should."

"Man, you're like one of those surprise birthday candles that doesn't go out."

"You saying you want to blow me?"

"I'm saying—" Cedric looked at Tony who had his arms crossed, waiting. "Okay, I met a woman. Her name is Ellie."

"Now we're getting somewhere! Where did you meet her?"

"On the street corner."

"A hooker?"

Cedric blinked twice. "You see? You can't be serious for even a minute."

"Can too. Okay, tell me about her. What's she like?"

Cedric sighed. "She's cool, she's mysterious, she's spunky, she's intelligent, and she's beautiful. Other than that, she's no big deal."

"More importantly, when are you going out?"

"We kind of already went out, sort of. We had coffee at Starbucks. One moment we were talking about her co-worker's birthday and the next, she was desperate to find out what material my shirt was made of." He took a bite of his food and thought about her. "It was the weirdest thing. She's crazy, that's got to be it. But I can't get her out of my mind, so that makes me crazy too, right?"

"I don't see what the problem is."

"The problem is …" Cedric sighed. "I'm an idiot."

"No."

Cedric nodded.

"You shut her down?"

"Yeah, pretty much."

"Damn. You need to quit doing that, it's time to move on."

"I've been telling myself that for a while now. Hopefully one day I'll listen."

***

Cedric was looking forward to his volunteer training at the library. He'd had his background check and fingerprinting completed and was ready for the next step. The more he thought about it, the more excited he got.

Cedric had fond memories of his mother reading to him and he knew how important it was for children. He loved so many of the classics: *Cat in the Hat, James and the Giant Peach, Green Eggs and Ham, Charlie and the Chocolate Factory, Charlotte's Web*, and hundreds more. He just couldn't get enough and was thrilled he was able to contribute to these kids' lives and be a positive role model.

He was running five minutes late, so he'd have to wait to apologize to Ellie. His first training session was simply to watch Peggy as she read a few short books to a small group of three to five-year-old kids. He snuck into the back of the room, and Peggy acknowledged him with a wink and a smile as he sat down.

Behind Peggy, on the wall, was a poster with a quote from Dr. Seuss that said, "The more you read, the more you will know."

Peggy was a sight to see, so full of life and animated as she read *Grumpy Bird* from Jeremy Tankard. She was a natural.

Cedric took a few notes on her style and technique and imagined himself in her place, reading to these kids. He smiled.

"Looks like the Bird has a lot of company on his walk," said Peggy.

"I like the rabbit," said a boy.

Peggy nodded. "Me too. It's good to make friends."

"I like the beaver," said a girl.

"Me too," another girl agreed.

"Animals are very cool." Peggy smiled and turned back to the book. Ten minutes later, she finished reading the book, closed it, and smiled, as the kids clapped with appreciation.

"I hope to see you next week," she said, hugging a few of the kids as they left. She straightened out a few of the chairs and then looked up at Cedric.

"Well?" she said. "What did you think?"

"I definitely could relate. I woke up grumpy this morning." Peggy laughed. "But seriously. You were amazing and the kids loved you."

"Well, I'm sure they're going to love you too."

Peggy filled Cedric in on the next step, which would be watching her during a one-on-one reading session.

"Those are even more special," she said. "You develop a wonderful connection with the child and watch them as they develop an excitement, a passion for reading. Occasionally, I even hear from someone I read to fifteen or twenty years ago, thanking me for the time I spent with them. Some say that early passion for reading helped them in school and got them into college. It's a wonderful feeling."

"I'm sure it is. I can't wait."

After Cedric said goodbye to Peggy, he walked through the library, promising himself he would first—before anything—apologize to Ellie.

He had barely walked a few feet before he spotted her talking to a slim, good-looking man in the Tech Center, an Internet room with fifteen computers. It was the same guy who was a fan of women's two-piece ensembles.

Julio.

He didn't want to talk with Ellie while she was with Julio, so Cedric stopped in the reference section, grabbed a book, and waited. He peered around the corner to get a glimpse of Ellie. Still talking with Julio. They laughed together about something, and he felt a ping of jealousy. Where did that come from? He felt odd. It was as if he were spying on Ellie. Was he in the eighth grade? Soon, Cedric was sizing up Julio. Who was this guy? Did he have a thing for Ellie?

Julio's clothes were impeccable from top to bottom. Shirt tucked in with precision. Pants falling at the perfect length over the shoes. Hair styled and gelled. Not a wrinkle on his clothes or on his face. Obviously he used moisturizer. Waxed eyebrows. Had to be gay. At least Cedric hoped he was.

Ellie and Julio left the Tech Center and were standing in front of the glass door, talking. What were they talking about? Didn't look like they were working.

Cedric moved behind the next rack, closer. He slid a couple of books over to try to see through, but there were books on the other side still blocking his view. He reached through to slide the books out of the way and—

Holy crap.

There they went, crashing to the floor. Fifteen books. Maybe twenty. At least he didn't kill anyone. The good news was, Cedric could now see Ellie and Julio perfectly through the space in the shelf. The bad news was, they could see him too.

Ellie whipped her head around after she heard the books fall.

"What's going on over there?" she asked Julio, pointing to the books on the floor.

Julio turned to look. "I don't know, but someone is going to die. I just organized that section."

"I'll take care of it," she said.

Ellie walked over toward the bookshelf. She saw a pair of green eyes watching her through an opening as she approached. Then the eyes disappeared. Odd. Kids, she thought.

She picked up the books from the floor, put them back on the shelf, and walked around to the other side to tell the kids the library was not a playground.

A man stood against the shelf and was holding a book close to his face. He looked suspicious. There was no possible way he could be reading the book with it so close to his face.

"Can I help you with something?" asked Ellie.

The man turned a few pages of the book before answering. "Not at all, Mate," he said. "Bugger off!"

Bugger off?

"Please be careful. You knocked over some books and it's very difficult to find replacements for some if they get damaged."

"Sorry!" His accent seemed to be getting thicker by the minute.

The man turned his back to Ellie. Her gaze dropped down to his backside and she noticed how well he filled out those jeans.

"Quit mucking around now," said the man. "Chop chop."

Ellie was well aware the man was not British. He had a horrendous accent. Something seemed familiar about him too. She leaned over to try to get a look at his face, but he covered it well with the book. A book she now knew was called: *Knickers in a Twist: A Dictionary of British Slang* by Jonathan Bernstein.

What a jackass.

"So." Ellie was ready to play his game. "You're from England?"

"That's right, mate."

"Nice. I've always wanted to go there. What part are you from?"

"London."

"Of course, it's the first city I would have thought of as well. I hear you Brits are proud of the Southampton Spigot Festival. Have you been?"

"Yes, of course. Who hasn't? It's … it's …" He flipped another page over in the dictionary before answering, "…the bees' knees."

"Oh come on … the bees' knees? Nice try. There's no such thing as the Southampton Spigot Festival. I just made it up. Drop the act and turn around."

The man was quiet for a moment as Ellie stared at his back, waiting.

"Jolly good." He took the book away from his face and dropped it down to his side. Then he slowly turned around.

No. Way.

Cedric.

Chapter Nine

Cedric couldn't comprehend what he had just done. It was like his body and mind were pre-programmed to perform idiotic functions whenever Ellie was in the vicinity, and he'd done it again.

"You going to say something or just stand there?" asked Ellie, her hands on her hips.

She was pissed, but even so, she still looked like an angel.

A very pissed off angel.

"Great," she said. "You've lost the ability to speak."

She wore a turquoise summer dress with spaghetti straps. The dress stopped just above the knees, showing off her smooth olive skin and legs.

"I'm not sure what the problem is. I'm just looking at books."

She stared at the bookshelf in front of them. "In this section here?"

"Yes."

"Hmm. So, were you looking for something in particular in the … Parenting section? Thinking of having a baby soon? That might be difficult since … You. Don't. Date."

Cedric stared at Ellie, unable to form sentences.

"Cat got your tongue?" she asked.

"I …"

"And while we're having this one-sided conversation, let me tell you—I saw your online dating profile. You told me you don't believe in online dating. Explain that one."

"That's impossible. It wasn't me."

"You calling me a liar?"

"No. I'm saying you're mistaken."

"Mistaken?" She turned to leave. "Right."

Cedric went with the first thing that popped in his head. "Go out with me."

She stopped and turned around. "You must be insane. And you're a lying bastard." She looked around the library and then muttered. "Pickles."

"I want to go out with you. On a date."

"First of all, you don't date. Remember? And you think I'm the kind of girl who goes out with a guy like you?"

Cedric shrugged. "Yes." Ellie looked like she wanted to kick him in the balls so he stepped out of reach. "I mean, no. I think you are the kind of girl who would go out with a man who's like me. Kind. Considerate. Not crazy at all. And I wasn't lying, I was just confused. And I'm not a bastard either. Well, technically I am since I don't have a father, but—"

"I must be getting some bad karma. Maybe from something I did in a past life."

Cedric grinned. "Karma is why I met you."

"What is that supposed to mean?"

"Good karma. We had to meet."

"Serendipity?"

Cedric nodded. "I'm John Cusack."

"I will punch you if you tell me I'm Kate Beckinsale."

"You're a hundred times more beautiful than her."

Ellie smiled and then erased it immediately. "Nice try. You lied." She turned again to walk away.

"Yes, I lied," said Cedric. Ellie stopped and turned back. "Not about the dating, though. I lied about having a meeting with a customer when I left Starbucks." He stuck his hands in his pockets. "The truth is, I haven't been letting people into my life. It was a defense mechanism. Self-preservation. So, I apologize for that. I admit, I have a few issues that I'm trying to work through, and you can help me. Go out with me."

"I already have plans."

"I didn't even say when."

"Fine. When?"

"Tomorrow night."

"Busy."

"Saturday."

"Not possible."

"Sunday."

She pretended to think about it. "No can do."

"Monday."

"Root canal."

Cedric cocked his head to the side. "Are you serious?"

"No."

He laughed. "God, I like you even more. Tuesday."

"No can do. You done?"

"Wednesday?"

"You're running out of days. And I need to get back to work. Cheerio." Ellie turned and walked away, leaving Cedric standing there.

Ellie joined Julio in the Tech Center, and they both watched Cedric as he walked out the door.

Julio smiled. "I'll have an order of that with a side of naked."

"You shouldn't be looking. You have Hugo."

"I'm loyal to Hugo one hundred percent. Doesn't mean I can't look and enjoy."

"The guy drives me crazy. The weird thing is, he doesn't date, but he just asked me out."

"No, no, no, sweetie. That's excelente."

Ellie smiled. "I love when you speak Spanish."

"Gracias. So when's the big date?"

"We're not going out."

Julio put his hands on his hips. "Explain."

"Why would I go out with him?"

"Um … because you *want* to. And I saw the way you were eyeballing him as he left. You're definitely attracted to him."

"True. But he's a liar. God, the odd thing is … even though he makes me mad, I still wanted to grab him and kiss him like crazy."

"Not that odd. I had the exact same thoughts."

Six hours later, Ellie was ready to go home to get ready for her next date. The entire day was a blur; she couldn't even recall what she'd done at the library. She had nothing but recurring thoughts of Cedric all day.

Julio approached and smiled. "Another date tonight?"

She nodded. "But I need to get Cedric out of my mind. It wouldn't be fair to Swayze if I was distracted and not fully present."

"Swayze?"

"Please don't start."

"His name is *Swayze?*"

Ellie nodded and frowned. "He was born the same year as the movie *Dirty Dancing* and his mother used to be a professional dancer."

"What is it with your dates and their names?"

"I have no idea." She laughed. "Dick, Buck, and Swayze."

Julio smiled. "Sounds like a gay law firm."

Chapter Ten

Two crappy dates and one crappy non-date with Cedric in one week. It wasn't a very good average, but Ellie was hoping to change that tonight with Swayze. He suggested they meet at Opa, a tasty Greek restaurant on Lincoln Avenue. She loved Greek food and was looking forward to the evening.

Ellie waited outside of the restaurant on the sidewalk—it was crowded inside. She already had blown a thousand dollars she could have had from Grandpa Frank for the library, for her promotion. This was her last shot. Five hundred dollars was still a lot, and the money would be put to good use. Time to get motivated.

Do it for the promotion. Do it for the promotion. Do it for the promotion.

She pulled her phone from her purse. 7:03 p.m. The tardiness rule was in effect, of course. More than five minutes late and she would leave.

No exceptions.

A man approached, looking as if he was searching for someone. She remembered Swayze had dark hair, but was blanking on his other features at the moment.

The man smiled. "Hi."

"Hello," said Ellie, matching his smile. "Are you Swayze?"

He laughed. "Swayze?"

"Okay. Guess not."

"If that was my name, I'd kill myself. In fact, maybe that's why Swayze isn't here. You might want to check the alley behind the restaurant for a body." The man laughed as he walked off.

Great. Another dick.

Thank God that wasn't Swayze. The man had enough grease in his hair to fry ten pounds of potatoes. Ellie checked her phone again. 7:05.

Time to go.

Ellie turned and walked straight into something that smelled very nice.

Cedric grinned. "What are the chances?"

"Pretty good, considering my luck."

"Would we be talking about good luck or bad luck?"

The words "bad luck" were on the tip of Ellie's tongue, but she didn't have the energy to be mean, so she shrugged.

"I'm going to go ahead and guess good luck. You looked like you were waiting for someone."

Ellie avoided eye contact with him and didn't answer.

Cedric frowned and looked sincere. "Got stood up?"

Ellie nodded and was ready to crawl under a rock. Why did she always have to tell the truth?

Cedric shrugged. "His loss."

Sweet. Cedric had something that resembled feelings.

"Technically, he's late. But I've waited long enough."

Cedric studied Ellie for a moment. "What's your cutoff for waiting?

She didn't answer.

"I usually give people twenty minutes," he continued. "I think that's reasonable. I get that cushion from my friends, since I'm notorious for being late."

Those words ended any possibility of the two of them ever hooking up. Tardiness wasn't something she tolerated. Ellie still didn't answer and Cedric just stared at her. His gaze dropped to her mouth.

She wished he wouldn't do that, make that sexy grin. The conflicting feelings set in again. She wanted to run, but she also wanted to know what his kisses were like.

"Well …" Cedric looked at his watch. "I've got five after seven on my watch. So, he was supposed to meet you at what, six-thirty? Thirty-five minutes late?"

If her legs would just start moving, she'd be home in no time.

"Six forty-five?" he continued.

Ellie didn't answer.

"Please don't tell me you were supposed to meet at seven."

Ellie grimaced.

"Seven o'clock? He's five minutes late? God, you're strict. You could get a job working for the North Korean government." Cedric laughed. "A smart girl like you hasn't heard the expression, better late than never?"

"I prefer 'Better three hours too soon, than a minute too late.'"

"Who said that?"

"William Shakespeare. A wise guy like you should know that."

"Well … 'A fool thinks himself to be wise, but a wise man knows himself to be a fool.' Also by Shakespeare."

"So, you admit to being a fool? Good to know." She turned and walked away, not looking back. She needed peace. Comfort. Support.

She pulled her cell phone from her purse and pressed number two on the speed dial.

"Hi, sweetie," answered Grandpa Frank. "How are you?"

"I was contemplating killing someone."

"Does this mean you're coming over?"

He knew her so well. "Can I?"

"Of course. See you soon."

Ellie rang Grandpa Frank's doorbell and waited. What a night. It was bad enough Swayze didn't show. But then running into Cedric was like someone pouring lemon juice on an open wound. She had to remain positive and believe her luck was going to change. But for the moment, she needed a drink and some comforting from her favorite person in the world.

The door opened and Ellie was greeted with that familiar smile and a wonderful hug.

"There's the most beautiful girl in the world," said Grandpa Frank. "Come in."

They went to the kitchen and he grabbed the lemonade from the fridge.

"I think I need something stronger."

Grandpa Frank laughed. "You're in luck, I have an open bottle of cabernet."

"Great."

He poured two glasses of wine and they retreated to the living room. Ellie sat down on the couch, let out a deep breath, and took a sip of her wine.

Grandpa Frank grabbed his checkbook from the bookshelf and opened it. "Okay, first things first … where are we with the challenge?"

Ellie didn't answer.

Grandpa Frank looked up from his checkbook. "You must have at least gone on a second date with one of them."

Ellie took another sip of her wine. "Technically, the third guy didn't show up so I get to have a replacement date."

"Didn't show up? Or you wouldn't wait for more than five minutes?"

Ellie smiled. "How am I supposed to defend myself when you know me so well?"

He laughed as Ellie pulled the list from her purse and stared at it. "Do you think I'm too picky?"

"Maybe a tad. I think you can meet someone without the list."

Ellie laughed. "Coincidentally, I did meet someone who didn't match much on the list, and I can't get him out of my head."

"You see!"

"I keep running into him everywhere, but he said he doesn't date."

"Well, give it time. You never know what life has in store for you." He stared at the list. "I'd be happy to tear that up for you."

"Not yet. I'm going to try one more date with it. If nothing comes of it, I promise I will burn the list and try the Grandpa Frank approach."

Grandpa Frank smiled. "That's my girl."

***

"What are you wearing?" asked Tony, before Cedric could say hello.

Cedric stretched and switched the phone to his other ear. "Are you seriously asking me that?"

"You know I love black."

"If you tell me you're naked, I'm hanging up. What time is it?"

"Hammer time."

"Oh God."

Cedric was pretty certain Tony's mission in life was to drive him crazy, not to mention wake him up in the morning as many times as possible. Cedric made a mental note to start turning his phone off at night.

He sat up in the bed and dropped his foot to the floor to scratch Tofu on his side. "Did you have a reason for calling or was it just to annoy me?"

"Two things. One, the Tax Collector is on vacation. That's good and bad. Good because he's not going to sell the property until he gets back. And bad, since you can't talk to him until he gets back. So, you just have to have patience."

"Patience is my middle name. So, what was the second reason for calling?"

"I'm in a donut mood and was going to pick one up before I meet you. You want one?"

"Chocolate old fashioned."

"Okay, you got it."

Tofu turned completely over on his back and extended his legs into the air.

Cedric laughed and rubbed him again with his foot. "I want to be a dog. Tofu has a good life, don't you boy?"

"You just want to be a dog so you can lick your own balls."

"Can we have just one conversation where you don't talk about private parts or sex?"

"You need to get laid."

"I'm hanging up now. See you soon."

Saturday mornings meant the farmers' market for Cedric in downtown Willow Glen. Compared to his regular customers online, he didn't make a lot of money there, but he loved being around the people. So did Tony, who was always there with Cedric.

Tony took one end of the banner and unrolled it with Cedric. They attached it to the two canopy poles with large clips. It was a bright green banner with images of garlic and white letters that said: *Papa George's Heirloom Garlic.*

Cedric stared up at the banner, deep in thought.

"You remembered."

Cedric nodded.

It was the anniversary of Papa George's death. Some of Cedric's fondest memories as a child were of him attached to his grandfather's hip at the farm and at the flea markets as Papa George sold garlic to just about everyone who came by.

"You were the youngest salesman in history."

Cedric smiled. When Cedric was five years old, Papa George allowed him to hand the bag of garlic to the customers. Not too long after that, he got to give them their change. At the age of ten, Cedric was pretty much running the show, stocking the display, taking money and giving change, and thanking customers as Papa George sat back, smiling proudly, reading the paper, doing crossword puzzles, and occasionally napping.

"I couldn't wait for each Saturday to arrive. It didn't seem like a job to me."

"Does it now?"

"No, but it was special back then. I do it today, in his memory. That's why I want to get that farm back and make a garlic museum there. It's the right thing to do, plus it's what my mom wanted."

"It's going to happen."

"I hope so."

When Papa George died, Cedric was crushed. Papa George left the business and his farm in Gilroy—everything—to Cedric. It was difficult at first for Cedric to focus on work. He would sometimes get caught up in the busy day of selling, then by habit turn around to see the smile on his grandfather's face, only to realize again that he wasn't there anymore.

"A lot has changed since then," said Tony.

"Yeah, but I think he'd be proud of what we've accomplished.

"Absolutely."

Cedric made sure there was no way he would ever forget his grandfather, so he added a caricature of him to the company logo, website, and marketing materials. He was an amazing man with a passion for garlic and he loved sharing it with people.

Tony grabbed a crate from the back of the truck, and set it on the table. He pulled off the top, exposing the baskets of fresh garlic. He pulled the baskets out, one by one, and placed them on the table.

A woman approached the booth, wearing a tie-dyed Bob Marley shirt and a giant triple-loop nose ring that hung underneath her nostrils.

She stared at the garlic and smiled. "They look good. How much?"

"Six dollars for a basket," said Cedric. "We'll be open in just a few minutes, if you don't mind." He smiled back at her.

Tony leaned into Cedric. "She likes you, man. Did you see that smile she gave you?"

"I'm pretty sure she was smiling at the garlic."

Tony stacked more garlic and continued to speak, but Cedric mentally blocked him out. All he could think about was Ellie. He couldn't get her out of his mind. Her smile. Her feistiness. As Cedric picked up a garlic bulb he dropped, he looked over toward the next aisle, and there in front of a table of organic jam was a woman with her back to him. He had a strange feeling about her. She had wavy brown hair.

Everything about her—including the green skirt—reminded him of Ellie. "No way."

Tony looked around. "What?"

"Nothing. Start selling, I'll be right back."

Cedric walked over toward Ellie, trying to figure out what he would say when he got there. Apologize again, that would be first thing.

Don't be an idiot. Remain calm.

His heartbeat accelerated as he approached her from behind. He tapped her on her shoulder and smiled. "Hey."

She turned around. "Hi."

The woman wasn't Ellie. Not even close. She was at least fifty years old and missing a bottom tooth.

"Sorry. I thought you were someone else."

"That's okay. I get that all the time. People think I look like Julia Roberts."

More like Julia Child.

Cedric turned to walk back and saw Tony grinning as he approached.

"Going for the older women now, are we?" Tony asked. "What's going on?"

"I thought she was someone else."

"Ellie?"

Cedric didn't answer. He started pulling cherries from the other crates and placed the baskets on the table. He straightened the sign that said: *Cherries for Children. 100 percent of the proceeds go back into our community.*

"We can play this game as long as you want," said Tony. "I have stamina and you know I'm right."

A man smelled a bulb of garlic and turned to walk away.

"Impossible that you don't like them," said Cedric.

The man stopped and turned around. "I know I'll like them. Some other day, perhaps. I only have enough money for the apricot jam I need to pick up for the Mrs."

Cedric smiled and threw the man a bulb. "This is on the house. Come back and see me again."

"Definitely. Thanks." The man smiled as if he'd won the lottery.

"I thought you were going to stop doing that," Tony said.

"There are worse habits to have."

An older man approached and Cedric waved. "Hey, Joe."

"Cedric. How's the kindest man I know?"

"Maybe I should be asking you that." Cedric handed him a basket of cherries.

"You'll be blessed beyond your wildest dreams."

"I already am."

Tony watched the man walk away with the free cherries and sighed. "Okay, I'm going to pretend I didn't see that. You could be missing the opportunity of a lifetime with Ellie. Why don't you give her a chance?"

"Let's not talk about her anymore. I don't want to … never mind"

"What?"

"Nothing."

"Tell me."

Cedric knew Tony wouldn't stop pestering him so he decided to tell him. "Okay. Remember that woman I met at the meet-up for vegetarians?"

"Of course. You said you liked her yams."

"No. *You* said that."

"Yeah, okay." Tony nodded. "Maybe I did. Anyway—"

"Anyway … after I told you I met her, she never came to the meet-up again."

"So."

"The same thing happened with the woman who owned the jewelry shop. I told you about her and then she sold the place and moved to Alaska."

Tony put his hands on his hips. "So, you're saying that I'm jinxing you, is that it?"

"I'm just saying—hell, I don't know what I'm saying."

"Call her," says Tony. "Quit being a pussy."

"I don't have her number."

"Where does she work?"

"The library."

Tony stared at Cedric in disbelief. "God no. Please don't tell me she's a librarian."

"Okay. I won't."

"With sexy librarian glasses?"

"She doesn't wear glasses."

"It doesn't matter. Get your ass down there and bang her. I'll cover for you."

"That's not what I want."

"Have you turned gay on me? That's every heterosexual man's dream … a quiet librarian by day, sexy nymphomaniac by night. She sets her glasses on the bedside table, lets her hair down, and BAM! Time to get busy."

"I told you, she doesn't wear glasses. Plus, she's not like that. And you are the reason why women think we only have sex on the brains."

"If you don't go down there, I will."

"Calm down, I'm going there this afternoon."

Cedric had another training session today, a one-on-one session with a boy. He was looking forward to it, but just the thought of seeing Ellie again made his hands sweat.

"Great. But take it slow and don't worry so much. If by chance it doesn't work out with her, I've already put Plan B in place for you."

"What are you talking about?"

"You'll see."

"Tell me."

"Okay, I didn't want to tell you yet, but … I signed you up for online dating last week."

Cedric froze. "Seriously?"

"Man, you're popular. You have a boatload of women who want to meet you. I've been communicating with them. Two or three hours a night. It's fun."

"You're pretending to be me?"

"Consider me your agent or the middleman. I'm pre-screening them for you … then you can take over."

Cedric took a moment to mull things over. Now it made complete sense. That's why Ellie acted that way in the library. She saw his profile online and thought he was dating. No wonder she was pissed off. Cedric paced back and forth, thinking about what Tony did. How could he? He didn't even ask.

"You screwed me over on this one," said Cedric.

"What are you talking about? This is a step in the right direction."

"No. This is a step into Hell. One of the reasons why Ellie is pissed at me is I told her I didn't date. I also told her I didn't believe in online dating. I couldn't understand why she said I was lying and was so adamant about it. Now I understand, she saw my profile. She called me a lying bastard, because of you."

Tony ran his fingers through his hair and let out a breath. "Shit. Sorry."

"Take me off of the website. Now."

Cedric watched as Tony pulled his phone from his jacket pocket. He sat on the tailgate of the truck with his head down, working on his phone. Cedric helped a customer who bought three baskets of cherries and placed three new baskets in their place.

"Okay," said Tony. "I deleted your profile."

Cedric didn't say anything.

"Sorry. You know I only had the best intentions."

"I know."

"Just tell Ellie what I did. Or better yet, I can."

"No. I'll figure out something."

"You like her a lot?"

Cedric nodded.

"Well, then don't give up."

He wasn't going to give up yet. He just hoped she hadn't already done so.

Chapter Eleven

"This is disgusting." Ellie sprayed the self-checkout machine with cleaner and wiped it down with a handful of paper towels. "It just seems like common sense to me that you don't put your drink on top of a machine while you're using it. Or even when you're not using it!"

"Since when do teenagers have common sense?" asked Julio.

Ellie nodded. "Good point."

"Speaking of common sense, I think it's time you threw away your list."

Ellie let out a deep breath. "Believe me, I've been very close to doing just that."

Her dates with "The Dick" and "The Buck" were a disaster. Maybe it was a good thing Swayze never showed.

Then there was Cedric Johnson. Mr. I Don't Date. Mr. Incredibly Kind and Generous.

Cedric was driving her crazy and he wasn't even there.

Pickles!

Her heart skipped a beat watching Cedric through the window as he approached the entrance.

Ellie grabbed the spray bottle and paper towels and plugged the machine back into the outlet. "I'll be back. "

"Looks like your lover boy is here."

"He's not my lover boy. What is he doing here?"

"Volunteering, of course."

Ellie swung around to face Julio. "What?"

"You didn't know?"

Hell no, she didn't know.

Julio smiled. "He's sweet, isn't he?"

"Like sugar. Gotta run." She turned and—

"Ellie!" Peggy said, stopping her in her tracks. She glanced over Ellie's shoulders and smiled. "And Cedric!"

Ellie turned around and tried to avoid eye contact with Cedric. She pretended to inspect the spray bottle. Good quality plastic, that's for sure.

"You two have met, already, right?" asked Peggy.

"Yes, we have," said Cedric. "Nice to see you again, Ellie." He held out his hand.

Nice trick. Now they have to touch and her girly parts were going to twitch.

"Nice to see you again too." Ellie shook his hand.

Twitch. Twitch. Twitch.

Damn.

Julio held out his hand. "We haven't officially met. Although I did talk with you when you came in the other day. I'm Julio."

Cedric shook his hand. "Nice to meet you."

Ellie was pretty sure some part of Julio was twitching too.

"I need to run to a meeting with the event director at the San Jose Museum of Art," said Peggy. "I'll try to check in on you later." She turned to Cedric. "If you have any questions, ask Ellie. She knows the reading program better than anyone. She created it."

Cedric's eyes widened, a smile forming on his lips. "I'm impressed."

Peggy nodded. "You probably don't know this, but we had an amazing children's area, but there was a break-in recently and hundreds of books were destroyed and vandalized."

"What a shame."

"It is. We have a fundraiser in a couple of weeks and hope to raise enough money to replace the books. Maybe you can attend?"

"Sounds great."

"You are the best! Isn't he something, Ellie?"

Peggy winked at Ellie. What was she up to?

Ellie forced a smile. "He certainly is."

"Do you have *The Very Hungry Caterpillar?*" asked Cedric. "It's one of my favorites."

Ellie felt a flutter in her belly. "I love that book."

"Sounds like I won't have to worry about you two," said Peggy. "You're the perfect match!"

Did she just say that? Someone needed to wipe that grin off of Cedric's face.

A few minutes later, Ellie and Cedric sat on two small stools directly across from Jose, who was happily sitting on a Kermit the Frog pillow; his legs were crossed and his hands folded neatly on his lap. Ellie smiled at Jose and noticed his eyes were bright and wide open as he rocked back and forth. Must be in eager anticipation of the reading, Ellie thought. This was clearly a child who loved stories and couldn't wait to get started.

"I love books," said Jose.

"That's what I heard," said Ellie. "Are you ready, then?"

"Yes please."

"Great, let's get started."

As Ellie opened *The Very Hungry Caterpillar*, she couldn't help but notice the clean, refreshing smell drifting over from Cedric, kind of like that white tea and jasmine body wash she used to use. She wanted to lean in for a closer whiff, but knew it wouldn't have been appropriate.

She read for a few minutes from the book, and then paused to ask Jose a question or two. Interaction was key to get a child's imagination going.

"The caterpillar sounds hungry, doesn't he?" asked Ellie.

"Yeah. Maybe he wants a hot dog with ketchup and mustard."

"Maybe he does."

"Or mac & cheese. I like mac & cheese."

"Do you?"

Jose nodded.

"So do I," said Cedric.

Ellie did a double take at Cedric.

"Or a cookie," said Jose.

"Sure," said Ellie. "A cookie is possible too."

"His mommy can give him a cookie, but he has to be a good caterpillar."

"Of course he does. Well, let's see what he finds." Ellie went back to the place she marked in the book and continued reading.

"Where do baby caterpillars come from?" asked Jose.

Great.

Ellie was not prepared to talk about the birds and the bees, let alone the reproductive processes of butterflies. Especially in front of Cedric.

Ellie smiled at Jose and then looked at Cedric. She knew the answer, of course, but didn't want to get into it. Maybe she could just continue with the story and Jose would forget about it.

"They come from butterfly eggs," said Cedric as Ellie's mouth hung open. "The butterfly lays the eggs on the bottom side of leaves so they don't get wet from the rain. They're very smart."

Where the heck did Cedric get *that* from? What else was he hiding?

"Are butterfly eggs like Easter eggs?" asked Jose.

Ellie turned to Cedric to see if he was going to respond to that one as well.

Good luck!

"No," answered Cedric. "Easter eggs are a lot bigger and much more colorful. But they do have something in common. Do you know what it is?"

"No," said Jose.

Neither did Ellie.

"Butterflies like to lay their eggs in March and April. And that's when Easter is."

Jose's eyes opened wide. So did Ellie's.

Very impressive. Cedric was good with children too. She pictured him as a father and had a feeling he'd be a great one. He was kind and sincere and down to earth.

Pickles!

Ellie applied the brakes on her positive thoughts about Cedric. He was a liar and she had to think with her head, not her—

"Is he your boyfriend?" asked Jose.

"Not yet," answered Cedric, grinning.

Ellie shifted in her chair. She felt her body temperature rising.

"Do you like to kiss?" asked Jose.

"Absolutely." Cedric bent down to high-five Jose. "Do you know the world record for the longest kiss?"

"Okay!" Ellie's hands flew in the air. "That's enough questions for now. Let's see what the caterpillar does next."

Twenty minutes later Ellie and Cedric said goodbye to Jose. Ellie moved the two stools against the wall and placed the book on the shelf.

Ellie tried to act professional and pretend there was nothing happening between her and Cedric. "So, do you have any questions about anything?" She stood there anxiously, tapping her fingers on the side of her leg, waiting for an answer.

Cedric smiled. He was getting to know Ellie well. She had a lot of cute nervous habits. His favorite was probably the one she was doing at the moment…that finger-dance on the side of her leg. Very cute.

Crap.

He just realized he'd been staring at her thighs for the last twenty seconds or so. Ellie's finger-dancing on her leg stopped, and Cedric slowly lifted his gaze to her eyes. She did not look happy.

Busted. Again.

Cedric scratched the side of his face and shrugged. He wondered if his nervous habits were as obvious as hers. He wanted to apologize to her for his random acts of stupidity whenever she was within a fifty-mile radius. He opened his mouth, hoping a few sensible words would come out.

"Ellie …"

Well, okay, one word. That was a start. Ellie held up her hand to stop Cedric, as if she knew what he was going to say.

"Cedric, let's not get distracted here."

He stared at her lips. "I …"

"In fact, can you email me your—"

Cedric kissed her.

And it was the most amazing kiss.

Then Peggy walked in and Ellie slapped Cedric.

Crap.

"Oh," said Peggy. "I—"

"I'm very sorry," said Cedric. "I shouldn't have done that. I'll go now."

As Cedric left the library, he caressed the side of his face and smiled. He'd gladly take another ten of those slaps for just one more kiss from Ellie.

Chapter Twelve

"He kissed me in the library!" said Ellie. "That's my place of work and it's completely inappropriate." Ellie forked some noodles on her plate. "I'm up for the biggest promotion of my life and if that kiss has repercussions, I'll kill him with my bare hands."

Grandpa Frank laughed. "You're not overreacting a bit?"

"You don't go kissing people in their place of work."

"Well, I don't know about that. Things happen in the moment of passion and sometimes you just can't help yourself. I kissed your grandma in the malt shop … a few times."

Ellie stopped chewing.

"Don't look so surprised. I wasn't a prude, you know."

"I know, but …"

"Is it about the promotion? Or is it something else?"

Grandpa Frank knew her so well.

No. It wasn't about the promotion, now that she'd thought about it.

The real issue was … she enjoyed the kiss, and she didn't want it to stop. That scared her, because she still wasn't sure about who he was. She was attracted to Cedric that was for sure. He was witty and charming, but she had a lot of unanswered questions and doubts about him.

Ellie smiled. "Have I ever told you that you're a wise man?"

"Yes." Grandpa Frank chuckled. "But I don't get tired of hearing it."

"I enjoyed it. The kiss."

Grandpa Frank nodded.

"And I slapped him."

Grandpa Frank grimaced. "Poor guy. I guess this is one of those times where we men don't understand you women. Why would you slap him if you enjoyed the kiss?"

Ellie shrugged and fidgeted with the salt and pepper shakers. "Nervous reaction, I guess."

"Okay …"

"Peggy was standing there too. I wanted her to know it wasn't my idea to kiss and I would never think of doing that in the library."

"Now we're getting somewhere."

"I should pay you for your services. You can become a pro."

"I think you're figuring this out on your own."

"I guess I'm scared."

"Fear is not good. It can paralyze you."

"You're right."

Ellie stared down at Grandpa Frank's plate. He still hadn't taken a bite of his food.

"Speaking of fear, you still haven't touched your food."

He smiled. "Touché."

Grandpa Frank picked at the Mongolian Delight dish he ordered, moving the food around with his fork, like a five-year-old.

"Just try it."

He wrinkled his nose. "How could this not be meat? Looks like meat to me."

Ellie patiently smiled. "It's supposed to look like that. It's made of soy protein."

He played with the food a little more and forked a few pieces of vegetables—along with the meat-looking thing—and stuffed them in his mouth and chewed. He gave no indication of whether he liked it or not. He grabbed another forkful and ate it. Then a little more. And a little more. "It's got to be meat."

"There's a reason the sign on the building says Vela Veggie. This is a vegetarian restaurant. Do you like it? Yes or no?"

He nodded. "Not bad." Then he took another bite. And another. And another.

"For someone who thinks the food is 'not bad' you sure are eating rather quickly."

He smiled. "Okay. I like it."

"You see? You opened yourself up to something new and look at the positive result." She took a bite of her pineapple-fried rice and moaned. "Oh God, I love this stuff."

Grandpa Frank forked another bite into his mouth. "Obviously they add some type of addictive ingredient to the food. That must be illegal. Now I can't stop."

Ellie laughed. "I wish you would use that enthusiasm to meet someone new."

"I'm seventy-five years old, Ellie. There isn't a lot of inventory on the market for me, and most women my age can't keep up with me anyway."

"Well, you may have a point there. But that's because you're a stud, grandpa. You've been walking an hour a day for the last forty years. Before that you used to run. You just need to meet someone younger. Then, they'll be able to keep up with you. Maybe."

"I won't rule it out. Never say never." He ate the last bit of food on his plate. "But I won't hold my breath either."

Ellie stared at his empty plate. "Since you enjoyed the food so much, we are going to celebrate by having dessert."

"Makes sense. We celebrate the food by eating more food."

"Why not?"

Grandpa Frank chuckled. "Where did you meet him? The amazing kisser."

"His name is Cedric and I saved him from being hit by a UPS truck. Then we talked at Starbucks."

"What do you like about him?"

"He's handsome, intelligent, funny, and sweet." Ellie shrugged. "I thought we had a connection ..."

"But?"

"But ... as usual, Dr. Jekyll turned into Mr. Hyde and that was that. He lied to me, basically. He told me he wasn't dating, but I saw his profile on the dating website."

"What did he say when you asked him about it?"

"He denied it, of course."

"Maybe it was just a little white lie. Sometimes people lie to protect others, you know that. I don't think that's so bad."

"I agree. The weird thing was, he was so adamant about not being on the website. If it weren't for the proof I saw, I would have believed him. In fact, he was looking at me like *I* was lying."

"Something sounds odd."

"Yeah." Ellie heard the front door of the restaurant open and was hit with an odd sensation and the need to turn around to see who it was. A man walked by her with flowers toward the open-air kitchen where the chefs were preparing the meals. Something seemed familiar about him. And there was no mistaking a butt of that caliber.

Oh God. Could it be?

The owner of the restaurant looked up and smiled as the man handed her the flowers. They did that cute European-kiss-on-each-cheek thing and followed it up with a hug. That's when Ellie saw his face clearly and froze.

Cedric.

"You okay, sweetie?" asked Grandpa Frank. "You look like you've seen a ghost."

"Uh …" Ellie leaned over and grabbed the wine list that was on the table. She opened it and hid behind it, praying Cedric did not see her.

"Wine? Now? What happened to dessert?"

Ellie spoke in a soft voice. "Shush. The man we were just talking about, the man I slapped, is here and is now talking with the owner of the restaurant behind you."

Grandpa Frank started to turn around.

"Don't you dare move; he'll notice! Okay, okay, this is the worst possible scenario ever. I need to get out of here. We need a distraction. Then I'll run out the door … and possibly just keep running until I hit the border of Mexico."

Grandpa Frank laughed. "What's the big deal if he's here?"

Ellie ignored his question. "Do you have any grenades on you from your army days?"

Grandpa Frank chuckled again. "Of course, I always happen to keep a few in my back pocket, just in case."

"God, if he sees me I will die."

"Why don't you just go and talk to him?"

"Grandpa, he lied to me."

"I understand, sugar, but there must have been a reason. Look at you. The last time I saw you this worked up was when that singer announced he was gay." Grandpa Frank scratched the side of his face, thinking. "What was his name?"

"It doesn't matter. And I wasn't worked up."

"You tore his posters off of your wall and said you'd never love again."

"I was fifteen. Please focus, Grandpa, I'm in crisis mode here."

"How about if I focus on the dessert menu? Maybe you should focus on it too and pick something."

She peeked over the wine menu and watched as Cedric and the woman smiled and laughed, occasionally touching one another on the arm or shoulder.

Cedric walked toward Ellie.

Ellie kept her entire head hidden behind the wine menu as Cedric walked in her direction toward the door. Her menu was shaking in her hands, and she had the urge to throw up into it.

She could feel heat from a human being right next to her face, and there was the sweet smell of a man's cologne in the air. Tommy? Armani? Whatever it was, it made her temperature rise.

She was about to drop her menu, when she heard his sexy voice.

"When you're done hiding behind the wine menu and I've left the restaurant, I highly recommend trying a glass of the Horse's Ass from Sonoma County. You'll probably agree they named it after me. But also like me, it's very good … if you give it a chance."

Ellie heard the door open, the noise from the street, then the door closing.

Grandpa Frank laughed as Ellie kept the menu held up against her face.

She whispered, "Is he gone?"

"Yes," said Grandpa Frank, still chuckling. "He's gone."

Ellie lowered the menu and let out a loud breath. "What was that about?"

Grandpa Frank smiled. "That was a gentleman, in my opinion. Apologizing in his own unique way."

***

What a pleasant surprise for Cedric, seeing Ellie. She was lovelier than ever, and he was pleased with the way he handled himself. He'd apologized and would do so again the next time he saw her, maybe even follow that up with a gift. As he walked to his car, he felt good about his progress. More and more, he was ready to allow a woman into his life, and he wanted that woman to be Ellie. This time, he hadn't acted like a fool.

Cedric's smile disappeared when he spotted the ticket on his windshield.

"Not again …"

He pulled the ticket from his windshield and looked for today's infraction.

"What?"

He did a double take and read it again. "Expired registration. No way in hell."

Cedric's registration didn't expire for another six months, he was sure of it. He walked to the back of the car and—

"Come on!"

The registration tag on the plate was from last year. Someone had peeled off the current tag. He'd heard about people stealing the tags and sticking them on their cars so they didn't have to pay for their vehicle registration, but he never thought he'd be the victim of such a theft. He knew it was another easy fix; he just had to pay for a replacement tag.

But still, he didn't like his recent string of bad luck. Hopefully it wasn't going to continue.

Chapter Thirteen

"A slap is not as bad as a kick in the jewels," said Julio. "But I agree with Grandpa Frank. He was definitely apologizing. Looks like you're back in the game!"

"His profile disappeared from the dating website."

Julio smiled. "Looking again, were you?"

Ellie shrugged. "Maybe I just happened to notice."

"Just happen to notice … uh huh."

"Obviously that means he's seeing someone if he removed it. He seemed close to the owner of the Vela Veggie. They were all touchy-feely. Maybe he's seeing her."

She hoped not. She wasn't sure about Cedric but still wanted to keep that option open, just in case.

"Victoria Vela? Not possible."

"Why not?"

"Married."

"You sure?"

"Yes. Her husband is a psychologist. I don't remember his name."

That was good to know, but maybe it was something else.

"Must be having an affair," she said. "I saw them kiss."

"On the lips?"

"No."

"If you saw them in a juicy lip-lock, that would be different. Cheek kisses are innocent." Julio leaned over and kissed Ellie on the cheek and smiled. "See?"

Ellie laughed. "You're not taking this seriously. He's got to be seeing somebody. He's not on the website anymore."

"Here's something you may want to consider. Maybe he's not on the dating website because of you."

"Right."

"You never know."

Ellie took a sip of her wine and thought about Cedric. "Dating should be a lot simpler than this. Like the way my grandpa Frank met my grandma in the malt shop. So sweet."

"Very sweet. Ooh, a malt for dessert sounds even sweeter, don't you think?"

"You be a good boy and you may get a treat. I have a surprise."

"I love surprises."

Ellie studied Julio as he grabbed another slice of pizza. He looked so relaxed on the couch, like this was a regular thing they did.

"This was such a great idea," she said, grabbing another slice of pizza and taking a bite. "We should do this every week."

"And you thought having a gay best friend was a cliché. Ha!" Julio took a sip of his wine, smiled, and touched Ellie on the arm. "Just mention wine and pizza together in the same sentence and I'll come running."

Ellie wasn't sure why she hadn't thought of it before, having Julio over. She was seriously lacking in the friends department, but always enjoyed his company at work. They had a lot in common. They loved the same food, the same wine, the same movies, even the same men. Speaking of which …

"When are you going to see Hugo again?"

Julio let out a sigh. "Not for a few more weeks. He's still in Japan."

Ellie didn't know how he could do it. "That has to be difficult."

"It is, but I know it's temporary. He's going to start his own consulting firm so he can set his own hours and be closer to home."

Ellie rubbed his shoulder. "Well, I guess that means I get to enjoy you even more until that happens!" Ellie smiled and popped the movie into the DVD player. *You've Got Mail.*

"That you do." Julio pointed to the TV. "Just to let you know, I'm a crier."

"Me too!" Ellie wasn't sure why she was so proud of that.

When the movie was over, Ellie and Julio both wiped their eyes and got up to stretch.

"I love when Tom Hanks comes around the corner with his dog and Meg Ryan sees him," said Ellie. "That part gets me every time."

"Me too," said Julio.

"Ben and Jerry's?"

"I think I love you."

"Yeah. I wish."

They laughed and Ellie went into the kitchen to get the ice cream. She came back a couple of minutes later with two big bowls of ice cream and two spoons. "You want to see who I'm going out with tomorrow night?"

"Why are you still on that dating site? Go after Cedric."

"I have to keep my options open, and you know I don't like to flake on people. Do you want to see my date or not?"

"Yes."

"Okay." Ellie grabbed her laptop and set it on the coffee table in front of them. Her mouth was too full of ice cream to speak so she just pointed to the man on the screen. "Be nice."

"That's him?"

She nodded.

Julio leaned forward and frowned. "Okay, this is not going to do. We need larger pictures." He leaned forward and looked at the man. "Not bad, not bad. Although … I'm surprised you don't have something on your list about toupees."

Ellie leaned in for a closer look. "You think that's fake?"

"Honey, his hair comes from a factory … or previously belonged to another person … or an animal. Guaranteed."

"No way, Julio Jose."

"Yes way, Ellie May."

She looked closer. "I don't know, I guess I'll find out tomorrow. Anyway, he seems interesting. He owns an import business, he likes animals …"

"Especially that porcupine that's keeping his head warm."

She laughed. "Stop. Let's not judge him. He does match a lot of the things on my list that I'm looking for. So there."

"Speaking of which…" Julio stuck out his hand "I do need to see this infamous list."

Ellie got up and grabbed it from the end table and handed it to Julio. "Don't laugh."

"I can't promise that." Julio glanced over the list and laughed.

"Hey." Ellie tried to grab the list back.

Julio held it out of her reach. "Damn, girlfriend, I thought I was picky."

"Okay, give me the list."

"Number one … punctuality? I bet if you were to survey a thousand people, no, make that a million people, not one of them would have punctuality as their number one preferred trait in someone they wanted to meet. You have honesty at number two. Honesty *below* punctuality. Something is askew here."

"You know why."

"Yes, I know why, but your tardiness that day was not the reason for your mother's death."

"Yes it was."

Julio held up his hand. "Okay, let's not get into this again."

"I agree." It was something Ellie did not like to discuss, so she was glad he dropped the subject so quickly this time.

"What's the latest on your fundraising?"

"Peggy said she would update me soon, but I think I'm doing pretty well. I've sold forty-five bricks."

"Great!"

Ellie smiled. "Now if I can just make it to a second date tomorrow with Jim. It's my last shot at an extra five hundred from Grandpa Frank. Every bit helps."

"You can do it, girl!" Julio glanced at Ellie's list again. "I do see a problem with a particular item here, though."

"What?"

"You say you want a man with a full head of hair, but you don't specify if the hair has to be real. That, my dear, is a big fat hairy discrepancy."

She lunged forward. "Give me the list!"

The next evening, Ellie was ready for her fourth and final online date. If this date didn't work out, she was going to go home, tear up her list, cancel her membership to the dating website, and become a nun … or a lesbian. Maybe Julio could give her advice on the latter.

Fortunately, Jim seemed like he had the most potential out of all of the men she'd seen online. He was tall, attractive, ran a successful import business, volunteered at church, loved his mother, owned a dog, and matched most of the criteria on her list.

Ellie met Jim at a cute French Restaurant in Mountain View. It was located inside of a converted Victorian home, and it was charming and romantic. The clock on the wall said six thirty on the dot when he walked in the door carrying a bag and some flowers.

Right on time. So far, so good.

He kissed Ellie on the cheek and handed her flowers.

"They're beautiful." Ellie stuck her nose in them. "And they smell so wonderful."

"The grass withers, the flower fades, but the word of our God will stand forever."

Did he just frigging quote the Bible?

Strike one!

She was pretty sure that was the fastest strike she has ever given.

As they were escorted to their table, Ellie couldn't help but notice Jim was carrying a bag. She admired the interior of the restaurant, the beautiful colors, the rattan bistro chairs, tables with cabriole legs, and the carved oak hutches against the wall. She glanced out the window at the fountain on the lawn, with its four small sprouting bronze lion heads. "I love this place. Great choice."

"Bless you, child."

Ellie raised an eyebrow.

"Sorry. Old habits are hard to break."

Ellie had no idea what he was talking about. She shifted her focus to the romantic setting and the good-looking man she had seated before her. He had dark brown wavy hair and wore a charcoal gray tailored Armani suit with an off-white dress shirt and platinum oval mother-of-pearl cuff links. His silky red tie was bold and gave him energy, not that he needed any more. Her eyes drifted back up to his hair. If it was fake, it was good quality.

"I brought a bottle of wine, if you don't mind the waiter opening it."

"That sounds wonderful."

Jim grabbed his bag from the floor, stuck his hand inside, and pulled out a bottle of wine, handing it to the waiter.

The waiter smiled. "You're aware of the corkage fee?"

"Of course," said Jim.

"Great." The waiter opened the bottle.

Ellie shrugged. "Sorry, I don't know much about wine. Even though I do enjoy it, I usually just get whatever the employee at Costco recommends."

"Not a problem. I took the liberty of pre-ordering the tasting menu for both of us when I arrived. I hope you don't mind. We'll get to sample a variety of things from the chef. Should be fun and tasty."

"That sounds wonderful."

She liked that Jim was a take-charge kind of guy and not indecisive like most men she knew. He seemed like a nice guy too, not too many issues. Heck, they've made it this far and he only had one strike against him.

They raised their glasses and Jim smiled. "To life and love."

"Very nice. Cheers." Ellie clinked his glass and raised the glass to her mouth, but Jim obviously wasn't done with his toast.

"Love is patient. Love is kind."

"Ain't that the truth?" Ellie raised her glass again to her mouth.

"It does not envy. It does not boast. It is not proud."

"Why would it be?" She was seriously ready to taste the wine.

"It is not rude. It is not self-seeking."

"Thank God!" Were they in Bible study? Can a girl get a sip?

"It is not easily angered. It keeps no record of wrongs."

Ellie kept no record of anything. She was still trying to find some receipts she needed for this year's taxes. But there might be a record of Jim's death if she couldn't have some wine and food soon. She tried to distract him from continuing. "I'm surprised the food isn't here yet. Where's our waiter?" She pretended to look around, but then lit up when she saw the waiter actually walking their way with appetizers. "Speak of the devil."

Jim raised an eyebrow.

"Sorry."

The waiter set the platter down on the table and pointed to the first two items. "Scallops over puff pastry with saffron and cream cheese, paired with our tortellini with garlic, cream, and porcini mushrooms. Enjoy."

"Oh we will!" Ellie reached for the spoon to serve herself, but before she could get her fingers on it, Jim grabbed her hand.

"First let's pray, Ellie." He bowed his head and closed his eyes.

She had nothing against prayer, but…in the middle of a romantic restaurant?

Strike two!

"Dear Father, Lord Jesus, you are my light, my savior, my love, my life …"

Ellie reluctantly closed her eyes and felt guilty, thinking she hadn't been to church since the sixth grade. Who knows when her last confession was? Maybe this was her punishment.

Payback is a bitch!

"Thank you for bringing us together on this absolutely perfect evening. It never ceases to amaze me, your daily miracles. I know I'm a miracle. Ellie is a miracle too."

Ellie was sure it would be a miracle if they got a chance to sample the food before midnight.

"Please bless this food and use it to nourish our bodies."

I could use some of that nourishment right now, God. I'm starving over here!

She opened her right eye slightly to peek at the platter on the table while Jim continued his mini-sermon. Her stomach growled and she placed her free hand on her stomach, as if such a gesture would actually stop the noise. Nice try, the growling got louder and louder.

"You are the master, the messiah, the mediator, the minister, the messenger …"

She couldn't take it any longer. Ellie opened her eyes and quickly used her free hand to grab one of the puff pastries, jamming it in her mouth. She chewed quietly, but at a good pace. How divine, how delicious. She tried to chew faster since she had a feeling Jim was wrapping up his evening service and would be passing around the collection basket soon.

Just a few more chews, a swallow, and … done.

Wonderful.

And there it was … complete satisfaction. Incredible. That should hold her off for a few more minutes. She smiled and enjoyed the wonderful taste in her mouth.

"In Jesus' name … Amen."

"Amen!" Ellie clinked his glass, took a sip of wine, and piled the food on her plate. At least if things went anymore south from here, she would have been able to enjoy something.

Jim smiled. "You like food, that's good. One day, God willing, you'll be eating for more than one."

She nearly choked. "Yes." She stabbed the next pastry puff with her fork and wondered if this was another guy obsessed with having babies. Was he related to Chuck the Buck?

"I saw in your profile that you were never married, which is great."

"Oh? Why is that?" She wanted him to continue to talk while she stuffed her face.

"I recently realized that marriage was important to me. I quit the priesthood because I found out that I did not want to take a vow of celibacy after all."

She nearly choked again on her food, this time more violently, and had to bang on her own chest to get some of it to go down. "You were a priest?"

"Yes. Are you all right? You're turning red."

"I'm fine." She chewed the rest of the food in her mouth and then drained her glass of wine. "Please continue." She held out her glass, knowing he'd be smart enough to get the hint. He grabbed the bottle of wine and filled her glass.

"I put in a lot of time with my studies. Eight years with the seminary after high school. Then six months as a deacon. Once

I was ordained, I thought I was where I was supposed to be in life. Something was still missing, though. And when the bishop saw me at a weekend retreat looking at a woman's behind after she dropped her pen, it was over. I was never placed with a parish. Everything happens for a reason, and I now believe the reason was … I needed to have a woman in my life. I'm hoping that woman is you, Ellie."

"Wow, that's … amazing." She eyed the tortellini. "Especially after you dedicated so much time." She forked three pieces of tortellini and put them in their proper place. Her mouth. She wanted to eat as much as possible in case she had to make an abrupt exit.

"I was attracted to your profile when I saw your picture, Ellie, but also saw you were never married."

"No. Never." She forked more tortellini fearing strike three was rapidly approaching.

"Never felt the need or never met the right person?"

"Never met the right person."

"Good, good, good. No long term boyfriends either?

"No." She wondered where he was going with this.

He smiled. "Good, good, good. Look, I need to ask you something very important."

Oh God, please no. I have a bad feeling about this. Please don't ask me anything. If you do, it will probably mean strike three. Can't I at least get to the main entree on a date? Can't you see how skinny I am? I want to eat more food.

"Ellie?"

She held her breath. "Yes?"

"Even though I gave up the priesthood, I still have certain values, so I need to know."

"Yes?"

"Are you a virgin?"

Strike three!

"It's nothing to be embarrassed about. But before we proceed any further with things, I hope you won't be offended if I have my doctor check your hymen. You know, just to make sure everything's still intact."

It certainly was a sight to see. Too bad there wasn't anybody there to capture it with a camera; it would have easily made one of the top videos on YouTube.

Wine shot out of Ellie's mouth and nose like a geyser, spraying the table, the food, the flowers, the floor, the curtains, the passing waiter, and Jim's Armani suit.

She grabbed her napkin and jumped up to pat dry his face. "I'm so sorry. I didn't do that on purpose."

"I hope not."

"But if you must know, I'm not a virgin. I'm thirty-one years old and it shouldn't be a surprise to you."

"I was just hoping."

"I'm going to go. I hope you find what you're looking for."

Twenty minutes later, Ellie was at home on the couch in her pajamas with a cup of tea in her hand, thinking about the disaster that was her dating life. She had come to the conclusion she was trying too hard.

Way too hard.

From now on, she wasn't going to force things. Wasn't going to be so picky with that damn list. In fact, she was going to tear it up, but she'd wait and give Grandpa Frank the honor. Maybe this was happening because she was supposed to give Cedric a shot.

Of course. Her thoughts returned to *him*.

Damn him.

Even when she was on dates with other men, she had thought of him occasionally. That had to mean something.

The phone rang and Ellie grabbed it from the coffee table and checked the ID. Grandpa Frank must have ESP; he always knew when she needed to talk.

"Hi, Grandpa."

"Hi, sweetie. Are you doing okay?"

"You knew I needed to talk!"

"… Of course."

"Well, it was another bad date, but it's not the end of the world, right?"

She waited for a response from him.

"Are you there?" she asked.

"Yes. It's just … you didn't check your messages?"

"No. I saw the light blinking, but I wanted to get out of my clothes and … why?

"I'll be right over."

"Okay." She was confused. "See you soon."

Ellie hung up and stared over at the answering machine. Grandpa Frank didn't sound like his normal jovial self. Something was wrong.

She stood and walked over to the answering machine where five messages awaited her. She rarely had messages on her home phone. What was even odder was the first four messages were hang-ups—the person or persons didn't even leave a message. The fifth and final message would explain everything.

"Hi, Ellie, this is Ranger Warren Viders from Yellowstone. I tried calling a few times today, but was unable to reach you live."

Now she knew where the hang-ups were from, but Ellie didn't like the tone of the man's voice. Something happened.

"I feel bad leaving this information on your machine, but you needed to know as soon as possible. Your brother, Derek, ran his car off the road and crashed into a tree."

Oh God. She backed up slowly, leaned against the wall, and stared at the machine.

"And … he didn't make it."

Ellie felt a painful tightness in her throat as a tear fell, landing on her slipper. She slid down the wall until her butt hit the floor, continuing to stare at the machine.

"Derek and I had become good friends over the last couple of years and I'm in shock right now. I can't imagine how you are feeling, and it pains me to call you and tell you this with a message. I left a message for your grandfather as well, since Derek had listed you both as emergency contacts. Please call me when you can so we can make some decisions. I'm so sorry, Ellie."

A minute later, Grandpa Frank entered, his eyes red. "My princess," he said, holding out his arms for her. Ellie jumped up and fell into his embrace, squeezing him, not wanting to let him go.

Chapter Fourteen

It had been four days since "the Slap Heard Around the World." Cedric had left Ellie four messages on her cell phone this week, but she hadn't returned any of his calls. What she didn't know was he wasn't going to give up so easily. He pulled out his cell phone and dialed Michael as he stood in front of the library.

"Hey," said Michael. "I've only got a minute. What's happening?"

"Oh, just staring at the front door of the library."

"Another training?"

"No, not today. I'm here to ask Ellie out."

"Man, you've got some serious balls."

"I'm not giving up. There's something between us. I can feel it."

"And can you still feel that slap?"

Cedric had to admit it was a damn good slap—it was a surprise he didn't have a permanent hand-mark on his face. But he knew the truth and how she felt. "She kissed me back. She leaned into me and enjoyed it just as much as I did. Well, okay, maybe not as much. That was the best kiss of my life."

"Then why did she smack you?"

Cedric had wondered the exact same thing. He'd replayed the scene over and over again in his head. "Good question. I think it has something to do with her boss, who walked in on us during the kiss. Maybe Ellie didn't want Peggy to think she initiated a kiss at work."

"That's a good possibility. Look, I have to run. Stop by for dinner on Sunday and you can fill me in on the latest. Sam and Lucie are coming over and I'm going to fire up the barbecue. Six o'clock."

"Sounds good."

Cedric pocketed his cell and entered the library, looking for Ellie. He stood at the information desk for a moment, tapping his fingers on the counter. A body popped up from underneath the counter and scared the hell out of him.

Julio.

Cedric jumped back. "Whoa, nice trick. Can you also pull a rabbit out of a hat?"

"I'm not sure what you mean. Is that the same as kissing someone between the rabbit ears?"

"Uh …" Cedric was positive that Julio was referring to something sexual, but he didn't want to go there.

"What can I do for you?" asked Julio.

"I just wanted to speak with Ellie for a moment."

"Didn't get enough abuse the last time you saw her?"

Julio knew about the slap.

"Don't look so surprised. Ellie tells me everything."

"Of course. Makes sense."

"Anyway, she's off today."

There goes that plan.

"I thought she worked Wednesday through Saturday."

"Normally, she does, but …"

Cedric waited for Julio to finish the sentence. Maybe he needed help.

"But?"

"I guess I can tell you. Ellie's brother died. The memorial is today."

No wonder she didn't call him back. She had bigger things to deal with.

"God," Cedric mumbled.

It's the most horrible experience a person can have, losing a loved one. He wondered how she was doing and if she had someone to console her. He wanted to be that someone.

"How is she doing?" asked Cedric.

"Not so good. I wish I could be there with her, but someone had to hold down the fort here since she and Peggy are at the memorial."

Cedric looked around the library, deep in thought. "Do you mind telling me where the memorial is being held?"

"At that funeral home in downtown Campbell." He looked at his watch. "I don't remember the name of the place, but it's happening right now."

Cedric smiled. "I know the place. Thanks."

"No worries. Oh, and if you see a tall guy who looks like a cross between Christopher Walken and Brad Pitt, try to avoid him. That's Ellie's ex and he is a world-class loser."

"I know exactly who he is and that's good advice, thanks."

One minute later, Cedric was sitting in his car with the engine idling, contemplating his next move. Stepping inside the funeral home would bring back painful memories. Maybe he could just drop off some flowers and a card—let her know he was thinking about her.

He shook his head. "That's bullshit. It's not enough."

When Cedric's mom and girlfriend died, the cards and flowers from friends and acquaintances came pouring in. Most of them said the same thing: sorry for your loss; she's in heaven now; she's in a much more peaceful place; she's with us in spirit; she's looking down on you right now, smiling. Cedric now knew how they felt. It's an awkward situation and nobody should have to go through it. He wanted to give Ellie more. He wanted to physically be there for her and let her know everything was going to be okay.

"Don't be a pussy. Go."

He had to stop thinking about himself, like Michael had told him. He had to do it for her.

"Let's do this."

Cedric's mind was made up and he felt good about it. He put the car in drive and headed toward Campbell.

He stopped by Citti's Florist and found a beautiful gardenia plant in a rustic flowerpot that transmitted peace and happiness. He was also able to find a nice card to go with it. The closer he got to the funeral home, the better he felt about the decision he'd made.

***

With card and gardenia plant in hand, he stood outside of the funeral home staring at the front door that was open. This was going to be harder than he thought.

"You can do it. Do it for her."

An older woman with white hair stood at the entrance and waved him over. She handed him a memorial card. "Please come in, don't be shy. The service is still going on."

Cedric forced a smile and felt embarrassed. "Okay."

"There's room in the back row, if it makes it any easier. The presence and support of the friends and loved ones is beneficial to those who are mourning."

She's seen a person's hesitation before, obviously. Death was not easy to cope with. There were probably more than a few people who skipped the service and just sent a card in the mail. Cedric had contemplated the same thing in the library. But the woman was right. It would be beneficial to Ellie. The more support the better.

The woman held out her hand and Cedric grabbed it. "I'm Gladys." She led him inside. So sweet and so calm, Cedric instantly felt relaxed.

"Thank you, Gladys, you're very kind. Do you have a pen I can borrow?"

"Of course." Gladys reached into a drawer and grabbed one for him.

"Thanks. I'll get it back to you on the way out."

"Not necessary. Those are handouts."

Cedric smiled and entered the sanctuary, looking around. The room was packed and all eyes were on the slideshow upfront.

He sat in an open seat in the last row and placed the plant on the seat next to him. It was amazing how many people were there, but Ellie was nowhere in sight. The slideshow continued as the guests sniffed and cried. A silly picture appeared on the screen of a man dressed up as a pink pig on Halloween, bringing a few people to laughter.

Cedric filled out the card, occasionally looking up at the slideshow. He finished writing and slid the card in the envelope, just as the slideshow ended. A woman stood and walked toward the podium.

Ellie.

"Hi. I'm Ellie, Derek's little sister."

She looked around the room as she fidgeted with her necklace.

"I don't know what to say today except…" she looked down for a moment, trying to regain her composure "…Derek was an angel."

Cedric recalled being in that exact same spot, trying to find the words to express how he felt about his mom and about his girlfriend. It was the most difficult thing he had to do in his entire life.

Ellie cleared her throat and continued.

"He wasn't like a brother to me. He was more like my best friend. He used to call me almost every day when I was down at UCLA. He knew how hard it was for me to be away from home. If it weren't for him, I probably would have given up. Nobody knew he called me. That's the way he was, such a giving person, and he didn't make a big deal about it. He never expected anything in return, and he never bragged or boasted about anything."

She looked down and sniffled, obviously trying to hold back the tears. Then she smiled.

"Well, unless you count how he used to always say that former President Gerald Ford had been a park ranger at Yellowstone … just like him. I think he may have told me that a thousand times." Many of the guests laughed. "He loved his job. But it was tragic how he died."

More people sniffled and Cedric started to get misty-eyed himself.

"He spent his days protecting the wildlife at Yellowstone, so it was sort of ironic he swerved off the road to avoid hitting a bison and ended up crashing his car into a tree. But he didn't suffer, that's a good thing, and he had a chance to do something he was passionate about."

Ellie wiped her eyes and struggled to get out her last few words. "I'm running out of family members."

Cedric watched as a tall, well-built man rushed to Ellie.

Vlad.

What the hell was he doing here? Vlad put his arm around Ellie as he leaned into the microphone. "Thank you for coming. Please help yourself to refreshments in the next room." He pulled Ellie closer and then kissed her on the top of the head.

Then the unexpected happened. Vlad made eye contact with Cedric in the back row and winked at him. Then he kissed Ellie again.

This time on the lips.

That kiss on the lips was equivalent to someone slamming a sledgehammer into the side of Cedric's head, the energy drained from his body.

Shit. Were they back together? It happened when people were vulnerable, he knew that, but could it be?

Cedric stood to leave, but glanced one more time at Ellie, feeling dejected. He watched as Ellie turned and entered the room behind the podium. Vlad glanced over to Cedric and walked in his direction.

Great.

Getting in Cedric's face, Vlad asked, "What are you doing here?"

Cedric didn't answer. He wasn't dumb enough to start something with a cop—especially one with a chip on his shoulder. Add to that they were inside of a funeral home. Today was about Ellie mourning the death of her brother, and he was going to respect that and take the high road.

Cedric walked past Vlad toward the exit.

"I'm talking to you, asshole." Vlad pushed Cedric in the back, knocking him into a row of chairs before he fell to the floor. Pouncing on Cedric, Vlad put him in a headlock. "Do you know who you're messing with?"

"Yes," said Cedric, trying to break free. "Your name is Vlad and you're Ellie's psychotic ex-boyfriend."

Vlad tightened the grip on Cedric's neck. "Let's see how funny you think you are when you have a broken neck."

"What's going on here?" asked Gladys, covering her mouth with her hand. "This is a place of mourning and you're disrespecting the memory of a loved one."

From his uncomfortable vantage point on the floor, Cedric could see Ellie approaching and she did not look happy. "Are you kidding me? What are you doing?"

"He doesn't belong here," said Vlad.

"And you do?"

"I came to pay my respects to your brother."

"My brother hated you, Vlad."

Vlad unlocked his arms from Cedric's neck and got up. He brushed off his pants and took a step toward Ellie. "Okay, then. I came to support you."

"And this is how you want me to remember the memorial of my dead brother? By wresting like barbarians on the floor? You two should be ashamed of yourselves."

You two?

Not good.

"Please leave. Both of you. Out."

"I love you, Ellie," said Vlad.

"You have a funny way of showing it. Get out."

Vlad brushed off his pants and walked out the door.

Cedric stood up and rubbed his neck. "I'm sorry, Ellie. Let me just straighten this out." He picked up the chairs that were tipped over and grabbed a couple of programs from the floor. He was aware Ellie was watching him, but he didn't look at her. He finally straightened out his shirt. "I'm truly sorry."

Ellie pointed to the door. "Out."

***

Cedric popped inside the gelato shop for a scoop of his favorite Strattiatella. Hopefully that would relax him as he tried to get over what happened at the funeral home.

Ten minutes later, he approached his car and stopped, scratching his chin.

Odd. The car seemed to be tilted lower on one side. He went around to the passenger side of the car and saw what he was hoping not to see. A flat tire.

He checked out the tread on the tire, searching for a nail or screw or something but didn't find it.

"What the …"

Someone slashed his tire.

He looked over at some of the other cars to see if anyone else had slashed tires, but the other cars looked okay.

"Someone's messing with me," Cedric said to himself.

Vlad. It had to be him. Of course he had no proof.

Cedric threw his keys, phone, and wallet inside the car on the passenger seat and removed the spare from the trunk. After he jacked up the car and slid the flat tire off, a convertible Corvette pulled alongside him.

"What a shame," said Vlad from inside the car. The look on his face couldn't have been any cockier. "Looks like someone has a flat. How did *that* happen?"

Cedric didn't respond and continued to change the tire.

"You know I have the power to make your life a living hell."

Cedric continued working.

"Stay away from Ellie." Vlad laughed and took off, his laughter fading in the distance.

What the hell did Ellie see in that guy? One thing was for sure, Vlad had something to do with the flat tire and the tickets.

Cedric finished putting on the spare tire, got back in the car, and rubbed some hand sanitizer on his hands before he noticed that the contents of his wallet had spilled out over the passenger seat. As he retrieved his ID, credit cards, and other various items, he eyed the chronic fainter's business card.

Owen Fitzpatrick.

The thought of tennis popped into his head, but was immediately erased after Cedric saw Owen's occupation. Private Investigator.

Cedric grabbed his phone and dialed Owen's number.

"Owen Fitzpatrick," he answered.

"Owen, it's Cedric Johnson, do you remember me?"

"Cedric! Of course I remember, good to hear from you. You changed your mind about tennis?"

"Yes, and I know it's last minute but I wanted to see if you were available this evening to play."

"I'd love to."

"Great. And just so I don't blindside you with it, I have a … situation. Maybe you can help me with it."

Owen laughed. "Not a problem. I happen to specialize in *situations.*"

Chapter Fifteen

Ellie couldn't believe it: two grown men wrestling on the floor of the funeral home.

"I'm sorry, Ellie," said Gladys. "I should have been paying more attention."

"Don't be silly. There was nothing you could have done. It was just a case of too much testosterone in one place. A simple castration for both of them will take care of the problem."

Gladys laughed. "It's good to see you still have a sense of humor. It helps in times like these, but only one castration is necessary. The man in the black polo shirt was on his way out and didn't instigate it."

Ellie smiled. "Thanks Gladys, that's good to know. Thanks for everything."

"My pleasure."

Ellie should have known Vlad started it. Cedric didn't seem like a violent or unstable person. Odd, maybe, but that was nothing to be worried about.

"My little sunshine." Grandpa Frank approached and kissed Ellie on the cheek. "Don't worry about your brother. He's in a peaceful place now. No stress. No traffic."

"I know. He's with mom and Grandma now. I know he's not suffering, but I certainly am."

"Grieving is normal. Just because we've done it before doesn't make it any easier, does it?"

"No."

He smiled. "Go join everyone in the other room and get something to eat."

She kissed Grandpa Frank on the cheek. "Thanks, I will. You're the best."

Ellie saw the beautiful pot of gardenias on one of the seats in the last row.

"How beautiful." She smelled the gardenias and then opened the small envelope attached to the pot, pulling out the card.

Dear Ellie,

I'm not always the best in expressing myself. No doubt you've heard the expression, "Actions speak louder than words." Well, I did some research at my local library (wink wink) and discovered the number one thing I could do for a person who lost a loved one. Please see the back of my enclosed business card for the answer. And no, it's not a fifty-eight hour kiss! (Although I could easily be talked into it)

Sincerely,

Cedric (the horse's ass with the horrendous British accent)

Ellie pulled the business card from the envelope and read it.

Cedric Johnson. Owner - Papa George's Heirloom Garlic.

She turned the business car over and smiled as she read it out loud.

"This card is good for one free thirty second hug. There is no expiration date. Void where prohibited."

Ellie felt a warm feeling pass through her veins when she read it. That was sweet and so different. She needed that hug badly.

She was surprised when she saw Cedric this afternoon, because it seemed as if he cared. But that fracas with Vlad left a bad taste in her mouth.

She read the card again and smiled when she read the horse's ass part. He was obviously trying to make her smile during a difficult time. Maybe he's not such a bad guy after all. The truth was, even when she was mad at him or confused, she still wanted to kiss him badly. That kiss they shared in the library was off the charts.

Ellie froze when she thought of the kissing, as something horrible popped into her head.

Cedric saw Vlad kiss her. On the lips.

Pickles!

She visited with the guests for an hour and proceeded to clean up, putting paper cups and plates in the garbage can. She admired the flowers and arrangements on the counter. She picked up the gardenias from Cedric and smelled them again. But how did he know she loved them? They seemed to comfort her. She felt peace as tears streamed down her face.

Grandpa Frank entered the room. "Now, now. What's going on in here? It's going to take some time, you know." He put his arm around Ellie and smiled.

Ellie sniffed and wiped her eyes. "You know it's not about Derek. It's Vlad. He won't leave me alone."

"That man was never good enough for you."

"I know that now."

"Just say the word and I'll chop off his nuts and stuff them down his throat. You know I have Mafia connections."

"Sure you do." She cracked a tiny smile and wiped her eyes.

"I used to do Sunday barbecues with the Corleone family."

Ellie grinned and sniffed again. "The Corleone family was fictional."

"Oh." He thought for a moment. "Did I say Corleone? I meant … *Mor*leone. Yeah. Either way, Vlad's testicles are history."

"You always know how to make me smile, but that won't be necessary. He'll get what he deserves."

Grandpa Frank smiled. "Karma?"

"Yeah. Karma is going to bite him in the ass."

"That's my girl. Well, I have a surprise for you."

"What is it?"

"You may want to look up the meaning of 'surprise' in the dictionary. Can you come by the house?"

"Of course."

"Great. See you soon."

Grandpa Frank kissed Ellie and left. Ellie wiped down one of the counters and then picked up the envelope from Cedric again. She pulled out his business card, called the number on it, but it went straight to voicemail.

"Hi, this is Cedric Johnson and you've reached Papa George's Heirloom Garlic. I'm not available at the moment, so please leave a message. Have a great day."

"Hi, Cedric, this is Ellie. I found out you had nothing to do with what happened with Vlad at the funeral home. I'm sorry I kicked you out. Obviously, I'm a bit sensitive and … well, I don't want to ramble on your voicemail. I just wanted to say thanks for the gardenias and the card. That was sweet of you. Can you call me? I want to clear some things up."

Ellie left her number and disconnected, wondering if he would call back. Then she drove to Grandpa Frank's house.

She leaned against the back of the couch in Grandpa Frank's living room waiting for him to return from the bedroom with the surprise he'd mentioned at the memorial. She loved surprises but wasn't exactly in the mood for one at the moment. She knew Grandpa Frank was probably just trying to make her feel better, and she felt grateful to have him in her life. But it would take time to get through what had happened to Derek.

He yelled from the other room. "There's fresh squeezed lemonade in the fridge."

"Thanks." Ellie went to the kitchen.

She poured herself a glass and took a sip before spotting the box on the kitchen table filled with picture frames. She felt some tightness in her chest as she peeked in the box and saw pictures of Grandpa Frank with Grandma Esther. "I don't understand. What are you doing with these?"

Grandpa Frank entered the kitchen with a small wooden box in his hand, carrying it as if something inside was very fragile. "I guess it's time for some changes. I didn't take all of the photos down."

Ellie didn't say anything. She just stood there with a dazed look.

Grandpa Frank rubbed her back. "I know what you're thinking and no, I'm not going to forget your grandmother. She will always be a part of me. I'm just going to replace a few with something more current. Pictures of you, for example."

Ellie pressed her palm to her heart. "You scared me for a moment."

Grandpa Frank rubbed her back. "That was a beautiful memorial. You did well and we'll always have those wonderful memories of your brother."

Ellie nodded and felt her eyes burn. "He was always there for me, the best brother I could ask for." She wiped her eyes. "I hope I was able to show him how much I appreciated him."

"Believe me, he knew. He was always talking about how proud he was of you and how he always heard a smile in your voice when he talked with you on the phone. He loved you so much."

Ellie cried and Grandpa Frank pulled her close. She sniffed a few times, pulled away from him, and let out a nervous laugh as she wiped her eyes. "Good thing I don't wear a lot of makeup or I'd look like a monster right now."

Grandpa Frank chuckled. "Never."

Ellie sorted through a few of the frames and smiled when she saw the old photo of Grandpa Frank's wedding day. "What year did you get married? I can't remember."

Grandpa Frank smiled. "1955. July 17th to be exact. Did you know I almost didn't make it to the wedding?"

"Is this another one of your famous tales?"

He chuckled. "We were living in Anaheim at the time. It was one of the hottest days of the year, around one hundred and ten degrees. Some wise guy had the bright idea of opening a theme park a few blocks from the church.

"Disneyland?"

Grandpa Frank smiled, nodded, and set the wooden box on the table. "It was a big deal and Ronald Reagan was there to introduce Walt Disney to the thousands of people in attendance. The grand opening was the same day as our wedding and the traffic was bumper to bumper. They didn't expect it, obviously. In fact, people were walking faster than the cars. So, that's what I did. I walked to my wedding, in the heat."

Ellie inspected the photo again. "That's why you have tomato cheeks in this photo. How far did you walk?"

"Ten miles."

"Come on."

"Okay, maybe two. But it felt like ten."

"How late were you?"

"Forty minutes."

"Wow. Did Grandma freak out?"

"That would be an understatement. She called the police and tried to file a missing-persons report."

Ellie laughed. "No way."

"She even called the local AM radio station and asked if they could announce on the air that she was missing her fiancé."

"Did they do it?"

"No. They asked her if she had a question about nuclear energy and she hung up on them." He smiled. "She was something."

"I miss Grandma."

"There's not a day that goes by I don't think of her. I got her right here." He patted his heart with his hand.

Ellie wiped her eyes. "So sweet."

Grandpa Frank kissed her on the forehead. "Can't help it if I'm an old sentimental fool."

"Does this mean you're going to start dating?"

"It means … I'm open to the possibility."

"That's wonderful." She lost her smile when Grandpa Frank grabbed the wooden box from the table. "Please don't tell me you have Grandma's ashes in there."

"Of course not."

"Thank God."

"I keep her in the closet underneath my loafers." He winked. "This box did belong to her, though. I have something for you. I've always wanted to give it to you, but I wasn't sure about the right time. Then I got to thinking, anytime is the right time."

He opened the wooden box and set aside some cards and papers. Then he pulled out a velvety heart-shaped box and handed it to Ellie.

Ellie smiled at Grandpa Frank and slowly opened the box to reveal a silver necklace with a silver hummingbird pendant. "Oh my. It's … beautiful." She studied it for a moment. "Why does this seem so familiar to me? Did Grandma wear this often?"

"When you were a baby, she used to wear it when she watched you. It was her favorite necklace. But then you figured out how to grab things and put them in your mouth, so she put it away and forgot about it. I had it cleaned, just in case you felt like putting it in your mouth again."

Ellie laughed and felt tears welling up. "You're the best. And I love it. Thank you." She kissed Grandpa Frank and hugged him.

"Allow me," he said, undoing the clasp. Ellie turned around and Grandpa Frank wrapped the necklace around her neck, clasping it. She looked down to admire it and placed her palm over the hummingbird, as if she were protecting the bird.

She took a deep breath and then let it out slowly. "The hummingbird symbolizes joy and peace."

"I'm not surprised you knew that."

Ellie smiled. Grandpa Frank always knew how to make her feel better. The memorial for Derek was perfect, very touching. And seeing Cedric there was definitely a pleasant surprise; the gardenias and card were lovely. Ellie wondered about Cedric since he hadn't returned her call yet. Hopefully he wasn't mad at her for throwing him out of the funeral home. Or worse, hopefully Vlad didn't scare him off. She felt bad blaming Cedric for the incident, but would apologize to him when they talked.

"So you like it?" asked Grandpa Frank.

"I love it. And as long as we're in the gift-giving mood, I have something for you." She opened her purse, pulled out a folded piece of paper, and handed it to him.

He squished his eyebrows together as he unfolded the piece of paper. Then his eyes lit up. "The list."

Ellie shrugged. "I guess it's time to try dating the Grandpa Frank way."

"Very good. I'm proud of you."

"Got any matches?"

"My granddaughter, the pyromaniac." He pulled a lighter from one of the drawers and held the list over the sink.

"Too bad we don't have any ceremonial music."

"It would have been a nice touch." Grandpa Frank flicked the switch on the lighter and moved the flame toward the list. "Hunk of burning love?"

"Come on baby, light my fire."

They watched the list burn, and Ellie couldn't help but think that everything was going to be fine.

"I still won't tolerate tardiness, though."

Grandpa Frank nodded. "One thing at a time."

She took a deep breath and her thoughts drifted back to Cedric.

Of course.

Chapter Sixteen

Cedric had a light schedule for the rest of the day. First was a Skype videoconference with a company in San Diego that provided packaging materials for shipping. He wanted to find a more lightweight, cost-effective, and eco-friendly way to ship his garlic products around the country. After the meeting, he dropped off garlic samples to two Bay Area chefs who had heard wonderful things about his heirloom garlic and potentially wanted to use it in their restaurants exclusively.

He went home and changed, fed Tofu, and took him for a quick walk before meeting Owen for tennis. When Cedric arrived at the park, he found Owen lying on the grass, face up, in front of one of the tennis courts. "Holy crap, not again."

He knew he didn't have to do mouth-to-mouth, Owen had told him that much. But he didn't tell Cedric what he *should* do. Cedric reached for Owen's wrist to feel for a pulse.

Owen jumped up. "Mother Mary, you scared the bejesus out of me."

Cedric let go of his wrist. "Sorry, I thought you passed out."

"I was meditating."

"I didn't know people meditated with their mouth open."

Owen shrugged. "Okay … there's a possibility I fell asleep."

Cedric laughed.

They stretched before they played, and the tennis game didn't last long—a little over an hour. Cedric felt exhilarated, reconnecting with that passion he thought he'd lost over the years.

Owen wiped his forehead with a towel. "For someone who hasn't played since high school I'm impressed. You did very well."

Cedric was dripping with sweat. "I don't think I've ever run so much in my entire life."

"We're almost at the same skill level, though. You just need a few more sessions to get back into the swing of things. I hope we can play again."

"Absolutely. I'd love to."

"You said you had something going on?"

"I'm interested in a woman, and it seems her ex is a psycho."

Owen nodded. "I've had more than a few cases with psycho exes. What's he doing?"

"Well, I don't have any proof it's him, but ever since he saw me with Ellie, I've received two tickets. He's a cop and I'm pretty sure he had something to do with them. And someone slashed my tire right in the middle of the day. There's no way this can be a coincidence. He drove by as I was changing the tire and the way he looked at me led me to believe he had something to do with it."

"What's his name?"

"Vlad Cunnings."

"I don't know him. Do you still have the tickets?"

"Yeah. In my car. Give me a minute." Cedric went to his car and pulled the tickets out of his glove box. He returned and handed them to Owen.

Owen inspected the tickets and laughed. "That was easy."

Cedric moved closer and inspected the ticket on top. "What?"

"Read the last name of the officer who gave you the ticket, next to the badge number."

Cedric looked for the box with the officer's name and his mouth fell open. "Cunnings. I knew it. I didn't even think to look for his name there."

"Be careful. If he's bold enough to cut your tire in broad daylight, you need to watch out for that guy. I've seen his type before and it usually doesn't end well."

Cedric pulled his car into his driveway, hopped out, and jogged to the front door. The plan was to pick up Tofu and go straight to Michaels's home for the barbecue. He opened the front door of his house, and Tofu made a beeline for Cedric.

"Arf. Arf, arf, arf."

He smashed into Cedric's legs, his tail spinning like a propeller, and his mouth wrapped around his favorite toy, the stuffed squirrel. Cedric closed the door behind him and scratched Tofu on the head.

"Hey, buddy, drop it, time to go for a walk. Then we'll go see Michael and Veronica."

Tofu dropped the toy and licked Cedric's hand as he clipped the leash on the dog. He just wanted to do a quick loop around the block, hoping Tofu would poop before they got in the car.

Not this time. Tofu seemed more interested in getting in the car, and Cedric had to practically pull him down the street.

"I shouldn't have told you about visiting Michael," he told Tofu. "Okay, I give up. Let's go back."

"Arf." Tofu agreed it was the best plan.

They returned back to the house, and Cedric grabbed a bottle of wine from the kitchen.

As Cedric drove, his cell rang. He hung the blue tooth on his ear and answered the phone. "Hey, Tony."

"Hey. Have you been to the online auction website for the property recently?"

"No, why?"

"I just went to the website you gave me and Papa George's old place has disappeared from the list."

Cedric swallowed hard and waited for Tony to continue.

"Are you there?"

"Yeah. Please tell me this is just a screw-up that will be corrected."

Tony let out a sigh. "I don't know. I sent an email to the Webmaster and the County Tax Collector. We'll find out soon enough. It could be just a glitch."

"I hope so."

Twenty minutes later, he pulled up to the house.

Cedric's friends, Michael and Veronica Vela, lived in Monte Sereno, a quaint city just outside of San Jose, where the average home price was over two million dollars. Just a drop in the bucket for the psychologist and his restaurateur wife, who owned his and her Teslas.

Cedric pressed the button and grinned as the doorbell projected the chimes of Westminster throughout the house. Tofu sniffed the door and wagged his tail in anticipation, obviously happy to be there. And who could blame the dog? If Michael and Veronica gave Cedric half of the treats they gave Tofu, he would probably be sniffing the door too—and be about fifty pounds heavier.

Tofu barked again, waiting impatiently for someone to open.

"Don't get your hairy panties in a bunch. You won't go away hungry." Cedric scratched the top of Tofu's head. "*You* are a spoiled doggie, you know that, right?"

"Arf," admitted Tofu.

The door swung open and Veronica smiled as Tofu ran right by her. "Hey, you." She hugged Cedric. "You're late."

"You're surprised?" Cedric handed her the bottle of wine. "Sorry. I was trying to get Tofu to take a crap before we got here."

She laughed. "And were you successful?"

"Not at all. He was in sniff-mode and didn't deliver the goods, but I brought one of *these,* just in case we get lucky." Cedric pulled a plastic poop bag out of his pocket and waved it in the air."

"You may not need that. The last time he took a poop in the backyard, he buried it so well, we have yet to find it."

"Sorry." Cedric followed Veronica through the house to the backyard.

"No worries." Veronica stopped next to the granite island in the kitchen and grabbed Cedric's arm. "By the way…" Veronica glanced through the screen door to the backyard, and then back to Cedric "…not sure if Michael told you but Sam and Lucie are here."

Sam and Lucie were two of the coolest people and Cedric enjoyed their company. They were fun, positive, and passionate, and had no problem with public displays of affection. Cedric loved watching their connection.

"Yeah, he told me they'd be here. Why are you looking at me that way?"

She crinkled her nose.

"Crap." Cedric tried to keep his voice low. "Soledad is here?"

Veronica nodded. "I guess Michael didn't tell you that part."

"No. The sneaky bastard failed to mention that important detail."

Veronica laughed. "In his defense, he didn't know until this afternoon she would be coming."

"Guess he didn't feel it was necessary to update me."

"Probably afraid you would've canceled."

"I would have."

"Well, then." She squeezed his arm. "I'm glad he didn't tell you."

Lucie and Sam had the best intentions in their effort to set-up Cedric with their friend, Soledad, but it just wasn't going to happen. Cedric tried not to judge people, but sometimes you just don't click with someone, no matter how hard you try.

"You think she's pretty, right?" asked Veronica.

"Of course, even a blind man could see that, but I need more."

She smiled and nodded.

Cedric wanted great conversation and a woman who wasn't afraid to speak her mind. Soledad agreed with everything Cedric said, didn't matter what they were talking about. She never offered her own ideas or opinions and that got boring. Ellie, on the other hand …

Cedric should have known his thoughts would drift to Ellie again. The woman had enough personality and intelligence for ten people.

"Where did your mind just go?" asked Veronica. "That was some grin on your face."

Cedric laughed. "Maybe I'll tell you later."

"I hope so."

They stepped down into the backyard and smiled as Tofu lay on the grass with all four legs in the air while Lucie rubbed his tummy. "You little cutie. I'm taking you home with me. Cedric will never ever know."

"Oh yes I will," said Cedric. "And I wouldn't know what to do with the extra room in my bed. That flea bag is a serious bed-hog."

"Arf." Tofu protested.

"Okay, sorry, you're not a flea bag. But you *are* a bed hog."

"Arf."

"Liar."

"Extra room in your bed?" Soledad said, quickly moving in on Cedric.

She doesn't waste any time.

She bit her lower lip and tried to look sexy as she kissed Cedric on the cheek.

Nope. Not doing it for him. Little Cedric was out cold. In a coma.

"Hi, Soledad," Cedric said, looking around the yard.

Michael and Veronica had the kick-ass backyard—to die for—complete with full outdoor kitchen, pizza oven, swimming pool and jacuzzi, a lawn area under the king and queen palm trees, a bronze fountain with dolphins that appeared to be jumping out of the water, and a state-of-the-art bocce court.

"Hey, Cedric." Sam grabbed a beer from the outdoor fridge and handed it to him. "How's the garlic biz?"

Cedric popped the top off the beer and took a sip. "It stinks."

Sam laughed. "I never get tired of that one."

Cedric and Sam clinked bottles.

Michael was busy working the barbecue. "Cedric, get your ass over here. I need a hand."

"Yes, sir." Cedric sent Michael a military salute. He set his bottle on the counter next to the barbecue, inspecting the salmon and chicken on the grill. "Looks great. You don't really want help, do you?"

"Hell no. Just wanted to say sorry for Soledad being here. Try to have some patience, and remember, it wasn't my idea. Here she comes. Act natural."

"So, Cedric," the vulture said, swooping down on him again, this time brushing her claws against his chest. "You said you'd call me after that wonderful chat we had last time."

Wonderful?

Thank God, Veronica came to the rescue. "Dinner is served." She balanced three platters of food and set them on the patio table. "Caprese salad with avocado, pasta with white wine, garlic and mushrooms, and garlic bread."

Veronica was an amazing chef and she loved to cook for others. It didn't matter if she was in her restaurant or at home. Michael brought the platter of salmon and chicken from the barbecue and placed it on the table.

Michael turned to Cedric. "How's the volunteering going at the library?"

Veronica's eyes opened wide. "I didn't know you were volunteering."

"Well, technically, I haven't started yet. I just finished the training."

"What will you be doing?" asked Lucie.

"Reading to kids."

Veronica snuck a piece of chicken under the table to Tofu. "How fun."

Cedric smiled. "I'm looking forward to it. You know how much I loved it when my mom read to me."

"You were obsessed."

"I prefer to say I was eager."

Veronica laughed. "How often will you volunteer?"

"Just once a week to start. They have a book shortage in the children's section at the moment. Someone broke into the library and vandalized a bunch of books, tearing out pages, and marking up others with Sharpie pens. What were they trying to prove by doing that?"

Michael sat up. "That they were assholes."

"Yeah. Well, the good news is, the library is doing a fundraiser, so hopefully they'll be able to replace the books with new ones."

"When's the fundraiser?"

"Next week. You want me to send you the info?"

"Definitely. If we can't make it, we'll cut you a check."

"Us too," said Lucie.

Cedric wasn't surprised Lucie wanted to be involved. Not only did she have a heart of gold, she and Sam had a truck of gold. That happens when you win four hundred million dollars in the Powerball Lottery—although they chose the cash option and came away with a tiny check for two hundred and twenty-three million. They were two of the most generous people he knew. Sam and Lucie immediately gave half of their lottery winnings to their ten family members—eleven million each person.

Good people.

He looked over at Soledad to see if she was interested, but she was busy texting someone. Perfect. He didn't have to ask her.

Around forty-five minutes later, everyone had finished eating, and Michael stood up. "Cedric, grab a few of those plates. We'll let these lovely ladies relax."

"Good idea." Cedric hoped he would be able to fill Michael in on the Ellie saga.

"Don't I get to help?" asked Sam. He pursed his lips and fluffed his hair. "Or do you consider me a lovely lady?"

Michael waved him over. "Come on tough guy."

Veronica laughed. "Look at these macho men clearing the table. We've trained them well."

"Yes we have," Lucie said, laughing with Veronica.

Michael, Cedric, and Sam cleared the table and went inside.

"Okay, Cedric," Michael said, setting some plates on the counter. "Tell me the latest with what's-her-name. Ellie, isn't it?"

"Yes, and she's driving me crazy."

"That's a woman's job." Michael opened the dishwasher. "It's in their DNA."

Sam scraped leftovers from the plates into the trash. "It's also on their resumes. But God, I would be nothing without Lucie."

"You got that right, brother," said Michael. "So, have you gone out with her yet?

Cedric shrugged. "It's complicated."

"It's a yes or no question." Michael rinsed off the plates and handed them to Cedric to put in the dishwasher.

"Okay, remember I called you when I was outside of the library, getting ready to go in and ask her out."

Michael nodded and turned to Sam. "She's a librarian."

Sam smiled. "Nice."

"So," continued Cedric, "I go inside and she's not there. And her co-worker tells me she's at a memorial because her brother died."

"That sucks," said Michael.

"Tell me about it. So anyway, I go to the memorial, Ellie's crying, and next thing you know, I see her dick ex-boyfriend kissing her in front of everyone."

Michael scratched his head. "Was tongue involved?"

"He practically swallowed her head."

"At a memorial? No way, I don't believe it."

"I saw it. "

"Then what happened?" asked Michael.

"The ex got in my face and pushed me into a bunch of chairs. Then Ellie kicked us both out of the funeral home."

Michael laughed. "Your life is never boring."

"Never. She did call and leave me a message, apologizing for kicking me out."

Michael slapped him on the shoulder. "See? Did you call her back?"

Cedric shook his head.

"God. How much do you like her?"

"Too much."

"So what's the problem?" asked Sam.

"Her ex is a cop with a couple of screws loose. He doesn't look stable, plus, he may still be sticking his tongue down her throat. Is it really worth it?"

"Hell yes," said Michael. "It's probably not what you think. Talk with her. Be straight up with her and tell her how you feel. And ask her what's going on!"

Michael was right. Why speculate when you can just ask and find out the truth? Cedric wasn't going to give up so easily. Next time he saw Ellie, he would ask her out. Again.

Sam smiled. "Things will work out. And I look forward to the wedding."

Veronica entered. "What wedding?"

"No wedding," said Cedric. "But you'll be happy to know I'm officially interested in the opposite sex again."

"Great!" Veronica kissed Cedric on the cheek as Soledad came in.

"Glad to hear it," said Soledad. "I wanted to ask you something …"

Cedric's timing was always perfect.

"Cedric was just telling us that he's very interested in a particular woman at the library," said Michael, to the rescue.

Cedric wanted to kiss him on the lips.

Soledad looked as if someone just ripped the head off of her favorite Barbie doll and set it on fire. "Oh, that's … great." She glanced up at the clock. "Oh wow, is that the time? I better get running along, lots to do. Where is my purse?" She practically ran outside.

It looked like Michael was going to be getting another free round of golf. Cedric shot him a look that said, "I owe you, buddy." Michael winked and Veronica caught it.

"Okay …" Veronica eyed Cedric. "You're not leaving until I get the details."

After Soledad left, Cedric filled Veronica in on everything regarding Ellie from the beginning, including his idiotic behavior.

Veronica nodded. "Looks like you two have it bad for each other. I think you just need to get her alone and tell her how you feel. Don't beat around the bush. Lay it out there. Women appreciate honesty more than anything."

"And the ex?"

"Well, you definitely need to be careful there."

Chapter Seventeen

Ellie was on a roll, accomplishing and checking off one thing after another on her to-do list. The fundraiser was just a few days away, but there were still plenty of things to organize and confirm, in addition to selling more bricks. She was happy with her fundraising efforts so far, having raised over five thousand dollars.

She'd just about finished everything she wanted to do in the morning, so she took a moment to stretch, bending forward and touching her toes.

"Don't forget to breathe," said Julio.

Ellie stood back up and smiled. "If you see me turning purple, you know I forgot."

"Purple looks good on you."

"It's good to look on the positive side of passing out."

Julio grimaced. "How are you doing with your brother? I know how close you two were."

"I'm better. Thank you" she smiled. "I was just thinking about how he used to call me almost every day to check up on me when I went away to college. Just the sound of his voice helped me get through some rough days."

"I remember you told me it was hard."

Ellie nodded. "There was no way he was going to pass up being park ranger at Yellowstone and I understood that. I was sad to see him move away, but happy to see him doing what he loved." Ellie smiled. "He'll always be in my heart. Forever."

"Your brother?" Peggy asked, approaching with a slip of paper in her hand.

"Yeah," said Ellie.

"Well, I know you said you didn't want any time off, but let me know if you change your mind."

"Thanks. I'm good."

"Good, then. I have two more things to add to the list." She waved a piece of paper in the air. "Well, three."

"Okay."

"If you could confirm the arrival time of the photo booth and the band, that would be great." She handed Ellie the piece of paper. "And we never did receive this autographed 49er football helmet for the silent auction. We just need to confirm the whereabouts of the helmet and who's actually signing it. If it's not Kaepernick, hopefully we can get one signed by Joe Montana. And if I can meet Joe, even better!"

Julio held up his hand. "Me too."

Ellie smiled. "No problem."

"I appreciate it." Peggy turned to leave but Ellie stopped her.

"What was the third thing?"

Peggy stopped and turned back around. "What do you mean?"

"You said there were three things to add to the list. You only gave me two"

"Oh, of course. How could I forget Cedric?"

That got Ellie's attention. "Cedric?"

"Yes. Well, it's not actually something for the fundraiser. Cedric Johnson is here and—"

"Where?" Ellie looked around the library but didn't see him.

"In the children's area. He may need some hand-holding today."

Julio leaned into Ellie. "Some gland holding could be fun too."

Ellie smacked Julio on the shoulder. "Behave."

"All these years and you still haven't perfected your library voice," said Peggy.

"I'll work on that." Julio smiled as he walked off.

Because of Julio, Ellie was imagining Cedric on a deserted island. He just sliced the top off a coconut and was letting her drink from it. Then Cedric dropped the coconut to the sand, cupped her face, and leaned in to—

"Ellie?"

"Yes?"

"Please peek in on Cedric to see how he's doing. I forgot to tell him that he was going to be reading to a group of a hundred kids, which may be overwhelming for someone on their first day solo. I'm sure he'll be wonderful, but it wouldn't hurt to check."

"Of course."

Peggy leaned in and lowered her voice. "And I'll give you some unsolicited advice. I've seen the way you and Cedric look at each other, and you certainly didn't fool me with that slap after the kiss. Better snatch that man up quick. He won't last long on the open market."

Right. Like it was that easy. He hasn't returned her phone call.

Cedric was sending her a strong message. Not interested.

***

Cedric felt like he was going to throw up. Where the hell did all of these kids come from? There must be a thousand!

He paced back and forth trying to relax. He was going to be fine. He'd completed his volunteer training, including the one-on-one reading session, and was told he was ready to go. He'd asked Peggy if maybe he should do more training, but she'd said—with confidence—he didn't need anymore.

Still, his hands were sweaty and he was pretty sure he could feel his pulse trying to bang out of his neck. Most of the three and four year old kids sat on the floor in front of him in a few semi-circles, even though he gave them no such instructions. Others sat on the clover-shaped ottomans. They'd obviously been here before. Maybe they had high standards. He certainly didn't want to let them down. He wanted them to enjoy the story, but even more, he wanted them to be enthusiastic about wanting to learn to read. The thought brought memories of Cedric's mom and those unforgettable times when she would read to him. He suddenly felt a little more relaxed. Time to get to work.

Cedric smiled at the kids. "Welcome. Ready for a story today?"

The kids answered in unison, "Yes."

They crossed their legs and waited in anticipation, staring up at Cedric with their big beautiful eyes hungry for a story.

"Great. Let's get started."

Cedric opened the book *The Giving Tree* by Shel Silverstein and began to read. It didn't take long before he was lost in the story with them, alive and full of life. Every eye was glued to him, and it was the quietest roomful of kids he'd ever seen. Peggy taught him that it was good to pause the reading and ask the kids to predict and anticipate what was going to happen next.

"Wouldn't it be cool to have a tree as a friend?" asked Cedric.

Many of the kids agreed, but a cute girl wearing a dress covered with pink hearts raised her hand. "My dog is my best friend. His name is Bruno. He farts when my older brother gives him cheese."

The kids laughed and Cedric smiled, even more relaxed. "Interesting. Trees don't eat cheese so we won't have to worry about that. But they love water, though."

"Water doesn't give you gas," said the girl.

"That's good to know since I was getting thirsty." Cedric made a funny face.

The kids laughed again and Cedric felt connected to them. He imagined having his own children and reading to them every night. His confidence was coming back. For two years, he'd shut women out of his life, but things were going to change. No more denying himself the pleasure of having a wonderful woman in his life. The thought of Ellie crept into his head.

Lovely Ellie.

In his peripheral, Cedric sensed the presence of someone, but didn't want to look and get distracted.

Was it her?

Maybe she was checking up on him to see if he was doing okay. He knew he shouldn't look, but he couldn't help it. He waited until he reached the end of the paragraph and then shot a look in that direction.

Ellie.

Looking like an angel.

And oh, crap, he lost his place in the book.

He felt his cheeks burning and his heart rate going up. Idiot.

What a rookie mistake. Cedric paused, took a deep breath, and then continued with the story. Another minute passed and Cedric stopped reading, looking around at the children. "What would you do if you had a tree like this?"

A girl with ponytails and a Cinderella T-shirt raised her hand. "I would hug it."

Cedric smiled. "That's sweet. I'm sure the tree would like that very much."

After the reading, Cedric strolled through the library with only one thing on his mind: find Ellie and ask her out. This was going to happen today. Right now.

He approached the Tech Center and spotted her inside with the last person he wanted to see. Vlad. Ellie turned and saw Cedric. She said something to Vlad, who also turned and saw Cedric.

She came out of the room, leaving Vlad inside. "Hi. How did the reading go? I peeked in on you and it looked like the kids were enjoying it."

"It was amazing." Cedric looked over Ellie's shoulder at Vlad, who was staring back.

Ellie shrugged. "He just showed up. There's nothing I can do, it's a public place."

"I want to go out with you and—"

"What are you doing here?" said Vlad.

Ellie turned to him. "I told you to stay in the Tech Center."

"And let this bozo make a move on you? I don't think so." Vlad turned to Cedric. "I asked you a question. What are you doing here?"

"I'm a volunteer here, that's what. What about you? Looking for a book on good manners?"

Vlad got in Cedric's face, and Ellie used her arm to wedge herself between them. "Stop, both of you. You're acting like children."

You're? Cedric was wondering what the hell he did.

Ellie pointed to the door. "I have things to do so please leave."

Cedric held up a finger. "I—"

"Please," Ellie said, cutting Cedric off. "Leave."

Chapter Eighteen

"Not again!" Cedric had just hooked the ball into the Pacific Ocean.

Michael threw him another golf ball. "Try it again and aim for land this time. It's the part on your right that's not wet."

"Very funny."

Most people would cut him some slack since he was playing on what many would argue was one of the greatest golf courses in the world. Pebble Beach.

"Focus," said Michael. "No pressure."

"Right. No pressure …"

The most famous golfers in the world stood and played exactly where Cedric was standing, but the pressure Cedric felt had nothing to do with the difficulty of the game or history of the golf course. The problem was his mind was not on golf at all, and it hadn't been all morning. He was still thinking about Ellie.

"I screwed up," said Cedric.

"Just hit the ball and we'll talk about it as we ride."

"I mean, here I meet one of the most amazing women ever and I do stupid things in her presence."

"I know. Hit the ball."

He thought of Ellie's beautiful smile and the way she smelled, and his shoulders instantly relaxed. He scooted up closer to the ball, took his swing, and smacked it down the middle of the fairway.

"There you go!" Michael watched Cedric's ball roll to a stop. They hopped in the golf cart and drove toward the middle of the fairway. "By the way. Thanks for this."

Cedric turned to Michael. "Are you serious? The last couple of years haven't been easy for me, but you and Veronica have always been there. That's worth a hundred times more than this round of golf."

Playing at Pebble Beach was not a regular occurrence for Cedric. A round of eighteen holes was priced at a whopping five hundred bucks a person. Cedric had promised Michael six rounds of golf at the local community course for all of the time he'd spent at his office, but he asked Michael if he'd prefer to have one round at Pebble instead. "No brainer," Michael had answered.

After they finished, Cedric took a deep breath and admired the crashing waves and the two cypress trees next to the last green before they turned and headed to The Bench, an open-air restaurant overlooking the last hole.

As they ate, Cedric looked at his scorecard. "The first hole was a disaster. Two through seven a little less horrific. It depended on what I was focused on at the time. Whenever I thought of how I was an idiot around Ellie, I either hit the ball into the water or into the rough. So, I made a decision."

"To pull your head out of your ass?"

Cedric just stared at him for a few seconds and laughed. "Have you ever given that advice to someone during a consultation? Told them to pull their head out of their ass?"

"No." Michael, took a sip of his beer. "But I've thought it, though. More than a few times."

Cedric smiled. "Anyway, I decided to focus on something positive I could remember with Ellie, instead of the negative. And then I started playing well."

"What was the positive thing you thought of?"

"Her smile."

"That's it?"

"That just shows you how amazing it is."

"I doubt it's that powerful."

"Okay, maybe it's a combination of her smile and the way she smells."

The waiter returned to the table with the check and Cedric's credit card. "Thanks, gentlemen. Enjoy the rest of your …"

The waiter's words were interrupted by a group of three women practically running him over as they headed out of the restaurant. A man and a couple of teenagers followed the women. Another man ran by, awkwardly trying to remove a camera from his case at the same time.

Cedric signed the transaction slip and asked, "What's going on?"

The waiter shrugged his shoulders. "Rumor has it that Samuel L. Jackson is golfing on the eighteenth hole right now.

"Seriously?" asked Cedric, looking outside and noticing the growing crowd around the eighteenth hole.

"We get celebrities here all the time. Bill Murray. Michael Jordan. The Iron Chef."

"Who knew?" said Michael. "Hey, let's go outside and check it out. Maybe I can get a picture for my office."

Michael and Cedric headed toward the eighteenth green, where a wall of people was forming. They couldn't see Samuel, but everyone was talking about them.

"Can you see him?" asked a woman.

"Yeah," said the other woman. "He's got nice legs."

Cedric had no interest in looking at Samuel L. Jackson's legs. In fact, just the mention of the word *legs* had immediately returned his thoughts to Ellie and their time in Starbucks. Now those were some amazing legs.

He stared off into the ocean, imagining Ellie swimming there in a cute bikini and her legs coming out of the water occasionally to say hello. He would be waiting on the shore for her and then he would wrap a towel around her before reapplying sunscreen to those legs.

"Make love to me, Cedric," Ellie would say. "Here. Now."

His thoughts were so real and vivid, like he was there on the beach with Ellie. And Samuel L. Jackson was with them too. Wait. Why was Samuel L. Jackson on the beach with them? How did he creep into his daydream? He couldn't actually see Samuel, but he heard his voice.

"Fore Motherfuckers," Samuel yelled.

Now why would he yell that on a beach? Odd.

Cedric opened his eyes and didn't understand what was going on. He felt a bit hazy and his head was throbbing. He touched his forehead and then looked at his hand. Blood.

What the hell happened? Last he remembered he was daydreaming about being on the beach with Ellie and Samuel L. Jackson, and the next thing he knew, he was on the ground looking up at fifteen to twenty concerned heads hovering over him.

"Give him some room," said Michael. "Cedric, talk to me, man. Are you all right? What year is it?"

Cedric thought about the question for a second and looked confused. "How could you not know the year, Michael?"

A few people laughed as Samuel L. Jackson made his way through the crowd. He was now standing over Cedric, looking down at him, shaking his head. "Damn, did I do that? That's some seriously fucked up golf. Please accept my sincerest apologies."

Fifteen minutes later, Cedric felt much better, but the Golf Marshal recommended a visit to the hospital to check for a possible concussion. Fortunately, the Community Hospital of the Monterey Peninsula was just a quick drive up 17 Mile Drive to the other side of the freeway. As they sat in the waiting area of emergency, Michael flipped through the pictures in his phone.

"You should be ashamed of yourself," said Cedric.

"What?" Michael laughed. "What did I do?"

"There's proof on your phone of exactly what you did."

Michael flipped through a few pictures and then stopped on one of Michael smiling, giving the thumbs up. Directly behind Michael was Samuel L. Jackson squatting down as Cedric lay there, looking like he got run over by a truck.

"I'm one of your best friends, and I could have been dying, but the only thing on your mind was taking a selfie!"

"First of all, you were fine and secondly ... that picture is going on my wall."

"Glad you are able to celebrate my humiliation."

"That's what friends are for. Hey, at least we get another round of golf at Pebble out of it!"

"That we do."

Samuel L. Jackson felt so bad about hitting Cedric that he bought him and Michael a gift card, good for another round in the future. Cedric thought that was pretty classy of the man to do that, but next time he golfed, he would consider wearing a helmet.

"Before I got hit by that golf ball, I was day dreaming about Ellie."

"Life is short. Quit dreaming about her and do something."

That was the plan. Even if it killed him.

The next morning, as Cedric approached his booth at the farmers' market, Tony had his back to him and was eating cherries.

Cedric shook his head in disapproval. "You're eating the profits."

"Better than giving them away." Tony popped another cherry in his mouth. "Only a lunatic does that."

"Fine, I'm a lunatic."

"Oh my God! Your forehead!" Tony spit a cherry pit into Cedric's chest.

"That's very nice." Cedric wiped his shirt. "You're overreacting."

"You see stuff like that, the normal reaction is to scream or run. What happened?"

"Samuel L. Jackson hit me with a golf ball."

"You mean like *the* Samuel L. Jackson?"

Cedric nodded.

"Dude, I need to take a picture with your forehead."

Cedric's cell phone rang and Cedric eyed the number on the screen.

"Is that Ellie?" asked Tony.

"I don't recognize the number."

"Pick up."

Cedric stared at the phone. "I don't know."

"Don't be an idiot. You told me she was the coolest girl you've met. Answer it."

Cedric hesitated for a moment, but then decided to answer.

"Hello?" He didn't hear anything. He pulled the phone away from his ear to look at it. "Too late, it went to voicemail."

"I should kick your ass right now."

"First of all, quit being so dramatic. And secondly, you couldn't kick the ass of a flea." Tony gave him one of his serious looks. "Is that right?"

"Okay, you could kick the ass of a flea. Maybe an entire village of fleas. Happy?"

"Penis particle."

"Dingleberry."

"Cock cobbler."

"Nutsack."

An older woman approached and raised an eyebrow. She picked up a garlic bulb, smelled it, and put it back down, staring at Cedric, then Tony.

"Do you have any celery?" she asked.

"Sorry, we don't." Cedric pointed to the table. "Just garlic and cherries."

"That's too bad. I need to make some Bloody Marys. How about lemons?"

"Unfortunately not."

"Almonds?"

"You put almonds in Bloody Marys?" asked Tony.

"Of course not. That's disgusting."

Cedric scanned the tables looking for almonds even though he knew he didn't have any. "Hmm. Looks like we're out of almonds at the moment."

The woman scanned the tables again. "What *do* you have?"

"Just what's on the table."

She lifted the table cover of one of the tables to look underneath. "What do you have under there? You hiding any almonds or celery?"

"I assure you, if I had almonds or celery, you'd be the first one I'd sell them to."

"I certainly hope so." She roamed over to the booth next door without saying goodbye.

Cedric and Tony watched the woman talk with the man who was selling Kettle Corn. They could hear her ask the man if he had any celery or almonds.

"I think we should legally be able to shoot people," said Tony. "Someone's got to put them out of their misery."

"I think when they are in our presence, we suffer more than they do. Maybe we should be shot."

Cedric's phone beeped three times.

"Yes," said Tony. "Looks like Ellie left you a voicemail."

"You don't know that. It was a random number that could belong to anyone."

"Just listen to the damn message so we can find out."

"Fine." Cedric dialed his voicemail.

"Hi Cedric, this is Ellie. You know, from the library? Of course you know. Crap, I hope I don't start rambling again. Well, uh …"

Ellie paused, sounding nervous and Cedric grinned. Like she had to explain who she was. It's difficult to forget a person when you think about them twenty-four hours a day.

"Is it her?" asked Tony.

Cedric nodded.

"Yes!"

"Anyway," Ellie continued. "I already left you one message, but just thought I'd call and thank you again for the beautiful flowers and the card. And I'll definitely take you up on the free hug. Sorry I kicked you out of the library. I've been a little stressed. And I— Well, just give me a call, okay?"

Cedric saved the message and pocketed his cell.

"Well?"

Cedric smiled. "She wants to talk."

"Great!"

"Yeah, but—"

"You're thinking too much. Just talk with her."

"Right."

Tony slammed his hand on the table. "Look who's coming our way."

Cedric turned and saw Maria, the waitress from Piccadilly Pete's approach their booth. "You're a brave woman."

Maria smiled. "Thanks, but I can handle him."

"Yes, please," said Tony. "Handle me."

Cedric threw his palms up. "He's a good guy. He just hasn't figured out how to evenly-balance his testosterone output."

"How's my future wife?" Tony asked, leaning over to kiss Maria on the cheek.

"Not sure." Maria blocked his lips with her hand. "I can ask her next time I visit the zoo."

Tony laughed. "You see, Cedric? *That's* what I'm talking about. This woman is fan-fucking-tastic."

"She just insulted you."

"That's where you're wrong. This is our version of foreplay. This woman is a firecracker and she almost cracked a smile. She's enjoying this."

"I'll let you believe that," said Maria. "But the real reason is, I came here because I saw the garlic sign."

Tony grabbed three baskets of garlic, placed them in a bag, and handed it to her. "Complimentary garlic for the lovely lady. Enjoy."

Cedric almost fell over.

Maria smiled and grabbed the bag from Tony. "That's very kind of you, thank you."

Tony smiled. "Does this mean we are ready for our first kiss?"

"Check back with me in the year 2050."

Tony pulled out his smart phone and scrolled through it. "I'll put it on my calendar right now." He looked up. "Is ten in the morning good for you?"

Maria smiled and held up the bag. "Thanks again. See you at the restaurant."

"You can count on it." Tony pocketed his cell and watched her walk away.

Cedric let out a loud sigh. "Pete's going to be pissed off when she quits because of you."

"When she quits, he will be congratulating me and handing me a cigar because she will be pregnant with our first child."

"Okay, topic switch, please."

"I can do that. Let's talk about the hot librarian again."

"Please call her Ellie."

"As you wish. What's your next move?"

"I have no clue. We're kind of in limbo. There's an obvious attraction from both parties, but circumstances are getting in the way of us making any headway."

Tony pulled his cell from his pocket again and stared at the screen. "Hang on, I just got a message." He read the message and frowned. "Shit."

"What?" asked Cedric.

"The planned online auction for the farm has been canceled and will now be a private sale coordinated by the County Supervisor."

"That's okay, right?" asked Cedric as he grabbed three more baskets of garlic from under the table. "I mean, even if there are multiple offers, I'll top them all. I'll overbid if I have to."

"I don't know. According to this email from the Tax Collector's assistant, there are plans to sell it to a local contractor."

Cedric placed the garlic on the table and turned to Tony. "What?"

"That's what it says, but it says there are plans, not that they've already sold it. My advice is talk with the County Supervisor and get them to stop the sale."

"How am I going to do that?"

Tony considered the question. "Maybe you need to have that place declared a historic monument. There's so much history there, and that has to mean something to the county and especially the city of Gilroy."

Cedric scratched his chin. "That's brilliant."

"That's because it came from the mind of Tony Garcia. You'd better go now, though, before it's too late."

"Good idea. I'll be back."

Cedric made his way over to the County Supervisor's office on Hedding Street and took the elevator to the tenth floor. As he waited for the receptionist to finish up a phone call, he inspected the two aerial photos on the wall of Santa Clara County. The first photo was from the year 1960 with thousands of acres of farmland and trees visible in the shot. The second photo—from last year—showed the complete opposite, with hundreds and hundreds of buildings and thousands of houses where the farmland used to be. The only remaining farmland seemed to be in the south in Morgan Hill and Gilroy, near Cedric's farm.

"Amazing," muttered Cedric. "What a difference."

Next to the photos on the wall was a map of the districts in the county. He scooted over to get a closer look at the map and scanned south with his finger to the city of Gilroy.

"District one, there you are." He read the designation on the map.

The receptionist hung up the phone. "Can I help you?"

Cedric spun around. "I'd like to speak to the Supervisor for District One."

"Do you have an appointment?"

"No."

"Can I ask what this is regarding?"

"I'm inquiring about a farm in Gilroy that's going to be sold by the county."

"Just one moment." She picked up the phone and pressed an extension. "There's someone here inquiring about a farm in Gilroy." She hung up the phone. "You can head back. It's the second office on the right."

"Thank you." Cedric smiled and walked to the office, feeling hopeful. There had to be a way to stop the sale. Someone had to understand the history there and why a garlic museum was such a great idea and a wonderful tribute to the region known for its garlic.

Cedric peeked inside the office and saw a man with his head down, working on his laptop. "Come in." The man closed his laptop.

"Hi, my name is Cedric Johnson and I'm inquiring about a property in—"

Cedric froze after he spotted the desk nameplate.

It said Dominic Cunnings.

"You okay?" asked Dominic.

Cedric took a moment to speak. "Yeah. It's just … your name."

"Ah, that. I was named after a famous World War II pilot." He shrugged. "My dad is ex-military."

"No, I meant your last name. Would you happen to be related to Vlad Cunnings?"

Please say no.

"That's my brother, you know him?"

Yes. He's the biggest A-hole I've ever met. "He's a friend of a friend."

"What's your name again?" asked Dominic, now looking suspicious.

"Cedric Johnson."

"Cedric Johnson." Dominic sounded like he was trying to memorize the name. "You came about the farm in Gilroy, right?"

"Yeah. My grandfather originally owned the property. I'd like to buy it back and keep it in the family."

"Sorry, that property has already been slated to sell to a local contractor in order to pay the lien of delinquent unsecured taxes. You're too late."

"But it hasn't happened yet."

"No, but—"

"Look." Cedric let out a loud breath. "That property has sentimental value, as you probably might know. And there is historical significance not only for our family, but for the county, and the city of Gilroy as well. I want to build a garlic museum there and make it a historic landmark, since that's what it is. The garlic revolution started in that house."

Dominic seemed to be considering Cedric's plea. "Well, getting a property designated a historical landmark is not as easy as you think. It needs to be recommended by the State Historical Resource Commission and be officially designated by the Director of California State Parks. That's a detailed process, for sure."

"But it's possible."

Dominic nodded. "Yes, of course. It's possible." Dominic smiled and grabbed a pad and pen from his desk "I'll tell you what, give me your contact info and let me check into this. I can't make any promises. I'll get back to you as soon as I can."

"Great. Thank you, I appreciate it." Cedric smiled as he wrote his name and phone number on the pad and handed it to Dominic.

That's all he wanted. A chance.

Chapter Nineteen

"I think I've lost track of how many books you've dropped in the last hour," said Julio.

Ellie stared at the book on the floor, let out a loud breath, and picked it up. She placed it on the desk and removed another from the box. "I'm having a hard time concentrating."

"Thinking of Derek?"

"No, oddly enough. That was supposed to happen for a reason, a reason I may never know. And I may have another breakdown, but for the moment, I feel peace with what happened."

"I like that. Peace is good."

"Yeah. I was actually thinking about being Branch Manager."

"Ah." Julio sorted through a box of books. "You're the best person for the job and more than qualified. I've got every part of my body crossed for you. Quit worrying."

"Thanks, you're the best."

Ellie let out a deep breath and relaxed, her mind now back on Cedric.

The man looked so sweet and innocent as she watched him reading to the children a couple of days ago. As she watched him, she realized he was a natural, and the children seemed to be hypnotized by him. And when he asked the children a question, every hand in the room shot to the ceiling, ready to answer. Cedric was amazing and he surprised Ellie more and more.

She had a dream about him last night where they were both on the porch of their ranch-style home with his-and-her rocking chairs, smiling, holding hands, and reminiscing about the wonderful life they had together, their children, and their rapidly-approaching fiftieth wedding anniversary. Just the thought of that dream put a big smile on her face and a warm feeling in her heart.

"I like that smile," said Peggy.

"Thanks."

"But I need to tell you something."

Good news, good news, good news.

"Based on the latest total you gave me, you and Margaret Rossewood are tied."

Pickles!

Peggy rubbed her shoulders. "You still have time. Don't give up."

Ellie was on a roll with the list of donors who committed to buying bricks and thought she was doing well. Not well enough. But the worst part was she was running out of people to ask for donations.

"You have two wild cards you haven't used," said Julio, after Peggy walked away. "You need to use them."

Ellie narrowed her eyes. "What are you talking about?"

"Vlad and Cedric. They both have money. Ask them for it."

"No way. Not going to happen."

Julio handed her back the document. "What other options do you have?"

Ellie shrugged her shoulders.

"Honey, you know they would be happy to write you a check."

"I know that, but it's not the point. That check comes with strings attached. If I take money from Vlad, he'll assume we are back together. And I would rather be homeless and jobless before that happens. Actually, I'd rather be dead."

"Okay, then. What about Cedric? The man is loaded *and* he likes you."

"That would be taking advantage of the situation. I can't do that."

"You're not taking advantage. He's got plenty of money and he loves the library. You're simply asking him if he'd like to help replace the vandalized books."

"Look," Ellie said, letting out a loud breath. "Yes, technically, the money goes to replace the books. I get that, of course. But I'm trying to raise more money than Margaret to get promoted, so I have an ulterior motive."

"You're making a big mistake."

She couldn't argue with that. Maybe she was.

Julio smiled.

"What?" Ellie was not in the mood.

"Now's your chance to ask him. He's here."

She looked up and there he was, talking with Peggy.

Cedric.

With that sexy grin.

Her heart raced as she dropped another book, this time on Julio's foot.

"Ouch!"

Ellie picked up the book and brushed it off. "Sorry. I don't know why I'm so nervous, but I am. I have the sudden urge to pee."

Julio stepped back. "Here?"

"No, not here!" Ellie stepped sideways, did a quick turn, took ten steps, and then entered the women's bathroom. Once inside, she put her body weight against the door, forcing it to close faster than it normally would.

She let out a huge breath and then entered the stall. After she went pee, she washed her hands. Twice. Then she decided to help out the janitorial staff by picking up some tissue from the floor and wiping down the counter. Probably a good idea to clean the mirror too.

People can be so messy.

Ten minutes later, Ellie was tired of being in the bathroom, which was now practically spotless. She had to get back to her fundraising. She had a job to win, but her heart was still racing. Why was she so nervous?

It was just Cedric! No big deal! Just act calm and go back out there!

She checked her hair and her teeth in the mirror. All good. She slowly opened the door—barely an inch—and peeked through the opening.

Cedric sat on the edge of the desk, waiting. He looked in her direction and Ellie shut the bathroom door. She felt like she had to pee again.

Cedric stared at the bathroom door. He could have sworn he saw it open just a little. Ellie had been in there for well over ten minutes. What the hell was she doing in there? She had enough time to go number one and number two more than a few times. What did she have for lunch?

He watched as a large woman came from around the corner and pushed on the bathroom door to enter. The door only opened slightly and then it shut again. A loud thud echoed from inside the bathroom. The woman tried opening the door again, this time pushing hard and managing to get it open.

"Oh my God," she yelled, looking down at the floor. "Are you okay?"

Cedric jumped off the desk and ran to the bathroom, where he found Ellie on the floor with her eyes closed, grimacing. He squatted down to get closer to her. "Ellie. Are you okay? Ellie, talk to me."

Cedric noticed the red spot on her forehead; she'd obviously hit her head on something. He turned to the large woman. "Can you please go to the front desk and ask for an ice pack? And a first aid kit."

"Of course."

The woman hurried away as Cedric turned his attention back to Ellie on the floor. "Ellie, you hit your head. Can you hear me okay?"

With her eyes closed, she lifted her hand to her forehead and touched a bump that was growing over the red spot. "Ouch. Yes, I can hear you. Am I dead?"

Cedric laughed. "No."

"Well, this is embarrassing, so why don't you kill me then."

He touched her cheek and smiled. "You're going to be okay."

Ellie's eyes suddenly sprung open with a look of horror. "You have something growing out of your forehead."

"Look who's talking."

Ellie touched her forehead again. "Ouch." She started to lift herself up, but slid back to the floor.

"Whoa, whoa, not so fast. We're getting an ice pack for your forehead so just relax. There's no hurry."

"I want to sit up."

"Okay, but let me help you, though. Take it slowly and grab my hands."

Ellie let out a loud breath. "It's not necessary."

"I don't have cooties … if that's what you're worried about." Cedric grinned and pointed to her mouth. "You were almost going to smile."

"No I wasn't."

"I saw it."

"You're mistaken."

"Take my hands or you're not getting up."

"Fine."

"Thank you."

She grabbed both of his hands and Cedric felt a pleasant zap rocketing through his body. There it was again. Yeah, they definitely had something strong happening between them, no doubt. He felt it good this time. By the look on her face, she felt it too.

"You're …" Ellie didn't finish her sentence.

"Welcome?"

"… A very stubborn man."

"Ha!" said Cedric as the woman returned with an ice pack and Peggy at her side.

"You're the one who is stubborn."

"Are you two married?" asked the woman.

"No," said Ellie and Cedric at the same time.

"Ellie, are you okay?" asked Peggy. "What happened?"

"I'm not sure. I'm okay."

The woman handed the ice pack to Cedric. "I opened the door into her head, that's what happened. Knocked her right to the floor."

Cedric took the ice pack from the woman, broke the seal, and shook it to even out the ice inside. "She's going to be fine. Let's just put this against the bump. It may sting." Cedric leaned in to press the ice pack to her forehead. "Looks like we're going to have matching bumps. What are the chances?"

He adjusted the ice pack and she winced. "Ouch."

"Sorry."

"I can do it." She grabbed the ice pack from Cedric. "You can go."

"Looks like someone is in a hurry to get rid of me."

Peggy touched Ellie on the hand. "Ellie, he's just trying to help."

"It's okay, Peggy," said Cedric. "What Miss Stubborn doesn't know is that I'm taking her to urgent care."

"What? I don't think so," said Ellie. "I said I'm fine."

"I wouldn't doubt it since you're so hardheaded, but when I got hit in the head at the golf course, I was warned that no matter how good I felt, if I had foggy thoughts, any bit of nausea, a headache, anything, I needed to go get checked out. So, I went straight to the emergency. Better safe than sorry, right?"

"Absolutely, I agree," said Peggy. "Have you had any of those symptoms, Ellie?"

Ellie's eyes traveled from Peggy to Cedric, and then back to Peggy. She opened her mouth and then closed it.

"I don't have a headache," Ellie answered. "Just some pain in my forehead."

"That's good. Difficulty thinking? That's another one to watch out for."

She thought for a second and shrugged. "Not sure."

"Take my hands, Miss Stubborn. We're leaving. And don't say no."

Ellie stared at Cedric's outstretched hands. "No."

"Okay then. We do this the hard way."

Cedric reached down and with one swift motion, lifted Ellie off the floor and into his arms. Peggy and the other woman smiled as Ellie tried to climb out of his arms. He shouldn't have been having the thoughts he was having, considering she wasn't feeling well. But how could he not want to kiss the most beautiful, stubborn woman in the world? Even with that third eye growing on her forehead, she was amazing.

Cedric's left hand was on the outside of her right thigh, and his right hand supported her upper body on the side of her rib cage. She felt good.

"Watch your hands, mister." She glanced at his lips.

Cedric laughed. "Quit squirming or I'll throw you over my shoulder, or worse, drop you. You don't want a second bump on your head, do you?"

"Put me down, Mr. Stubborn."

"Not a chance, Miss Stubborn. Unless you promise me you'll walk quietly to my car so we can go. There's an urgent care clinic not too far from here."

"No!"

"Ellie," said Peggy. "There's no discussion here. You need to go. It's a precaution and I insist."

"Fine. Can you tell the caveman to put me down?"

Cedric laughed. "You promise you're going?"

"Promise."

"Good girl." Cedric put her down gently, and she immediately ironed her clothes with her hands.

"You're impossible."

"On the contrary," said Cedric. "I'm much easier than you think."

Chapter Twenty

Ellie was not a happy camper. She should have been concentrating on fundraising, but instead of contacting people, she was on her way to urgent care. All because she was playing hide-and-seek like a five-year-old. She wanted that promotion and there wasn't time to waste.

"This is inconvenient," said Ellie as they walked to the downtown parking garage. "I have a lot to do."

"It won't take long. I just want to be sure you're okay."

"Why do you care?"

Ellie felt his stare, but kept looking forward as they walked.

"I just do," he answered.

Ellie wondered what type of car Cedric drove. Based on Julio's Google search, the guy was loaded. Nothing worse than a materialistic man on a mission to have the most toys before he died.

He probably had a Ferrari or maybe a Maserati.

Cedric pointed in front of them. "That's me at the end on the right."

Ellie came to a halt and jerked her head back after she saw his car. "Oh …"

Cedric stopped and turned to her. "What?"

"Nothing," she lied.

No Ferrari. No Maserati. His car choice was a big surprise. A Toyota Rav4. Cute. Practical. Reliable. As they approached the car, Ellie stopped again and leaned an ear toward the car.

Cedric squished his eyebrows. "You sure you're doing okay?"

She pointed to the car. "You left your engine running?"

He cleared his throat. "I ... uh ... like to have the air conditioning on so it's a comfortable temperature inside for my boy."

Pickles!

Cedric had a kid. He never mentioned it. But what's worse was, he left him in the car! The man needed to be put in jail for child abuse. "Please tell me you're kidding."

"Why would I kid about that?" He gestured to the back window. "See for yourself."

Ellie peaked through the backseat window of the car and let out a big breath. She was staring at the cutest white dog, his tail swinging back and forth, obviously happy to see his owner. "Pickles! It's a dog."

Thank God.

"Of course it's a dog. What did you think it was?"

"I—"

"Wait a minute ... did you say pickles?"

She ignored the question. "What a cute dog."

"Careful. He'll use his cuteness to extract things from you. Cookies, treats, belly rubs ..."

Ellie smiled as Cedric opened the passenger door for her. She slid onto the soft leather seat and felt a lick on the back of her arm. And another. Then, more licks in rapid-fire succession. Ellie turned toward the backseat and was eye to eye with his dog, who was obviously pleased to meet her. "Aren't you a cute boy?"

Cedric got in and strapped on his seat belt. "His name is Tofu."

"Hello, Tofu. You are just the sweetest thing, aren't you?"

Ellie turned around and put her seat belt on as Cedric turned on the stereo. Music blasted through the car.

He turned downed the volume and looked embarrassed. "Sorry." He pulled out of the parking lot and stopped at the red light, tapping his fingers on the steering wheel, looking nervous.

"Barry Manilow."

"Huh?" Cedric glanced at the stereo and then back to the road in front of him.

"You were listening to Barry Manilow."

Cedric was silent for a moment and then pointed to the stereo system. "If that's what was on the radio, then … sure. I guess so."

She pointed to the stereo. "You're in CD mode. That means a Barry Manilow CD."

Cedric looked at the stereo, where it clearly showed it was in CD Mode. "Odd. Tofu, did you put that CD in there? Teach him a few tricks and the dog likes to show off."

Ellie reached over and turned the volume back on the stereo and heard Barry Manilow again. She smiled. "Mandy. I love this song."

Cedric stayed silent.

"Are you embarrassed?" Ellie asked.

"Oh look, the light's green. I guess I should go then." Cedric accelerated and didn't answer the question. He turned to the left to look out the window. "That looks like a new restaurant over there. Indian food." He tapped his fingers on the steering wheel again. "Yup, new restaurant for sure. I'll have to check the reviews on Yelp. I like food. Food is good."

Ellie leaned in toward Cedric to read his face. "You think you can fool me?"

Cedric let out a huge sigh. "Okay, I admit it. I was listening to Barry Manilow."

"There's no need to be embarrassed. I love Barry Manilow."

Cedric stayed silent.

"This isn't some sort of a macho thing, is it? You don't want me to know you listen to Barry Manilow because you're a man and men don't listen to Barry Manilow?"

Cedric swallowed hard. "Well … look at that, we're here. That was fast."

He pulled into the parking lot and took one of the reserved spots for patient drop-off upfront. Cedric was hiding something. Ellie knew it. But she'd have to wait to find out what.

"Just a minute." He got out of the car and ran around to the passenger side. He opened Ellie's door and she got out.

Ellie looked back at the car. "You're going to leave the car running again?"

Cedric nodded. "I try not to leave Tofu in the car, but if I have to, I leave the car running with the AC on. It can get hot in there and I don't want to take a chance."

Ellie had to admit that was so sweet.

The waiting room inside the Urgent Care Clinic was completely empty. The only noise came from the television on the wall. Cedric stood by Ellie's side as she checked in with the nurse, explained what happened, and handed over her insurance card.

"We have a standard concussion protocol," said the nurse after getting Ellie's information. "Follow me and we can take you through it. It's pretty straightforward."

Ellie turned to Cedric. "Thanks for the lift. I'll call someone to pick me up."

"I'll wait."

"That's not necessary." She felt guilty that she said it so harshly and tried to smooth it out. "Thank you, though."

Ellie disappeared behind the double doors with the nurse.

Cedric wandered around the waiting area with Ellie on his mind. Was she serious about asking someone else to pick her up? There was no way he was going to just leave her. It didn't even occur to him to do such a thing. Who was he, the mailman? Just drop off a package and then take off?

No way!

He wanted to make sure she was fine. He'd stay there all night waiting if he had to. That's what you do when you care about someone.

You're there for them when they need you.

Where did that come from? It shouldn't have been a surprise he cared for her that much. How could he care so much about her? They hadn't even been on one date. That needed to change, even though he still couldn't figure out what was going on between them. They needed to talk and clear up some things. A glass of wine—or two—would loosen them up, and then they could talk about things.

He stood underneath the television as the host of some show gossiped about a woman who was cheating on her husband. He reached up and turned the television off.

No use poisoning his mind.

He sat down and eyed the magazines on the table in front of him, leaning forward to shuffle through them.

Cedric grabbed the golf magazine, flipping through the pages. He stopped when he came across one particular article that caught his attention.

The Top 100 Celebrity Golfers

Curious, he checked the list to see if Samuel L. Jackson made the cut. Kenny G was number one on the list, which he thought was pretty odd. He just couldn't picture the jazz saxophonist golfing. Wouldn't his long hair get in the way?

As for Mr. Samuel L. Jackson …

Cedric smiled. According to the article, Samuel was the seventh best celebrity golfer in the world. Cedric felt the bump on his forehead and had to disagree. Maybe that day at Pebble Beach was not a good representation of his skills. Cedric couldn't help but think what a great memory he was given on that day. How many people could say they were almost killed by Samuel L. Jackson?

Fore motherfuckers!

Cedric threw the magazine back on the table, changing seats to face the reception area where Ellie entered.

Thirty minutes later, she walked out.

Cedric jumped up as Ellie stood there like a deer in headlights, staring at him. She obviously didn't expect Cedric to still be there.

"That was fast," said Cedric. "Everything's fine then, right?"

"Everything is good. They did a few concussion tests with my eyes and ears and balance. I passed with flying colors. The main thing was that I didn't have a headache. If I had one, that would have been a big warning."

"Anything else?"

"The doctor said that the only thing I have to worry about is a scary-looking bump on my forehead for a couple of weeks. That's it."

"Just like mine."

"Yeah."

Cedric watched as her gaze went from his bump down to his lips.

He grinned. "What are you doing?"

"What do you mean?"

"You were looking at my mouth."

"Right. Dream on."

He grinned. "I will. But for now, let me get you back."

"You don't have to do that."

"I know I don't have to, but I want to."

"Why?"

"Why not?"

"Not good enough."

Cedric scratched his chin and thought for a moment. "I'm doing it because of Tofu, okay?"

"You need to take me back because of your dog?"

"He was asking about you."

Ellie smiled. "I can't believe we're having this conversation. Okay, so, the dog was asking about me, and what did he say?"

"He said he liked you. Then he wanted to know how the hell I got so lucky to have a beautiful woman like you in my car."

Ellie looked like she was trying to hold back a smile. "And what did you tell him?" she asked as they exited the building.

"I told him I was pretty sure you liked him too, and as for the beautiful woman in my car, I said that I wasn't sure how I got so lucky. But I was hoping to get lucky again."

"This sounds very realistic … a talking dog."

"Not that crazy. You know there's a talking horse?"

"Of course, of course."

Cedric opened the back door. "I just need to let Tofu out for a pee. It will only take a second."

"Okay."

Cedric clicked the leash on the dog and he jumped out of the car, immediately pulling toward Ellie.

"You are just a sweetie pie, aren't you?" said Ellie.

"He drives me crazy sometimes, but he's not too bad."

After Tofu sniffed out the perfect bush to piss on, they headed back to the car.

Cedric turned up the volume on the stereo before he drove off, and Barry Manilow started playing.

His hand shot back up to turn it down again.

Ellie poked Cedric in the arm. "You have issues."

Cedric grinned. "You already knew that."

"It's just Barry Manilow." She reached over and turned the volume up. "Copacabana, great song."

Cedric didn't say a word, but secretly enjoyed the music. Two Barry Manilow songs later, they arrived at her house.

He walked her to the door and she turned to face him. "Thanks. I mean it. You didn't have to do that, but I appreciate it."

"Hey, no need to thank me. I did it for Tofu, remember?"

"That's right."

Cedric stared at her lips and, man, he wanted to kiss them. "I was wondering …"

"Yes. What were you wondering, Mr. Stubborn?"

He stuck his hands in his front pockets and eyed her lips again. "Are you in a slapping mood this evening? Because I was hoping—"

Ellie giggled. "Goodnight."

Cedric's shoulders slumped as he pulled his hands out of his pockets and ran them through his hair. "Right. Goodnight, Ellie."

He turned to walk away and Ellie stopped him. "Actually…"

Cedric turned around quickly, but didn't speak.

Ellie pulled his business card from her purse. "I think I would like to use my thirty second hug card now."

Cedric grinned. "I'd be happy to redeem that for you. And you're in luck, I'm having a two-for-one special this evening."

Chapter Twenty-One

Two things were making Ellie's hands sweat.

Number one, she found out from Peggy that she was losing the fundraising battle. She needed a miracle to win now. She had set up a table with a few bricks and an explanation of her project with the oak tree in hopes of grabbing a few last minute donations from some attendees with deep pockets. It was her last shot.

Yes, she could stay in her current job as librarian—and that wouldn't be such a bad thing, since she enjoyed it—but she had dreams of moving up and taking on more responsibility. She loved giving more and being more. Branch Manager was her ticket to do so.

Number two, Cedric.

It wasn't like they had a date or anything. She knew how he felt about those. She and Cedric were simply going to be in the same place at the same time. But being in the same room with him was not easy when all she wanted to do was kiss him again. Still, she had those conflicted feelings and unanswered questions about him.

She looked at her watch again. The event at the San Jose Museum of Art had started over twenty minutes ago and

Cedric was still nowhere to be seen. She just needed to relax and drink more.

"Would you like to trade that in for a new one?" The waiter asked, staring at Ellie's empty wine glass.

Bingo.

"That would be great. The red, please."

The waiter took her glass and handed her a full one. "Here you go."

"Thanks." Ellie immediately took a sip. More like a big gulp.

She scanned the room for Grandpa Frank, but didn't see him. He wandered off earlier into one of the exhibits. She sighed and took another sip of wine.

"Fancy meeting you here," said the familiar male voice behind her.

Pickles!

It was Vlad. The last person on earth she wanted to see.

"You look beautiful, Ellie. You always do."

Ellie spun around. "What are you doing here?"

Vlad jumped back. "Jesus Christ. What the hell happened to your forehead?"

"You know how to make a girl feel pretty."

"That lump would scare the hell out of anybody. Are you dying or something?"

"Are you seriously asking me that?"

Vlad waved his hand in the air. "Forget it. Sorry."

Ellie waited for him to say something intelligent.

"I'm a new man and I want to prove it to you."

Right. Like she was going to believe that.

"Look. If you've discovered life is not about power and money, that's wonderful. The next person you date will benefit from those changes. What we had is over and you just need to accept it and move on. I don't do second chances."

He caressed the side of her arm and smiled. "I can't accept that. I'm going to show you how I've changed. I'll prove it to you. Then we can be together again, the right way."

"I don't think—"

"I've already shown how serious I am by making a considerable donation this evening."

"What?"

That caught Ellie by surprise. She wanted to ask how much money, but she didn't have it in her.

"I care about you and I care about the fundraiser. I want you to get that job."

She stood there with her hands on her hips. "How did you know?"

"Does it matter?"

No. It didn't. He always had his way of finding out things and she certainly wasn't going to complain about his donation. She needed every penny possible if she were to get that promotion. Maybe now there was a chance.

"Thanks for your donation," she said. "I appreciate it. Now, if you'll excuse me."

Ellie turned and Vlad grabbed her arm.

"That's it?" he said.

"Please let go of my arm." She closed her eyes, hoping when she opened them he'd be gone.

Nope. Still there.

"Ellie, I love you."

Ellie shook her head in disagreement. "You love money more."

"I'm changing."

"Look, Vlad, I mean it. Thank your for the donation, but I stopped loving you a long time ago. Now if you'll excuse me, I need to use the restroom."

Ellie walked off before he could respond, but she knew he wouldn't give up that easily. She knew him too well.

Cedric felt his shoulders tighten as he entered the museum and decided rather quickly he needed a drink to take the edge off. Magically, a waiter appeared with a tray of white and red wine.

"Wine?" asked the waiter. "I have Chardonnay and Cabernet."

"Great," Cedric answered. "Cabernet, please."

The waiter handed him a glass. "Cabernet it is."

Cedric took a sip and tried to relax.

"Well, look who's here, Mr. Cedric in the flesh," said Julio, smiling. "Glad you could make it."

"I wouldn't have missed it," said Cedric, eying Julio's clothes.

Julio raised an eyebrow. "You like what you see?"

Cedric laughed. "Just admiring the clothes. You ever have an off day in the wardrobe department?"

"Never. I always dress to impress. Even when I'm naked, I wear a bow tie." Julio winked.

Cedric nodded, not sure how to respond. "Who doesn't?" He glanced around the museum. "How's the fundraising going?"

Julio frowned. "Not so good."

That wasn't the answer Cedric expected. He looked around the museum again. "Looks like a pretty good turnout to me."

"Oops!" said Julio, covering his lips with his fingers. "I thought you were talking about Ellie's fundraising."

"Aren't they the same thing?"

"Yes and no."

Cedric squished his eyebrows together. "I'm confused."

Julio looked around and then moved closer to Cedric. He grabbed his bicep and squeezed it. "I'm not supposed to say anything, but …"

"Just tell me."

Julio shrugged. "Okay, here's the deal, banana peel. Ellie has a little problem at the moment. Actually, it's a big problem. She needs a substantial donation in the next thirty minutes or she won't get the promotion she's after. End of story."

Cedric jiggled his head as if he were trying to shake water out of his ears. "I don't get it."

Julio let out a loud sigh. "Okay, listen to me very carefully. You must be inebriated, but I think you can do it. Ellie is going up against another woman to be promoted to Peggy's position, since Peggy is retiring. Are you with me so far, superstar?"

"Yes."

"Good. Ellie and Margaret are both equally qualified. So, the brains at the district office thought it would be clever—a bunch of idiots if you ask me—to give the job to the person who raised the most money for the fundraiser. Margaret Rossewood has raised more money than Ellie, so *Ellie* needs a big donation and fast … or she won't get the job. ¿Comprende señor?"

Cedric understood very well. He needed to help Ellie. "Sí."

"Good boy. Of course you know, the money goes to help repair the damage in the children's area."

Cedric nodded and pulled out his checkbook; he'd brought it just in case he wanted to bid on something in the silent auction, but this was even better. He wrote the check, folded it in half, and handed it to Julio. "This is an anonymous donation."

"Of course, thank you. Ellie is an amazing person and she deserves the best."

"I agree," said Cedric, smiling. "Oh, wait!" Cedric opened his wallet and pulled out a check from Michael and Veronica and another from Lucie and Sam. "Two more I forgot about."

"*You* are a good guy, Cedric, I knew it! You shall be rewarded for your kindness." He walked five, maybe six steps, and stopped, before screaming like a teenage girl at a Justin Bieber concert. He turned and ran back to Cedric, and practically knocked him over with an embrace. "You are fricking a-maz-ing!" He looked at the checks again. "Are you kidding me?"

"I told you it was anonymous."

"I haven't told anybody."

"But you looked at it."

"Somebody has to look at it, plus, when I give it to Peggy, she'll see your name on the check. I can't help that."

"Uh huh."

Cedric was feeling anxious. He took a deep breath, then a sip of wine, before wandering into the first exhibit room where "Pilgrimage" by Annie Leibovitz was on display. He recognized the photographer's name and remembered seeing a documentary about her life on television.

"Now I know where I've seen that name," said a male voice behind Cedric.

Cedric turned to find an older man with a kind face and full head of white hair. He looked rather elegant in his gray wool tweed blazer. Cedric noticed his wing-tipped shoes and they made him smile.

The man pointed to the photo and continued. "This photographer shot photos of some of the biggest celebrities in the world for *Rolling Stone Magazine* back in the seventies. Her most famous shot, which made the cover of the magazine, was of John Lennon naked, hugging his fully-clothed wife, Yoko Ono. Sadly, John Lennon was shot and killed hours after that photo shoot."

"That's sad," said Cedric.

The man nodded in agreement. "Looks like she wanted to go in a completely different direction with these photos."

The photos featured personal possessions of notable historical figures that Miss Leibovitz photographed on a journey through the United States and Great Britain between

2009 and 2011. Cedric took a sip of his wine as he stared at a picture of Sigmund Freud's couch.

"Yup," said Cedric. "That's a couch alright."

"I must be missing something here." The man analyzed the picture of the couch. "They call this art." He took a sip of his fruity-looking drink and nodded.

"But did you see who the couch belonged to?" asked Cedric.

"No." The man leaned in and tried to read the information underneath the photo, but the words were too small. He pulled out his reading glasses, put them on, read the placard, nodded, and then removed his glasses and slipped them back in his jacket pocket.

"Does that change your opinion of the photo?" asked Cedric. "Now is it art?"

"Hmm." The man scratched his chin. "Maybe." He stared at the photo longer. "Yes, yes. I think I get it now. When you know who owns the couch, your imagination takes over. Very clever. Your mind starts to wander, imagining what the rest of the room looked like, how many people sat on that couch, and if the couch is still in existence today. *And* … maybe what life was like during those times. I guess you could even imagine yourself on the couch, if you wanted to. That would be more fun, now wouldn't it?"

"Funny you mention it. That's exactly what I did."

"Good for you, a wise man." The man took another sip of his drink. "And when you imagined yourself on the couch, were you alone?"

"No."

"Very good. Present or the past?"

"Neither."

"The future?"

Cedric smiled.

"Ahh," said the man. "Albert Einstein said, 'Imagination is everything. It is the preview of life's coming attractions.' I agree."

"I like that." Cedric stared back at the couch in the photo and again, pictured Ellie sitting right next to him. They both had gray hair and were holding hands and smiling. It seemed so real. He wanted it to be real. "If only …"

"Of course, there's only one thing that could get in your way, though. One thing that would kill your imagination."

"What's that?"

"Fear."

"You're not the first person to tell me this."

"Fear paralyzes you. You can't dream or even make small changes with fear in the way. Fear will kill your heart and your mind."

Cedric turned to the man and stared at him as if he'd just discovered one of life's greatest mysteries. "That's deep." That's exactly what had been paralyzing Cedric for the last two years.

Fear.

Something shifted in Cedric's mind. He wasn't sure what had happened, but he felt an overwhelming sense of peace and relief. He smiled and held out his hand. "I'm Cedric Johnson."

"Frank Fontaine, pleased to meet you."

"Nice to meet you too." Cedric thought the man's name sounded familiar, but he was certain he had never met him before. They moved down to the next photo in the display. It was a shot of Emily Dickinson's only surviving dress.

Cedric frowned. "I'm going to pass on trying to imagine myself in that."

"You have to draw the line somewhere."

Chapter Twenty-Two

If Ellie's jaw were a broom, she could sweep the floor with it. That was how far it just dropped. She couldn't believe what she was seeing … Grandpa Frank talking with Cedric.

How did that happen? And what were they talking about? Just look at the two of them. Laughing like they're best friends!

Cedric looked mighty handsome in his charcoal gray suit, even from across the room.

Dang.

Once again, she thought of that kiss they shared before she slapped him, and the long hug after the hospital. She would be lying if she said she didn't enjoy them.

Peggy stepped up to the podium. "Ladies and gentlemen …"

Ellie turned and watched Peggy, who smiled and waved to a few of the guests as they moved closer to the stage. It was a much-needed distraction.

"Thank you so much for being here!" Peggy continued. "It means the world to us. I wish we didn't need to have a fundraiser like this, but I guess life is unpredictable and throws us a curve ball every now and then. The money we raise this evening will go toward replacing the books that were vandalized recently as well as the stolen computers. We were also hoping to have extra to use in other areas of our library."

Ellie glanced behind her to sneak a peek at Cedric. He was still with Grandpa Frank, watching Peggy speak on stage.

Cedric's eyes drifted to Ellie and she froze, not knowing what to do. Should she smile? Wave? Give him some type of acknowledgment? Before she could come to a decision, he winked at her and smiled.

She swallowed hard and spun back around, now feeling incredible heat in her face and ears.

Her timing was perfect. He caught her checking him out. Great. She tried to focus on Peggy's words, but they seemed to be garbled.

"I'm sappy to pronounce," said Peggy, "that thanks to your viscosity, we've more than secreted our fun blazing holes."

Okay. There was no way Peggy just said that. Ellie was obviously hallucinating and it was Cedric's fault. Him and that damn wink.

Ellie was pretty sure Peggy was talking about fundraising. She took a couple of deep breaths and tried to focus, since there was a good possibility Peggy was going to announce the new Branch manager.

"In fact," continued Peggy, "we had a very special anonymous donor who pretty much made damn sure we would be okay for the next five years. Yahoooo! Please enjoy yourselves and I'll be back with another special announcement later. Thank you very much."

The guests cheered and clapped and whistled as the band started another set of music. Now recovered from Cedric paralysis, Ellie worked her way over to Peggy.

"We did it!" said Peggy, hugging Ellie.

"Yes. What a wonderful evening."

Ellie lost her smile, along with the ability to move her muscles as she watched Grandpa Frank approach.

With Cedric.

"Ellie, sweetie, there you are. I wanted to introduce you to a nice gentleman I met in one of the exhibitions. Cedric Johnson, meet my granddaughter, Ellie Fontaine."

Ellie slowly held out her hand. "Nice to meet you."

Cedric accepted her hand and kissed it. Her knees wobbled just enough to scare her.

"Nice to meet you too … for possibly the tenth time." He grinned as she tried to pull her hand free. Of course, he didn't let go.

Peggy laughed. "You kids are so funny, of course they know each other. Cedric is a volunteer at the library." Peggy mouthed to Cedric the words "thank you."

"Is that right?" Grandpa Frank looked back and forth between Ellie and Cedric.

"Yes, sir," Cedric answered, still holding Ellie's hand.

"Ah. Ellie, is this the young man you told me so much about?"

Ellie felt heat rise up her neck to her face as Cedric raised an eyebrow and grinned. She tried to use her free hand to pull the other hand loose from his vise-like grip, but it was no use.

If she was being honest, she couldn't remember the last time she held a man's hand and it felt wonderful.

"I'll be a monkey's uncle," said Grandpa Frank. "Well, then I guess the only one who hasn't had an official introduction is me. I'm Frank Fontaine, Ellie's grandfather."

Peggy extended her hand and Grandpa Frank kissed it.

Peggy blushed. "Wonderful. What a pleasure to finally meet you! I'm—"

"Peggy Fleming." Smiling, Grandpa Frank said, "The pleasure is mine."

Oh. My. God.

It was clear to Ellie that there was something going on between Grandpa Frank and Peggy. Did she miss something? It was like an instant attraction. Could it happen that quickly? She thought back to the encounter on the street with Cedric and the UPS truck. She thought they had some sort of an instant connection, but then she was pretty sure it disappeared before the light turned green.

"Peggy, have you seen Sigmund Freud's couch?" asked Grandpa Frank.

Peggy giggled. "Why? Did he lose it?"

They both laughed as Ellie and Cedric stood there watching.

"Would you be so kind as to accompany me to the exhibition by the front lobby? There's something I would like to share with you that I think you will find very fascinating."

"I would love to."

And just like that, Grandpa Frank and Peggy were gone, leaving Cedric and Ellie together.

Alone.

Ellie glanced down at their hands, still locked together. "Can I have my hand back now?"

"Oh. Sure. I didn't realize I was still holding it." He grinned. "How awkward."

Right.

A waiter walked by with a tray of wine. As if Cedric and Ellie were both on a synchronized wine-drinking team, they simultaneously grabbed a glass of wine from the tray and took a sip.

They were silent for a few moments until Cedric decided to jump in.

"So."

"So."

Cedric grinned. "You drive me crazy."

"Me? What did *I* do?"

"All you have to do is be yourself, that's it. That would drive any man crazy."

"What does that mean?"

"Have you seen yourself? God, can we start with that hair of yours? Do you know how many times I've wanted to run my fingers through it?"

"Uh. No."

"Well, about a thousand times or so, okay?"

"Huh." Where did that come from? Ellie stared at his hands for a few seconds imagining them running through her hair.

"Did you know your eyes are closed right now?" asked Cedric.

Pickles!

"Of course I do," she lied, as she opened them.

"Right." Cedric laughed.

"You seem different this evening."

"I do?"

She nodded. "Something's changed."

"And do you like the change?"

Ellie shrugged. "Maybe."

"Maybe?"

More silence.

Ellie eyed him from head to toe. "What is it?"

He shrugged. "Maybe I finally know what I want."

Ellie blinked. It sounded like he was talking about her.

"Stop looking at me that way," said Cedric.

"What are you talking about?"

"You're licking your lips."

Ellie retracted her tongue. She had no idea she was doing that.

Cedric continued, "It makes me want to kiss you and break that world record we discussed."

"Is that right?"

"Yeah, but first we need to talk. Seriously."

Way to be a buzz kill, mister.

"Do we?" she answered, taking another big gulp of wine.

"Yes." He raised her two gulps of wine. "I'm tired of not knowing what is going on between us and jumping to conclusions. Let's just get this out in the open right now."

"Uh … okay." She took another sip of wine. And another.

"We have some sort of a chemistry. A connection. Do you agree?"

"Uh …"

"A simple yes or no would be fine."

"Yes."

"Good. But whatever *this* is, isn't going to happen unless we clear up a few things. Let me just spit it out. Number one … Are you seeing your ex again?"

"No."

"Do you plan to?"

"No."

"Do you still love him?"

"No. And wait! Hang on there. Why do you get to ask all of the questions?"

"God, you're so sexy when you pout."

"I don't pout!"

"If you say so. By all means, fire away." He stood there with a smirk on his face.

Such a cute smirk.

"You told me you didn't believe in online dating …"

"That wasn't a question."

"I wasn't finished. Haven't you ever heard of dramatic pauses?"

"Is that what that was?"

"Yes."

"Okay. Very nicely done."

"Thank you."

"But, back to the online dating thing … I misspoke. What I should have said was … online dating *probably* works for a lot of people, but *I* am not one of those people."

"Right. So … I saw your dating profile online. Explain *that*."

"Piece of cake," he said, smiling.

"Trying to think of a good lie?"

"Not at all. I know that question is related to why you were in such a stinky mood that day at the library."

"Stinky mood? You mean the day you turned into Austin Powers on crack?"

"Okay, I admit, that was horrific, but let's focus on one issue at a time. Back to the online dating thing. My friend, Tony, signed me up for an account and put my info on the website. He called it an "intervention." I called it stupidity and told him to remove the profile from the website. He did. Next question."

"So, just to clarify, it wasn't you, but Tony?"

"Correct. Never even logged in, not once. I did however threaten bodily injury to my best friend if he didn't remove it, sort of stupid considering he has a black belt in karate."

"The owner of Vela Veggie, I heard she was married. Are you having an affair with her?"

Cedric first stood there with his mouth open. Then he tilted his head to the side before laughter rumbled from his chest. "Victoria? Not. Even. Close. She's the wife of one of my best friends, Michael. I was there that night to say happy birthday, that's all."

Cedric pulled the wine glass out of Ellie's hand and set it down on the cocktail table, along with his wine glass, and then turned back to her, moving closer.

Ellie gazed over at her wine on the table and then back over to Cedric. "What are you doing? I wasn't finished with that."

"We'll get back to it in a moment. It looks like we are getting this cleared up faster than I thought, and I was just preparing things for our first official kiss, which should be happening momentarily."

Ellie tapped her fingers on the side of her leg and bit her lip. "First kiss?"

"Of course. And I wouldn't want to spill any wine on that beautiful dress of yours. This particular kiss won't be fifty-eight hours, though. I hope that's okay."

"I …"

"But it's going to be a damn good one."

Cedric moved closer.

Ellie blinked. "Okay, first of all … not gonna happen. And number two, you already kissed me once."

She had no idea why she said that; all she'd been thinking about was another kiss from him.

"The other kiss didn't count since I prefer not to be assaulted directly afterward."

Ellie laughed. "Oh … that. I'm sorry, but—"

"No need to get into it. I think we're good. Are we good?"

"Well …"

"Good."

Cedric took another step closer and she licked her lips. He put his hands on her waist and let his fingers slowly glide to her lower back. He pulled her forward and now they were completely touching, body to body.

Every nerve in Ellie's body tingled in anticipation. Why was she so nervous? It was like it was her first time. There was nothing to prevent this from happening now. They had crazy chemistry and the misunderstandings had been cleared up. She was ready now, she was sure of it. He was staring at her lips and she was certain it was going to happen any second. But why was he taking so long?

She let out a deep breath. "Are you going to kiss me or what?"

Cedric laughed. "You have to have patience."

"Forget patience." Ellie grabbed his neck and yanked him downward until their mouths met.

Chapter Twenty-Three

Cedric closed his eyes and enjoyed the moment as the woman he'd been thinking about practically twenty-four hours a day latched on to his body like a straitjacket and kissed the hell out of him. He pulled her closer and took control of the kiss—he liked to be in the driver's seat.

Based on what now poked Ellie in her abdomen, he was pretty sure there was no hiding how he felt.

Cedric had a major breakthrough and had let another woman back into his heart. He was past the point of no return. He wasn't shutting her down and he wasn't running.

He withdrew from the most amazing, sensual kiss of his life, smiled, and waited.

Ellie smiled. "What?"

"No slap this time. Things are looking up."

Ellie poked him in the chest. "I have a feeling you'll never let me forget that tiny slap."

It sounded like Ellie was going to keep him around for a long time, and he was definitely okay with that.

Cedric smiled. "Tiny? Just the sight of your hand gives me anxiety. You may have to start wearing gloves."

"You big baby." Ellie gave Cedric another kiss on the lips. "Thank you."

"For what?"

Did Julio tell her about the check? That was supposed to be anonymous.

"For distracting me. I was up for a promotion that I wanted and found out yesterday that the chances were very slim. I won't bore you with the story, but what I'm trying to say is, I'm happy. Things happen for a reason and if I'm meant to stay librarian for a while longer, that's okay. I do love my job."

"That's a good attitude to have, but it's not over until it's over."

Cedric grinned and Ellie cocked her head to the side, analyzing him.

"Friends," said Peggy, now back up on stage, talking into the microphone. Ellie and Cedric turned toward the stage. "This evening wouldn't have been possible without the help of someone very special. She put in countless hours helping me get everything in place. I just wanted to acknowledge Ellie Fontaine at this time and say thank you!"

Cedric applauded with the guests as Peggy waved Ellie to the stage.

"Excuse me," said Ellie.

"Of course," said Cedric.

"Don't go too far, though. Now that we've broken the stranglehold on our relationship, I want to go for that world record."

Cedric smiled as he watched Ellie join Peggy on the stage. He liked the way that sounded, "our relationship." She was something special.

Ellie was greeted on stage with a bouquet of flowers, followed by a hug and kiss from Peggy, who returned to the podium. "Ellie has been my support system at the library. She started out as a motivated intern, was a part-time librarian for three years, and a full-time librarian for the last five years. Many of you know I'm retiring and I've had a wonderful time managing the library for the last three decades. But it's time to pass the baton, so to speak. And it gives me *great* pleasure to present to you the new Branch Manager, Ellie Fontaine!"

"No." Ellie stood there like a deer in headlights as the guests cheered and applauded. A deer with its mouth open.

"Yes, Ellie. Congratulations. You've earned it and we know you'll do a fantastic job."

Ellie covered her mouth with her hands as tears streamed down her cheeks.

Peggy hugged Ellie again as Cedric whistled and cheered, along with the other guests.

He made his way toward Ellie and met her on the side of the stage as Peggy approached the podium again. "Please join us on the second level for coffee and dessert."

Ellie wiped her eyes and smiled before jumping into Cedric's arms.

Cedric kissed her and grinned. "Congratulations, Miss Branch Manager."

"Thank you." Ellie let out a deep breath. "I don't understand what just happened. I didn't think I was going to get the job. This doesn't make any sense."

Cedric wiped a tear from her cheek. "Life is unpredictable sometimes."

Ellie laughed and nodded. "Or maybe all the time."

Grandpa Frank approached and hugged Ellie. "That's my girl. Congratulations." He kissed her on her forehead next to her bump. "You know your mother would be proud of you."

Ellie smiled. "Thank you." But her smile vanished quickly as she put her hand over her heart, startled from the decibel-crushing noise getting closer by the second. She was pretty sure an African elephant had entered the museum and was charging her. She turned and watched as Julio ran directly at her, his arms waving in the air, screaming.

"Ellie, you did it! Congratulations!"

Julio hugged everyone, saving Cedric for last. He whispered into his ear. "You rock."

Peggy came down the stairs from the stage and smiled at Grandpa Frank. "Ellie, I want to introduce you to the new division manager before she leaves. Can you excuse us for a moment?"

Ellie turned to Cedric and caressed the side of his arm. "I'll meet you upstairs for dessert."

"Sounds great," said Cedric.

Cedric made a pit stop in the bathroom before heading upstairs. As he came out of the bathroom, his thoughts were still on Ellie and what an amazing woman she was. Kind. Intelligent. Funny. Beautiful. She had everything he wanted in a woman, and now that they cleared things up, nothing was going to stand in their way.

Except maybe the asshole approaching him.

"Cedric Johnson," Vlad said.

"In the flesh," said Cedric.

Vlad stared at the injury on Cedric's forehead. "Jesus Christ, you too? You and Ellie join some type of weird fucking masochistic cult or something?"

"Can I help you with something?"

"I saw you kissing Ellie."

"And what, you want to wrestle again?"

Vlad ran his fingers through his hair and moved in closer to Cedric so that they were almost eye to eye—he had Cedric in height by maybe an inch. He let out a stinky, alcohol-infested breath. Tequila.

"Don't fuck with me," said Vlad. "Stay away from her or you'll be sorry."

Vlad cracked his knuckles, obviously thinking it would intimidate Cedric. He couldn't be sure if Vlad was drunk, and he didn't want to test it. But Cedric wasn't going to be bullied either. He knew what he wanted now.

Ellie.

He was clear about that and nobody—especially Vlad—was going to stand in his way.

"You're threatening me," said Cedric. "That's sweet."

"You should take my warning seriously."

"Or else?"

"Or else I'll snap your legs off and shove 'em down your throat."

Cedric laughed. "You know that's not physically possible, right?"

"Obviously you don't know the power I possess."

"That's not true. The power of your breath could probably sedate an elephant." Cedric pulled a pack of mints from his pocket. "Mint?"

"Those car problems and the tickets? They're just the beginning." He pointed his finger at Cedric. "*You* ain't seen nothing yet."

Cedric blinked. Vlad just admitted to everything.

He watched in disbelief as Vlad walked out of the museum.

Cedric tried to shake off the negative vibe and headed upstairs to meet lovely Ellie.

He approached her and smiled at her. "What we have before us is intense."

"I'm just as overwhelmed as you are," said Ellie.

"Okay, let's take it slow and think about what we're getting ourselves into. It may not be worth it."

"You may be right."

Cedric laughed. "Okay, I've changed my mind. I just want to jump in, head first."

Ellie and Cedric eyed the eight-foot dessert table full of every possible type of dessert: cookies, cakes, pies, cream puffs, cheesecake, baklava, chocolate-covered strawberries, tiramisu, and wide variety of fresh fruit.

Ellie shrugged. "I'm not sure what to do."

Cedric laughed. "I have an idea. You pick three and I'll pick three. Then we'll share."

"That's romantic. You're scoring points with me."

"Good to know."

Ellie selected a serving of the tiramisu, a piece of blueberry pie, and a chocolate chip cookie.

Cedric chose a piece of baklava, the cheesecake, and some pineapple slices.

Grandpa Frank waved Ellie and Cedric over to join him and Peggy, who both looked mighty comfortable together.

"How are you kids doing?" asked Grandpa Frank. "Enjoying the evening?"

"Very much," said Ellie.

"Me too. How about you?"

Grandpa Frank smiled. "How could I not be? I was able to witness my granddaughter being recognized for her hard work, then get promoted. And I met her boss, who seems to be a very intriguing woman." Grandpa Frank winked at Peggy.

Cedric leaned into Ellie and whispered, "There's something going on there. Your grandpa may get some tonight."

Ellie pinched Cedric on his side and whispered back, "I'm visual."

Cedric laughed.

"You two make a cute couple," said Peggy. "Matching bumps and all."

Ellie smiled. "Thanks."

Cedric agreed with Peggy. He thought they were a cute couple too. He was pretty sure he was going to fall hard for Ellie, and fast. And they still hadn't had a date yet. He knew he had to change that and couldn't wait to get her alone.

He leaned into Ellie again and whispered, "I'm enjoying my time with you this evening immensely, but I just can't help but wonder when I'll see you again. Alone. We need to go on a real date, you and me."

Ellie leaned into Cedric's ear. "I agree. The sooner the better."

"Well, then, two bonus points for you."

"For agreeing?"

"For your enthusiasm. Do you do Sushi?"

Ellie smiled. "I do."

Holy crap.

Cedric was in trouble. Just the way she whispered those two words had him picturing the two of them on their wedding day.

I do.

"Sushi it is," he said. "Let's plan on six o'clock at Yuki Sushi. I may have to meet you there, though, if you don't mind. I can call you in the morning to confirm."

"Sounds great. Don't be late. I can tolerate a lot of things, but tardiness isn't one of them."

"Why would I be late?"

Cedric wasn't sure why he asked that. He always seemed to be running late.

Chapter Twenty-Four

The next morning, Ellie tried to stay busy at work and keep her mind off Cedric, but it wasn't easy. As she outlined a set of goals for her first year as Branch Manager, Julio coded and classified a collection of gardening books next to her.

It had been a wonderful evening last night. The drama between her and Cedric was merely misunderstandings, and now they were able to proceed forward getting to know each other. They had talked for hours at the museum and Ellie felt closer to Cedric.

And that kiss.

God, it was magical, and delicious.

Still, with the positives of the evening, something was bugging Ellie. He hadn't called when he said he would.

I can call you in the morning to confirm.

He did say the morning. It was 11:55 a.m. and the morning was just about over. Why hadn't he called?

She just had to deal with this head on. She could do it. She glanced at the clock again.

"How many times are you going to look at the clock?" asked Julio.

Good question. Ellie was obsessed, having looked at the clock at least a dozen times over the course of the last few hours. Maybe Cedric just overslept, they didn't leave the museum until very late. He overslept.

Yeah, that's it. Or not.

"He said he'd call in the morning to confirm Sushi for tonight. It's not morning any longer."

"Maybe he meant Hawaii time."

"Not funny."

"Don't worry. He likes you too much not to call."

Ellie hoped so. She glanced at the clock again.

"Stop that or I'll yank it off the wall and do my impression of the River Dance all over it."

"You don't even know how to do the River Dance."

"I'll learn and then I'll trample that clock. And you know what, Ellie May? Your obsession with the time has run its course."

"I'm not obsessed."

"Tell me that after Cedric arrives late to one of your dates. Tell me it doesn't drive you crazy. Then I'll believe you."

"No comment."

"And by the way, are you even sure your phone is on?"

"Of course it's—" Ellie's eyes darted back and forth between Julio and her purse. She reached over and pulled her cell phone out and touched the screen.

No power.

Julio giggled. "And I considered you the smartest woman in the world? Ha! You're going to get demoted to second smartest in the world."

"This isn't funny." She pressed the power button on her phone. A minute later the phone sounded. She had a message.

"Hi Ellie, it's Cedric. It's eight in the morning. Hope I'm not calling too early, but I couldn't help myself. Just wanted to tell you how much I enjoyed your company last night. And I'm also calling to confirm Sushi for tonight. I'm going to be out on a couple of appointments for work, so unfortunately I'll have to meet you there. Six o'clock at Yuki Sushi. See you then."

Ellie erased the message and the second message started.

"Hi Ellie, it's me again … Cedric. I forgot to say, wear something casual because we may go somewhere after sushi, if it's not too late. Also, you may want to bring some Chapstick with you because we're going to break that world record."

Ellie giggled and disconnected.

"I see things are okay," said Julio.

Ellie nodded and smiled. "More than okay."

***

Cedric's phone rang as he headed out to meet Ellie. He stepped back inside the house, closed the front door behind him, and answered it. "This is Cedric."

"Cedric, this is Dominic Cunnings, County Supervisor."

Cedric's heart started to beat a little faster. "Hi, Dominic. I hope you have good news for me." He ran his fingers through his hair and began to pace back and forth.

"I think you'll consider it good. Although it's not definite, I talked with a few people and there's a strong possibility we can make your grandfather's old property a historical landmark."

Cedric let a huge breath and closed his eyes. "That's great."

"Like I said, it's not a hundred percent, so don't go throwing a party yet or making any plans. There are lots of things that need to be done, but all signs are pointing in the right direction."

"That's good enough for me."

"Good. I'll be in touch soon."

Cedric disconnected and pumped his fists in the air. He walked outside, looked up into the sky, and smiled. "We did it, Mom."

As he drove to meet Ellie, Cedric couldn't help but feel like he was going to explode with excitement. His promise to his mom was going to happen. And now, he was on his way to meet Ellie. Amazing Ellie. Things couldn't be any better.

He slapped the steering wheel and smiled. "Yes!" But the excitement faded after he saw what was ahead of him on the road, the one thing he didn't want to see. Bumper to bumper traffic.

"No!" Cedric banged his hand on the steering wheel.

The traffic was at a standstill and the stoplight at the corner was flashing red. There was obviously a power outage or construction going on.

Why tonight? Cedric glanced at the clock. He was supposed to meet Ellie in ten minutes and there was no way he was going to get there on time. He remembered very clearly what she had said to him.

I can tolerate a lot of things, but tardiness is not one of them.

She was very adamant, but hopefully she'd understand he couldn't control the traffic.

He pulled out his cell phone to call Ellie and the call went straight to her voicemail.

"Hi Ellie, it's Cedric. I'm running late, but I'll be there as soon as I can. I'm sorry."

He disconnected. What an idiot. He was going to be late for his first date with the most beautiful woman in the world. Why didn't he allow extra time, just in case?"

He found an open spot on the street in front of Yuki Sushi. He looked at the clock again. Five minutes after six.

He unfastened his seat belt and watched as Ellie exited the restaurant. She was wearing black jeans and a turquoise top with something written in French across the chest. She was leaving and walking down the sidewalk rather quickly.

Not good.

"Hey," he said, trying to stop her. "Sorry for being late."

"I have to go." She continued walking.

"Seriously? I said I was sorry. And besides, you haven't even had a chance to translate your shirt for me yet."

She stopped and turned around. It was obvious by her expression that she didn't think that was funny.

Cedric shrugged. "Sorry. Please don't go. I've been looking forward to this."

"I told you I had a problem with tardiness. Time is precious."

"I called you to tell you I was running late. Does that count for something?"

"I don't have my phone with me."

"Come on, five minutes isn't going to kill you."

Cedric was pretty sure he saw her nostrils flare. This wasn't good.

"Five minutes killed my mom," she said.

"I don't get it."

"Of course not, you're just like the Austrians."

"What does that mean?"

"Napoleon Bonaparte said, 'The reason I beat the Austrians is they did not know the value of five minutes.' Just like you."

She got in her car and started the engine.

Cedric watched as she just sat there, staring at the steering wheel. He tapped on the window, trying to figure out how he could make everything better. "Hey, Ellie. Please don't go. This is just a big misunderstanding, whatever it is. But please tell me what's going on. Your mom died?"

She looked at him through the window for a few moments and then nodded.

"I'm sorry." He ran his fingers through his hair. "Mine too."

She turned to look at him and stared into his eyes for a few seconds, before opening the door and getting out of the car.

"Ellie, I like you. I promise you this is coming from the heart when I tell you …" Cedric looked into her eyes. "I just feel like giving you a hug right now. That's all I want to do. Is that okay?"

She didn't answer, but moved closer to him. He extended his arms and she fell into his chest. The hug only lasted a minute, but it was like a year of therapy. It was what they both needed at that very moment.

Cedric pulled away and smiled. "I'm trainable, you know. Just like Tofu."

"Maybe so, but Tofu is cuter." Ellie cracked a smile.

Cedric put his hand over his heart. "Oh! The dog is better looking than me. Okay, I'm willing to accept that."

"And he's kissed me more than you have. You are seriously slacking off and—"

Cedric cut her off and kissed her good.

Thirty seconds later, he pulled away and smiled.

Ellie still had her eyes closed and her mouth slightly open. "Not bad," she muttered.

"Ha! Not bad? Your eyes are still closed, so I think it was much better than 'not bad.'"

Ellie opened her eyes and blushed. "Okay, it was … outstanding. Just don't let it go to your head."

"Too late. By the way, I'll be having my very first sushi experience with you." Cedric grabbed her hand, smiled, and led her into the restaurant.

Chapter Twenty-Five

Ellie glanced around the packed restaurant, admiring the many happy faces and moving chopsticks. "I can't believe you're a sushi virgin."

Cedric laughed. "I'm a creature of habit. I have so many things that I enjoy, I didn't think it was necessary to try anything new."

Ellie smiled. "What made you change your mind?"

"You."

"Me? What did I do?"

"Let's just say you inspire me to get out of my comfort zone."

They sat and Cedric agreed to let Ellie order various items from the menu and a couple of beers. When the first order arrived, Cedric perked up and pointed to the plate. "What's that again?"

"California Roll. Avocado and crab. I wanted to break you in slowly."

Cedric awkwardly pick up one of the rolls with his chopsticks and then dropped it on the table. He tried again, this time dipping it in soy sauce, and squeezing it into his mouth. He nodded and chewed. "Love it."

"You need to mix some wasabi with the soy sauce and ginger."

"No, no, no. I had a friend who mistook wasabi for avocado and almost died after a spoon full. I'll start off slow, as you suggested. No wasabi."

"That's fine. I'm impressed with your enthusiasm so far."

They were silent for a spell and ate. Then Cedric broke the silence. "I want to let you know even though we're not talking, I'm still enjoying your company and think you're incredible. There, I said it." He grabbed another California Roll and dipped it in soy sauce.

"Likewise."

Vlad walked up, picked up one of Ellie's California Rolls with his fingers, dipped it in her soy sauce, and popped it in his mouth. "Mmm. So good. Just like you, baby." He licked his fingers. Cedric stood up and opened his mouth to say something, but Vlad cut him off. "Easy tiger. I just stopped by to say hello to Ellie. I saw her car outside."

"Judging by her body language, she doesn't look like she wants to talk with you."

Vlad inspected Cedric from head to toe and then shrugged, looking back to Ellie. "What are you doing with this guy, Ellie? You deserve better."

Ellie signed. "And you're better? Please leave."

"We all have flaws, Ellie." He grabbed a piece of her edamame and ate it.

Cedric stepped closer to Vlad. "Get out of here. Now."

Vlad laughed. "Okay, tough guy. But make sure you ask her to tell you about the time she killed her mother."

"You bastard." Ellie pushed Cedric out of the way and punched Vlad in the chest.

"Is everything okay?" asked the waitress. "You want police?"

"I *am* the police," said Vlad. "And I was just leaving."

Ellie and Cedric sat back down as Vlad walked out of the restaurant. The waitress placed another order on the table and Cedric pointed to it. "What's this one?"

The waitress smiled. "Spider roll."

As the waitress walked away, Cedric slid the plate in front of Ellie. "Don't know about this one ... spiders. Hmm. There's a Mexican place downtown that serves deep-fried grasshoppers."

Ellie forced a smile. "Spider Roll is just a name. There aren't actual spiders in it."

Cedric grinned. "Is that right? Please tell me more."

She could see what type of person Cedric was. Kind and compassionate. He obviously knew what just happened was embarrassing to her and he was trying to distract her. Sweet. She could kiss him for that. She also felt she needed to say something, to explain things. "He likes to torture me." Her eyes started to burn.

"Well, he's gone now. We can just pretend like it never happened."

Ellie wiped her eyes and forced another smile. "It's probably good for you to know the truth. He wasn't always an asshole. The change occurred after he started working on the force. It was like things changed and that was all he cared about. I didn't want to be with someone who valued money more than they valued their relationships."

"I get it, but it's the past and it's time to move on."

"Well …" She looked toward the door. "The problem is, my past doesn't want to go away." She took a sip of her beer and set it down.

"He'll get what's coming to him."

She nodded. "As for my mom, he's right. I blame myself for her death."

Cedric covered her hand with his. "You don't have to talk about it, if you don't want to."

"Thanks, but since we're getting to know each other, it's probably good you know. This particular story is connected to my … issue."

"You only have one issue? I'm impressed."

Ellie smiled and kissed Cedric on the cheek. "You're a doll." She took another sip of beer. "But let me tell you."

"Okay."

"I was tied up at work one day; we were preparing for a used book sale. I lost track of time and I didn't get my mom to the airport on time for her flight. She was going to see my aunt in North Carolina, who was very sick. Because of me, she missed her flight by five minutes. So … my mom had to take the next flight and—" Ellie pulled a tissue from her purse and wiped her eyes. "Well …" She thought for a moment. "Because I made her miss her flight, she got on the next one, and that plane crashed."

"I'm sorry."

Ellie wiped her eyes again. "They say that things happen for a reason, which I normally agree with. But, you know what? I haven't been able to figure out the reason for removing these precious people from my life."

"You can't blame yourself for those things."

"I can and I do. That's why Julio says I'm obsessed with punctuality. That's why I freaked out when you were late today. That's why I freak out when anyone is late. Five minutes was all my mom needed and she'd still be alive today."

"You don't know that. Something else could've happened. Anything could happen to us on any given day. I could have died from that golf ball hitting my head or I could even get hit by a UPS truck." Ellie smacked him on the arm and sniffled. "We can't predict the future and there are some things that are just out of our hands."

"I could have prevented her death, I know that. She died because *I* was late."

"I don't want to argue with you, but let me say this. The day I met you on the corner? I was on my way to an appointment and was running five minutes late."

"Right. I get it. You didn't die that day. I'm not saying something bad is going to happen every single time you're late. I'm just saying bad things can happen when you stray from the plan."

"And good things. Or amazing things. Or the best thing ever in your entire life."

"I highly doubt that."

Cedric scooted closer to Ellie and grabbed her hands. "Okay, I'm going to start again, but this time, let me finish what I have to say. Promise?"

"Promise."

"Okay. I had an appointment and I was running five minutes late. Now for me, I don't have a problem at all with being late, because if I *hadn't* been five minutes late that day, I wouldn't have met you."

Ellie sat there and stared at Cedric for a moment. A tear fell from her eye and she could see Cedric's eyes follow it as it traveled down her cheek.

"Now I know we've only just begun." He wiped her tear away. "And I know there's still so much we don't know about each other. But holy hell, I met you because I was late! And that's the best thing that has happened to me in years. So what do you have to say about that?"

Ellie sniffled and smiled. "Kiss me you fool."

Cedric kissed her on each cheek and followed it up with a kiss on the lips. "God, this is scary …"

"Death?"

"No. I was thinking about how good this feels. You and me."

"Yeah …"

"Pardon the urge, but I want to kiss you again."

"What a coincidence, I *want* you to kiss me."

Cedric kissed her and smiled. "Now I guess I need to eat some spiders."

Ten minutes later, they finished the last of the sushi and beers. Ellie felt much better and more relaxed, enjoying Cedric's company.

"This place is amazing and I definitely want to return," said Cedric. "But I want to take you somewhere else. Somewhere special. If we hurry, we can get there before it gets dark."

"Where?"

"It's a surprise."

"I swear, you're just like my grandpa Frank."

"Is that good or bad?"

Ellie pretended to think about it for a moment. "Good, I suppose."

"Good to know. I think he's a pretty cool guy. You okay with leaving your car here?"

"Of course."

"Great. We need to stop by my house and pick up a hairy boy who's going to be very happy to see you."

Fifteen minutes later, Cedric drove down Highway 101 South as Tofu sat on Ellie's lap, perfectly content being pampered.

Tofu reached up and gave Ellie's chin a lick.

Cedric looked at Tofu. "Hey, stop that."

Ellie laughed. "You jealous?"

"Hell yeah I am."

As they passed through Morgan Hill, Ellie said, "The outlets in Gilroy?"

Cedric glanced over to Ellie and then moved his eyes back on the road, laughing. "You think the outlets are the special place I wanted to take you to? Obviously, you've forgotten I'm a guy and most guys don't like shopping."

"Yes, I guess I forgot. You may need to refresh my memory."

"You just wait until I stop this car." Cedric turned into the farm.

"Promises, promises." Ellie smiled up at the countless palm trees along both sides of the entrance to the farm. "Syagrus romanzoffiana."

"Bless you. Kleenex?"

Ellie laughed. "That's the scientific name for queen palm trees. I just love them."

"And they are native to?"

"Is this another round of drill the librarian?"

"Yes. Your answer?"

"South America."

"More specifically, please."

"Northern Argentina. Eastern Brazil, and Bolivia."

Cedric parked in front of the garage, turned off the engine, and leaned into Ellie. "Very impressive. You've just won a hundred kisses."

Ellie pushed him away. "That's just not going to do. Double or nothing."

"Okay." Cedric thought for a moment. "Largest populated city in the world."

"Shanghai. Eighteen million and change."

"Smallest town in the U.S."

"Ha! Buford, Wyoming."

"Population?"

Ellie gave Cedric the 'you think I don't know this?' look. "One."

Cedric turned to Ellie. "One what?"

"One person."

"Impossible."

"No it's not."

"Yes it is."

"Nope."

"Yup."

Ellie watched Cedric as he ran his fingers through his hair, obviously considering the possibility of a town of one.

"God," he said. "The poor bastard must be lonely."

"Why would you assume the person is a he?"

"Because men can be idiots."

She smiled. "Well, I certainly can't argue with that. But, maybe … it's a woman who is hiding from those so-called idiots?"

"You need to stop doing that."

"What?"

"It's bad enough your beauty almost debilitates me. Add your intelligence into the mix and I'm just a blubbering mass of helplessness."

"So, I can take advantage of you?"

Cedric grinned. "Yes, please."

Ellie slid across and gave him a kiss. She wanted it too. She loved the conversations with Cedric. They were fun and energetic and stimulating.

Cedric broke the kiss and smiled. "Come on, time for a tour." He opened his door and Tofu jumped out, making a beeline for the chickens.

He grabbed Ellie's hand and walked with her through the garlic field. Ellie inhaled deeply and moaned as she exhaled. "Love that smell."

"Yeah. I never get tired of it."

"How many acres do you have?"

"Thirty. They give us around three hundred thousand pounds of garlic every year."

She looked around, considering the quantity. "That's amazing."

"We don't sell everything. Twenty percent of the harvest is saved to plant next year."

"Still, I'm in awe."

"Well, compared to the big time farmers, it's just a drop in the bucket. But I can't complain. I'm grateful for what I have."

Humble. Ellie liked that about Cedric. "How did farming in your family begin?"

"It started with my grandfather, Papa George," Cedric said proudly. "He discovered a variety of garlic on a visit to Spain many years ago and thought it was the most flavorful garlic in the world. He had never tasted something so bold—with a denser concentration of nutrients and minerals. The Spanish had been cultivating it there for centuries. He was so excited about it that he brought it here and planted it in his yard. Five years later, he bought a farm with a partner and became an instant garlic farmer. A few years after that, he outgrew that farm, sold it, and bought a bigger one. This farm. In fact, I'm trying to buy that original property to build a garlic museum there."

"That's wonderful."

"Papa George was a genius. He knew everything there was to know about farming. He nurtured the seeds over the years and now we are one of only two commercially grown heirloom garlic farms in the entire United States. That was long before Gilroy was promoted as the garlic capital of the world. But you probably know it's really not the garlic capital."

Ellie smiled. "China produces almost eighty percent of the world's garlic."

"Yeah, but who has the best garlic?"

"Uh … Cedric Johnson?"

"Well, technically, Papa George, but it's all in the family. It's something I'm very proud of, but to be honest, I have a lot of help."

"From who?"

"The Garcia family, consisting of my best friend Tony and his mom and dad, Antonio and Ana."

"Is this the same Tony who put you on the dating website?"

"The one and only. You'll meet him soon. In fact, I would like to apologize ahead of time for everything that he says and does."

Ellie laughed.

Even as they stood in the middle of the farm, admiring the acres of garlic, Ellie still had a hard time picturing Cedric as a farmer. More like a world-class athlete or swimsuit model.

Great.

The thought of Cedric half-naked had her craving another kiss and even more than that.

Cedric held her hand up. "Your hand is sweaty. You thinking about last night?"

Ellie blushed. "Maybe."

Cedric pulled her against him and kissed her. This kiss felt different. Better. More intimate. She was falling for Cedric, and it was getting more special by the minute. No turning back now. Not that she wanted to.

Cedric deepened the kiss and she wondered if it would be wrong to rip off his clothes right there in the field.

"Hola Cedric," came a yell from the guesthouse. "¿Qué tal?"

Cedric waved. "¡Muy bien! Traigo a una amiga conmigo."

No way. Cedric spoke Spanish. Ellie looked back toward the guesthouse at an older Hispanic couple holding hands. Obviously Antonio and Ana.

Ellie turned back to Cedric with her mouth open. "You're fluent?"

"Sí, señorita."

"I must say, the more time I spend with you, the more you impress me."

"I would have to say the same about you." Cedric kissed her on her head and walked toward the guesthouse to meet the Garcias.

After the introductions, Ana said, "Well, you must be a special woman, Cedric never brings women here."

"Never," added Antonio.

Ellie turned to Cedric. "Is that so?"

Cedric shrugged. "I guess you're a little bit special. Or a lot."

Ana waved them into the house. "Come. I'll prepare something for you."

"We just ate," said Cedric. "But thank you." He turned to Ellie. "We'll need to come back another day for breakfast so you can try Ana's chilaquiles. It's the most amazing thing in the world."

"Gracias, hijo." Ana kissed Cedric on the cheek.

Antonio pointed to the farm next door. "You have to take her to see the cherries. They're ready."

"Great idea. We'll see you later."

They walked down the path toward the cherry farm and Cedric grabbed Ellie's hand.

Ellie smiled. "Antonio and Ana are sweet."

"They're the best."

"Arf!"

Cedric and Ellie turned around and watched as Tofu ran toward them.

"Looks like someone was pissed off to be left behind."

Ellie laughed and bent down to stroke Tofu on his back. "Did you think we were going to leave you, Tofu? We wouldn't do that!"

It was happening again. Cedric was getting attached to a woman. Ellie broke through his crusty barrier and conquered his heart. And he loved the feeling. As he held Ellie's hand and led her to his cherry farm, he hoped her feelings were as strong as his. He smiled just thinking about how happy he was.

"What?" Ellie obviously noticed his smile.

"Nothing."

"Right. Nothing. You going to be one of those typical guys who hides his feelings or are you going to have some balls and say what's on your mind?"

Cedric laughed. "Well, since you put it that way, I'm going to show you my balls."

Ellie smacked Cedric on the arm. "You know what I mean."

"I like you." Cedric stopped in front of the first cherry tree and turned to Ellie. "A lot. And I'm enjoying our time together. Every moment gets better and better, and I hope you feel the same way about me. There. So take that! Balls!"

Ellie got on her tiptoes and kissed him on the lips. "I feel the same way, and I'm having so much fun." She looked over toward the giant tree standing in the middle of the cherry orchard. "I love that they left that giant tree in the middle of the orchard."

"Me too."

"Is that an oak?"

Cedric nodded.

"I guess it's time to have fun, then." She ran toward the oak tree, grabbed on to the first limb, and pulled herself up. Within seconds, she had disappeared.

"Don't tell me you like to climb trees?"

Ellie didn't answer.

"God." Cedric laughed. "You're amazing." He climbed the tree and joined her in the middle, kissing her. "This is crazy. I was known as Monkey Boy and now look at you. Monkey Girl."

Ellie pinched Cedric's arm. "You seriously did not just call me that."

"Monkey Girl," he said, laughing. "We both love to climb trees. How many adults can say that?"

"One billion, six hundred thousand?"

"This is not another round of drill the librarian. This is us. You and me."

"Arf!"

"Right, right," continued Cedric. "Tofu too. And if I'm not careful, I'm going to fall in love with you."

Cedric couldn't believe that just flew out of his mouth. It was so quick he had no time to stop it.

Crap.

He held his breath and hoped that wasn't going to scare her off.

Ellie was quiet for a moment and then finally broke the silence. "Why should you be careful about falling for me? You chicken?"

Good answer. Cedric kissed her again, enjoying how incredible her lips felt against his and how she felt in his arms. She was right. Why should he be careful? He was all-in. No turning back now.

"Not chicken. Monkey."

He kissed Ellie again and they jumped down from the oak tree. They held hands as they walked around the property, chatting, enjoying every minute. When it started to get dark, they went back to the house with Tofu to say goodbye to Antonio and Ana.

Ana hugged Ellie. "We want to see you again soon, Ellie."

Ellie smiled. "I'd like that."

Antonio hugged her too. "We have many stories of Cedric's past to share with you."

Cedric waved his finger. "We don't want to bore her with those."

Ellie smiled. "I have a feeling I won't be bored."

"Not a chance," said Antonio. "Remind me to tell you about the time he wore a girl's blouse and—"

"Okay!" Cedric hugged Ana and Antonio. "That's our cue to leave."

A few minutes later, they were back on Highway 101, heading back to San Jose.

Cedric glanced over to Ellie and then got his eyes back on the road. "So, I have two questions for you."

"Okay. Let me hear them."

"Number one, will you meet me tomorrow night for dinner? And, number two, do you do falafels?"

"Yes and no."

Cedric quickly glanced over to Ellie again. "Okay, how about—"

"Maybe I should clarify. Yes, I do like falafels, but I have a better idea."

"Okay."

"You come over to my house tomorrow for dinner instead."

Cedric smiled. "Even better. What did you have in mind?"

"*That* is a surprise. Seven o'clock. Don't be late."

No way in hell he was going to be late this time.

Chapter Twenty-Six

Cedric arrived at Ellie's place ten minutes before seven. She greeted him with a big smile and a kiss after she opened the door. Tofu ran right by her, sniffing and exploring his new playground.

"Very impressive. Mr. Tardy Pants is early."

"Thank you for noticing, Miss Smarty Pants."

Ellie giggled as they walked to the kitchen. "Already at the nickname stage, are we?"

Cedric nodded. "But Mr. Tardy Pants isn't gonna fly with me. I need something more masculine ... like Hulk or Rocky."

"Men and their egos. Okay, we may have to negotiate."

"I'm okay with that, Princess Leia." Cedric grinned and set a canvas bag on the kitchen counter. Ellie tried to peek inside the bag, but he pulled the bag back so she couldn't see inside. "Have patience. I brought three things for us humans and something for the hairy beast." First, he took out a basket of cherries and handed it to her.

"Oh, very nice." She placed them on the counter. "Thank you, Superman."

He laughed. "You're welcome, Wonder Woman." Next from the bag came a bottle of cabernet. "I hope you like red."

"It's my favorite, Hercules."

Cedric placed the bag on the counter and brushed off his hands. "Good to know, Elektra."

Ellie raised an eyebrow. "We may need to work on this nickname thing. We're going in the wrong direction. I take that back. *You* are going in the wrong direction."

"I'm not sure what you mean, Black Widow."

"Oh!" Ellie hit Cedric on the arm. "You're going to get it."

"I hope so."

They laughed and Ellie held up her hand. "You said you had three things for the humans and I only counted two."

Cedric pulled Ellie closer and grinned. "You are so wise. Miss Smarty Pants may be the right name for you after all."

Cedric was already enjoying himself. He knew something special was happening here and all he could think about was kissing Ellie.

She smiled. "It looks like you want to kiss me, is that the third thing? I wouldn't wait too long because—"

Cedric's mouth was on hers.

A few seconds later, Ellie interrupted the kiss and smiled.

"What?"

She pointed to the floor below them. "You weren't the only one kissing me. That tickles."

Cedric looked down and watched as Tofu licked Ellie's ankle. "Hey, find your own girl."

They moved to the kitchen table, where everything was already set. In the middle of the table was a large platter of—

Cedric jumped back. "No way."

Ellie narrowed her eyes. "What?"

"If those are ravioli from LaVilla, I'm going to kiss you again."

"Nothing but the best for Iron Man." Ellie closed her eyes and puckered up.

Cedric grinned and leaned in for a kiss. "Can I open the wine?"

"Please."

Cedric opened the bottle and poured two glasses. After they sat, Cedric raised his glass. "To the new library Branch Manager."

Ellie clinked his glass and smiled. "Thank you."

"And to new beginnings."

"Oh, I like that one." She clinked his glass again, took a sip, and served the food. After a few bites, she said, "What does Tofu like?"

"He already ate, thanks."

"Does he like any special treats?"

"This is where you find out I have a weird dog."

"Why?"

"He loves carrots."

Ellie jumped up and grabbed a carrot from the bottom drawer of the fridge and snapped it into a few pieces. Tofu heard the carrot-snapping sound and scurried to the kitchen, his paws searching for traction on the floor. Ellie laughed and placed the carrots in a bowl. "Here you go."

Cedric laughed, as they listened to a symphony of crunches.

"Did you know the carrot originated in Afghanistan over a thousand years ago?" asked Ellie.

"Had no clue, but I think that's pretty cool. The Middle East gets such a bad rap. I think some people don't realize the history there and the wonderful cultures."

"People see only what they want to see."

Cedric nodded. "Speaking of which … I want to see you."

"You *are* seeing me."

"No, I mean, a lot. Regularly. Hourly, if possible."

"Sure you won't get bored with me?"

"Not a chance."

"Good." She was silent for a few moments. "Can I ask you a personal question?"

"Go for it."

"You don't have to answer if you don't want to."

"I'll answer."

"Okay." Ellie took a sip of her wine. "When we were in Starbucks, you said your dad hadn't been in the picture for a while. Do you mind sharing what happened?"

Cedric let out a big breath. "There's not much to tell, actually. I never knew him."

"*Never* never?

Cedric shrugged. "I was conceived on closing night of the Venice International Film Festival."

"Seriously?"

"Yeah. My mom spent a summer in Italy. She met a man at the festival. He swept her off her feet. I am the little bambino who came from that romance. She tried to track him down, but all she had was the man's first name. Gino."

"Wow. We have so much in common. Two moms who died and two missing dads."

Cedric sat up and studied Ellie. "Really?"

Ellie nodded. "My dad disappeared when I was two. I don't even remember him." She rubbed the hummingbird pendant on her neck. "My mom said he had to leave, to keep us out of danger. I never understood why and she never elaborated."

Cedric stood up and kissed her on the forehead. "Sorry you had to go through that."

Ellie cracked a smile. "Thanks."

"How about changing the subject to something more exciting?"

"Like what?"

"Drill the librarian!"

"Ha! Give it up, you're never going to stump me."

Cedric grinned. "We shall see."

After three hours of talking and laughing, they fell asleep on the couch, Ellie wrapped up in Cedric's arms.

Ellie awoke the next morning with a stiff neck. She couldn't believe they fell asleep on the couch. She yawned and stretched and looked over to the kitchen. Cedric was cooking and, God, it smelled good.

Waffles? French toast? Her stomach growled, craving some of whatever it was.

"Make yourself at home," she said.

Cedric turned around and smiled. "Good morning, sunshine. I was just getting ready to wake you up. I hope you don't mind me fixing a little something."

Ellie stood and noticed the table set with plates and silverware, orange juice, toast, butter, jam, eggs, and coffee. "A *little* something? This is a buffet."

Cedric pulled her close, kissed her, and then turned back to manage the pancakes. "I was so impressed with how well stocked your fridge was, I got a little excited."

"You need to be careful, this sets certain expectations for the future."

"I'm up for the challenge."

She sat back in her chair and sighed as Cedric stacked the last pancakes on the platter. "I don't understand how you did all of this without waking me up. This is so wonderful."

"My pleasure."

Tofu entered the kitchen and wagged his tail.

Cedric looked at him with his hands on his hips. "You think you can just waltz in here and ask for food? Not on my watch."

Ellie smacked Cedric on the arm. "That's not very nice."

Cedric laughed. "Watch this. Tofu…spin for food." Tofu just stared at Cedric, wagging his tail. "Spin for food. Come on, you're making me look bad. Okay, let's try this one. Roll over for a treat."

Tofu dropped to the floor, rolled over, and then popped back up on all fours.

Ellie was impressed and clapped. "Yes! You taught him that?"

Cedric nodded. "Obviously the treat was more important to him than the food." Cedric reached into his canvas bag for a piece of rawhide and dropped it on the floor. "Spoiled doggie."

Ellie laughed. "How long have you had him?"

Cedric held his hands about ten inches apart. "Since he was about this big. I found him tied to a tree when I was on a hike in Quicksilver Park. I thought I'd heard a baby crying and went off of the trail. I ended up finding a scrawny little puppy. Don't know how long he'd been there, but it must have been a day or two, because he was pretty hungry and had fleas and ticks."

Ellie covered her mouth with her hand. "Who would do such a thing?"

Cedric shrugged.

She scratched Tofu on his head as he chewed. "Glad you found him."

"Me too. I called my veterinary friend in Texas and sent her a couple of pictures. She said he didn't look that bad and told me exactly what to do." Cedric smiled, proudly. "The rest is history. Isn't that right, buddy?"

"Arf."

Ellie laughed. "Guess it was meant to be."

"Definitely."

"How did he get the name Tofu?"

"A friend of mine owns a restaurant where I always eat tofu scrambles. He suggested the name and Tofu seemed to like it."

She gave Cedric a kiss and eyed the pancakes. "That's sweet."

"The pancakes, the story, or my mouth?"

"All three. Yummy."

After they stuffed themselves, Cedric cleared the table and stuck everything in the dishwasher. "I need to run and take care of some work, something I haven't been doing much of lately. I'll call you this afternoon to schedule our next rendezvous."

"I'd like that."

"Good!"

He kissed Ellie goodbye, tucked Tofu under his arm, and headed downstairs to his car.

Happy.

Yeah, that was an understatement.

Cedric had no more fears. He was one hundred percent sure about Ellie and it felt so exhilarating, he wanted to scream.

Unfortunately, his high was cut short by the siren behind him as he left Ellie's place. He looked in his rearview mirror and saw the motorcycle cop behind him. He pulled his car to the shoulder as he waited for Vlad to approach the car. Now, he had to be more careful. Vlad was in uniform and had the power. That just about made Cedric sick to his stomach.

"You were doing forty-five in a thirty-five," lied Vlad.

"I was actually going five miles *under* the speed limit so if you want to write me a ticket for going too slow, have at it. We both know the truth."

"You calling me a liar?"

"I'm not saying anything. Obviously, I can't do anything about this, so just write the ticket and I'll be on my way."

"Arf. Arf, arf, arf."

Tofu was obviously a good judge of character and didn't like Vlad either.

"Number one, watch your language. Number two, you're not getting off that easy. And number three, tell your dog to shut the hell up."

"Arf."

"I'm okay with numbers one and three, but you'll need to elaborate on number two."

Vlad took off his sunglasses and leaned into Cedric. "Leave Ellie alone. Don't even go near her again or you'll have no chance of getting your old Papa George's property."

Cedric's body tensed up and his eyes widened. He was hoping Vlad's brother wouldn't have a reason to mention Cedric. Obviously not.

Vlad crossed his arms. "I see I have your attention now."

"You can't do that."

"That's where you're wrong. My brother is in charge of the sale of that farm, but *I* control my brother, giving me the power to approve who buys it. So back off or you lose the place."

"You're pathetic."

Vlad grinned. "And don't go getting any bright ideas. I have you under surveillance and if you are anywhere near Ellie, your deal will fall through."

Cedric looked around and saw a man with sunglasses in a car across the street, staring at him. "Seriously? You're having me followed? You're a lunatic. She doesn't want to be with you. Can't you get that through your head?"

"Maybe she doesn't. But if I can't have her, neither can you. Stay away from her. You better not go to the library either."

"I'm a volunteer at the library, I have to go."

"Cancel it or Papa George's place will be torn down and I'll piss on the debris before they clear it away to build a strip mall."

Chapter Twenty-Seven

Cedric was in need of a serious kick in the pants—must be that hole in his heart that was sucking his energy dry. He knew Vlad was serious with his threat and there was nothing he could do about it. Ellie was the best thing that had happened to him in a long time and now he was just going to give that up? Ellie had left him a couple of messages, but he didn't return her phone calls and he felt like crap.

And Tony's cheeriness at the farmers' market wasn't helping matters any. "Maria fucking rocks my world. I told you when I met her in the restaurant that she was the one!"

Cedric placed a few more baskets of cherries on the table and turned to Tony. "Wipe that look off your face. How many times have you gone out with her?"

"Twice."

"And just like that, she's the one?"

"I told you. I knew it *before* we went out. I'm a changed man."

Cedric shook his head in disbelief. "This is very hard to believe." Cedric watched as a woman approached. He leaned in to Tony, looking to test him. "What about her? What if she said she wanted to sleep with you right now? Would you do it?"

Tony didn't even look up at the woman. "Not interested." He turned to grab another crate of garlic from the bed of the truck.

Cedric was impressed that Tony didn't even look at the woman. But maybe it shouldn't be a surprise. Whenever Cedric saw another woman, he thought of Ellie.

The woman smiled and picked up a basket of garlic and stuck her nose in it.

"It's the best," said Cedric, confidently. "I guarantee it."

"I believe you." She squinted her eyes at him. "You look familiar. What's your name?

"Cedric Johnson."

"Did you go to San Jose State?"

Cedric raised his eyebrows. "Yeah. What's your name?"

The woman held out her hand. "I'm Pamela Deville."

"Nice to meet you. DeVille? Like the Cadillac?"

She smiled, still holding on to Cedric's hand. "Just like it."

"Sorry, I don't remember you. What was your major?"

"I—" Pamela suddenly had a pained look on her face. "Oh God."

She looked like she was going to pass out.

Cedric wrapped his free hand around her back to hold her up. "Are you okay?" Pamela leaned forward and slammed her face against his chest. Cedric used more of his arm to get a better grip on her back so she wouldn't fall to the ground. "Hang on. I got you."

She pulled her face from Cedric's chest and blinked a few times. "I just got dizzy all of a sudden. That was weird. I'm sorry."

"No need to be sorry. You okay?"

"I think so."

"You sure? Can I let go of you?"

"Yeah, yeah, I think I'm fine." She stood up straight. "I was in a hurry this morning and skipped breakfast. That probably wasn't a good idea."

Cedric pointed to a basket of cherries. "Eat some cherries to get something in your system."

"No. I'll be fine, thank you."

"No charge."

"You're very kind, but no, I'll be okay." She kissed Cedric on the mouth and smiled. "Thanks, though, that was very sweet."

Cedric stood there, motionless. What the hell just happened? He wiped his mouth, disgusted that a stranger kissed him.

As she walked away, Tony slapped Cedric on the back. "Dude, you don't even have to try and girls just throw themselves at you."

"I don't care about her. I want Ellie." He wiped his mouth again. "The problem is, I can't have her because my promise to my mom is a priority."

"I'd take the girl."

"I can't go back on my promise."

"Vlad's a dirty cop and he uses his authority and the system for his own interests. That's bullshit."

"I agree."

An older woman approached the booth pushing a shopping basket on wheels.

"Good morning, Mrs. Grundog," said Cedric. "How's the family?"

She smiled and rubbed her belly. "The family is going to get bigger, Cedric."

"That's great." Cedric went around the table to hug her. "Number seven. That's a lucky number."

"We're lucky to have them." She eyed a few baskets of garlic, chose one, and handed Cedric the cash.

Cedric pushed the money back in her direction. "It's on the house. Congratulations."

She put the cash back in her purse. "You're too kind, Cedric. When are you going to meet a nice girl and settle down?"

"That's the million dollar question." He waved goodbye to her.

"I've got it!" Tony slapped his hand on the table. "Mr. Chronic Fainter."

"Owen? What about him?"

"You said he was a PI."

"And?"

"And you need to have him dig up some dirt on Vlad to use against him."

Cedric sighed. "It's not that easy."

"Why not?"

"Because it's not."

Tony slapped his hand on the table again and Cedric jumped.

"Quit doing that."

"Call Owen."

"No."

Tony held out his hand. "Give me the phone, I'll do it."

Cedric didn't answer.

"How much do you like Ellie?"

Cedric looked at Tony and shrugged. "To be honest, we're past the *like* stage. I'm falling in love with her."

"Then fight for her dammit. What does it hurt to call Owen? Nothing! If he says no, then no big deal, you've wasted a minute on the phone with him. Call him."

Cedric pulled out his wallet to retrieve Owen's business card. He dialed the number.

"Owen Fitzpatrick."

"Owen, it's me Cedric, got a minute?"

"Hello, Cedric. What's going on?"

"Remember my situation?"

"Of course."

"Well, would you by chance be free today sometime?"

"Absolutely. Where are you?"

"Right now, I'm at the farmers' market in Willow Glen, but I can stop by later."

"No, I'll come see you. I'll be there within the hour."

"Perfect, thanks."

Thirty minutes later, Owen approached Cedric's booth, smiling. "Beautiful day."

Cedric looked around. "That seems to be the mutual consensus because everyone is out."

Owen held up an empty canvas bag. "And a great day to buy cherries."

"They're on the house today, thanks for coming by."

"No worries. How can I help?"

Tony stepped forward. "Cedric is being blackmailed."

"Is that right?" said Owen.

Cedric shook his head. "Blackmailed is such a strong word. I'm trying to buy my grandfather's old property in Gilroy. Ellie's ex said if I wanted to buy it, there were certain guidelines that needed to be followed."

Tony waved his finger in the air. "That's bullshit. He told Cedric to quit dating Ellie or he'd have no chance of buying the property. He's a cop and his brother is the County Supervisor controlling the sale of the farm."

"That's blackmail indeed. Which County Supervisor?"

"Dominic Cunnings."

Owen nodded. "Ah, I've heard of him. He got in trouble a few years back for accepting gifts from a general contractor in exchange for favors. They slapped him on the wrist, he returned the gifts, and that was the end of that."

"Can you dig up dirt on him?"

"Tony watches way too much television," said Cedric.

"On the contrary," said Owen. "Some people make it easy. One case I was working on not too long ago, it took me exactly two hours to get evidence that the guy was cheating on his wife."

"Will you do it?" asked Tony.

Cedric grabbed Owen's canvas bag and placed two baskets of cherries inside. "You can't just follow him until you see something odd. That could take months and I don't have that much time." He handed the bag back to Owen.

Owen smiled. "Thank you. It helps if I know what I'm looking for. If you know about some of his illegal activities, that would be ideal."

"Ellie would know for sure," said Tony.

"No. If he finds out she was involved, there's no telling what he would do to her. The guy doesn't seem stable to me. Forget it, this was a bad idea."

"Can I get your card, Owen?"

"Of course." He pulled a card from his wallet, handing it to Tony.

"No, Tony," said Cedric. "I can't take the chance of losing the property."

"I'm just innocently asking a person for their business card."

"I know you."

Cedric had images of Vlad harming Ellie flashing through his mind and he shuttered.

Tony stuck the card in his wallet. "So, you're just going to—"

"Forget it, Tony."

Later in the evening, Cedric was at home, pacing back and forth in his kitchen. He stopped, took a sip of his coffee, and then continued with his pacing. Tofu's head followed him back and forth, like he was watching a tennis match.

"I'm going to get an ulcer from this anxiety." He looked over to Tofu. "Do you even know what anxiety is?"

Tofu wagged his tail.

"No, you don't. You're a dog and you only know how to eat, sleep, and poop. That's it. Am I right?"

Tofu jumped up and walked over to Cedric who filled his cup with more coffee. He picked up Tofu and scratched him on the head.

"I wish you could help me."

Tofu licked Cedric's ear.

"I appreciate the effort, but a lick is just not going to cut it. You need to learn to speak."

"Arf!"

"No dog talk. You need to learn to speak English."

"Arf!"

"Okay, you don't get it. Don't you have another body part to clean?"

Cedric's cell rang and he grabbed it from the counter.

"Hey, Michael." He set Tofu back on the floor.

"I just got your message. Did you make a decision?"

Cedric let out a loud breath. "No, but I've worn a hole in the carpet, so at least I'm doing something productive. Or maybe that's destructive."

"Sorry. I wish I could help."

"You can. Just tell me what to do so if I find out it's the wrong decision in the future, I can blame you."

Michael laughed. "You wish. Look, I know this is hard for you, but if it were me, I would choose a person over a property."

Cedric put his coffee cup in the sink. "But I'm not really choosing the property, I'm choosing the promise I made to my mom. Which happens to be the property."

"I know this may sound silly, but … why don't you talk with your mom? Go to the cemetery if you have to. You may not get the answer directly from your conversation with her, but you may receive a sign."

"What type of sign?"

"I have no idea, but there's usually a sign if you look hard enough. So, just watch for it and pounce on it."

Chapter Twenty-Eight

Two days ago.

Technically, two days, six hours and fifteen minutes.

That was the last time Ellie spoke with Cedric. It was such a wonderful time, followed by two days of doubt and uncertainty.

Ellie tried to concentrate as she scrolled through the list of borrowers with overdue books, but her mind was on Cedric. Why hadn't he called? She had left him two messages yesterday, but still … nothing.

"Ellie!" said Peggy, startling her just as she sat down.

Peggy was a smart woman and Ellie was sure it wouldn't take long before she—

"Are you okay?" Peggy rubbed Ellie's shoulder. "Did something happen?"

Ellie tried to force a happy face. "I'm fine, just not feeling that well. Maybe it was something I ate."

"Oh dear, I'm so sorry. I hope you feel better soon." Peggy handed Ellie another manila envelope. "This just arrived for you."

"What's this?"

"I don't know, open it!"

Ellie opened the envelope and pulled out the contents, which included a full-access pass for the annual American Library Association Conference, confirmation for five nights at the Hyatt Regency in San Francisco, and transportation to and from the event. There were even meal vouchers.

Ellie looked confused. "I don't understand."

"You are the most intelligent person in this building. I'm quite sure you do."

"No. I can't accept this. This was a lot of money, especially for the hotel."

Peggy laughed. "For some odd reason, you are under the assumption that I bought this for you."

"You didn't?"

"I'm kind, but I'm not *that* kind."

Ellie read the letter enclosed. "Congratulations, you're one of three randomly-chosen librarians in Santa Clara County selected to attend our annual conference absolutely free."

Peggy hugged Ellie. "This is wonderful!"

Ellie didn't respond.

"Where's your smile, Ellie? Obviously, this was meant to be. Look, it'll be good for you to be there as the incoming Branch Manager."

"They don't give people a lot of notice, do they?"

"What's important is you can go!"

"This is crazy. I mean, don't get me wrong. I would love to go. I was *hoping* to go. But with the cost of Derek's funeral services and his—" Ellie felt some strong emotions coming on quick and had to cut them off. She knew it wasn't just about the conference or Derek. Cedric had her torn apart as well. She had to hold it together. "I just figured I would have to wait until next year." Ellie glanced at the documents again. "This is tomorrow."

"I can have your shifts covered. Take the rest of the afternoon off to go home, pack, and get ready."

"It says there are two shuttles in the morning, one at seven and one at eight."

"Great! Go and enjoy! Because once you get started as Branch Manager, you'll be busy for quite some time. Don't forget your toothbrush. Have fun!" And with that, Peggy walked off with a spring in her step.

Ellie couldn't help but smile. Peggy was one of the most positive people she knew—well, besides Grandpa Frank. He and Peggy were a good match for each other.

Ellie was thrilled to be able to represent her county at the conference. Not to mention the amazing education sessions and author events she'd be able to attend. Just when she thought her life was turning to crap again, the universe threw something wonderful right in her lap.

Funny how things like that happen.

Why shouldn't she go? The conference was the perfect distraction that she needed to get her mind off Cedric. It wouldn't be easy, but a week away with twenty thousand people from all over the country was definitely a good start.

Seven hours later, Ellie was packed, parched, and pooped. She took a sip of water and then slid into her bed, barely able to keep her eyes open. What a day. Disastrous and wonderful. She checked her messages for something from Cedric.

Nothing.

It was as if he just disappeared.

***

The next morning, two chartered buses full of Silicon Valley librarians would leave San Jose, headed for the city by the bay, San Francisco. Ellie had arrived thirty minutes before the first bus so she could be in a front row seat, across from the driver—her preference so she could always see the road. Otherwise, she would get motion sickness.

After a smooth ride to the city, Ellie felt like a rock star, walking into the Hyatt Regency hotel, spinning around to admire the world's largest atrium and looking forward to a week immersed in all things related to libraries and books. She took a deep breath and smiled before heading to the reception desk to check in. This was just what she needed.

Ten hours later, Ellie felt wonderful and exhilarated after her first full day at the conference. A day that included a morning welcome, two sessions on children's books, an intimate networking luncheon just for library branch managers, and three afternoon author sessions.

Ellie made her way back to her room for a quick shower before heading to Eclipse, the hotel restaurant. The paperwork said the reservation for her welcome dinner was for seven, so she had exactly thirty-eight minutes. She hadn't even had time to think about Cedric during the day and that was a good thing. Upon entering the restaurant at exactly seven on the dot, Ellie was escorted to her table.

"Enjoy your dinner." The hostess gestured to the open seat at a table occupied by a man who looked exactly like—

Vlad.

Pickles!

Vlad grinned. "Hello Ellie, I brought you these." He handed her a bouquet of yellow roses.

"What is this?" Ellie asked, looking around, ready to blow a fuse.

"Flowers."

"I know they're flowers. What I mean is … what the hell are you doing here?"

"I come in peace."

Ellie turned to walk away and Vlad grabbed her arm.

"Please, Ellie."

"I'm leaving." She shook her arm loose and turned to leave.

"It's about Cedric."

Ellie stopped and turned around with her hands on her hips, waiting for Vlad to say more.

Vlad held up a large envelope. "He's not who you think he is and I have proof."

Ellie tilted her head and stared at the envelope. "What are you talking about?"

"Have a seat and I'll show you. You need to see this, to know the truth.

"Why should I trust what you say?"

"I told you at the fundraiser. I've changed. I'm a new man."

Vlad was hung up on money and power and stature and there's no way he could've changed overnight. His cruel behavior in the sushi restaurant proved that.

Still … what was in that envelope? She shook her head and slid into the chair. Maybe a little wine would be okay before she found out what was in the envelope and told Vlad to go screw himself. She held out her glass and Vlad poured.

"Thank you for joining me."

"Please just give me the envelope." She took a sip of wine.

"At least eat something. You must be starving, in that conference all day with barely a break."

The waiter brought some fresh sourdough bread with garlic butter, and Ellie broke off a piece and buttered it. She took a few bites and ate it. "How did you know I was here?"

Vlad opened his mouth to answer.

"Never mind. It doesn't matter, just give me the envelope."

Vlad handed her the envelope. "I'm sorry you have to see this."

Ellie untied the string around the clasp, opened the envelope, and pulled out the contents. Five 8x10 photos were inside. Photos of Cedric and a woman. In the first two photos, the woman and Cedric were talking. The second photo showed Cedric hugging the woman. In the last two photos, Cedric and the woman were kissing. The photos had a time stamp on the bottom.

With yesterday's date.

Ellie was numb, almost as if she had no emotion whatsoever. "You could have Photoshopped these."

"Seriously? Look at them, they're authentic."

Ellie shuffled through the photos a few more times, before putting them back in the envelope.

Vlad took a sip of his wine. "Have you heard from him recently?"

"No."

"Well, there you go. I'm sorry you had to find out from me."

"No you're not. You're enjoying this!"

"Please Ellie, there's no need to get upset with me. I have no ulterior motives. I just want to be friends."

"Friends?" Ellie laughed and took another sip of wine.

"I'm serious. Let's go up to the room and talk about this in private. You're probably tense from a long day. Take a hot bath and I'll give you a massage."

Ellie stared at him in disbelief. "We both know what usually happens after a massage. I should have known. You want to be just friends? Ha!"

The waiter returned. "Are you ready to order?"

"No thanks," said Ellie. "Just the check for the wine."

"Very well." The waiter walked off.

"No need, it will be charged to your room," said Vlad. "I mean—"

"Why would—" Ellie's eyes widened and she studied Vlad for a moment. "Oh my God. You set this whole thing up? The conference?"

Vlad didn't answer.

Ellie looked around the restaurant as she tried to piece things together. "I didn't win the conference pass and hotel, did I? You paid for it. This whole thing was your elaborate plan to try to get me back. Admit it."

"That just shows you how much I'm sorry and how much I want you back."

"God, you haven't changed a bit. You still think money can buy you whatever you want."

"I still love you, Ellie. Give me another chance."

Ellie stood up and dumped her wine onto his lap. "Not going to happen."

She went up to her room, changed into a T-shirt for bed, grabbed her cell phone and texted Cedric.

Obviously you're not into me anymore, but you don't have the balls to tell me. Goodbye.

Then she turned off the phone and the light.

On Sunday afternoon, it was time for Ellie to head home from the conference. Considering the disaster that was her love life, she still had to admit the week was out of this world, thanks to the conference. She'd met so many people and learned things that she could apply when she took over as Branch Manager.

She had planned on going downstairs early and waiting in line to grab the front seat again on the first shuttle, but couldn't find her phone. She emptied her suitcase twice and looked under every crack and crevice in the hotel room. Another glance at the alarm clock caused her to freak out—she was going to be late.

Ellie was never late.

She could always contact the hotel when she got home to see if they'd found her phone, but more importantly at the moment, she needed to get that first seat on the bus.

She flew through the sliding doors to the outside of the hotel, happy to see two buses waiting. Rolling her suitcase in the direction of the bus, she was sideswiped and passed by two young women obviously in a race somewhere.

How rude.

She wondered what could be so important that they would run into her and not even say a word. As long as they don't get on the—

Pickles!

They were getting on the bus.

No problem. There are plenty of seats on the bus and they will probably—

Double Pickles!

They were making themselves comfortable in the front seats. What are the chances? Ellie could take the second bus, of course, but that would mean she'd have to wait an extra hour for it to leave.

She stepped up into the bus and smiled at the two women. "Good morning."

"Hello," said one of the women, the other was glued to her cell phone, not even bothering to lift her head and acknowledge Ellie.

"Did you enjoy the conference?" asked Ellie.

"Very much," said the first woman as the second woman continued to surf the net for something. Ellie didn't like the vibe she was getting from the two women, but still needed to get that front seat.

"Sorry to bother you, but do you mind if I have one of these front seats? I get motion sickness if I don't sit in the front and it's not a pretty sight."

"Well …" The first woman looked to the other woman, shrugging.

"I'd rather not." The woman finally found her voice, but didn't give a reason. She turned her attention back to her phone.

"Oh," said Ellie. "Okay, well take care."

Ellie stepped down off the bus and headed to the second bus. She thought about the two women. If the situation were reversed, she would have given up her seat in a heartbeat. But what could she do, beg?

No. Not worth it.

There would always be selfish people in the world and she couldn't change that. Luckily, she had another option. She'd have to wait longer to go home, but it was better than getting sick.

The driver of the second bus was reading a book, but when he saw Ellie approaching, he opened the door for her. She left her suitcase at the curb and stepped inside the bus.

"Hey there," said the driver, smiling.

"Hi."

"Let me guess … either you want the front seat or you want to experience my award-winning personality."

"Both."

"Smart lady. Make yourself comfortable and I'll put your bag underneath."

"Thank you."

"My pleasure. We still don't leave for an hour, though. Hope you brought a good book."

"I'm a librarian, what do you think?"

The driver laughed. "Good point. What was I thinking?"

Ellie sat in the very front seat and took a deep breath. What a nice man, and it was no big deal waiting longer. Of course, if she'd been on time, she would have gotten the front seat on the other bus. She prided herself in being on time. Today's tardiness was a rare occurrence.

An hour later, with the bus completely full, Ellie was enjoying the view on Highway 280, the interstate that connected San Jose to San Francisco. No matter what was going on in her life, it would be impossible to not enjoy what many believe is the most beautiful freeway in the country.

About fifteen miles past Highway 92, the traffic started slowing down. A couple of minutes later, their bus was completely stopped on the freeway. Nobody was moving, not even an inch.

"Not good." The driver grabbed the microphone to talk over the PA system to the passengers. "Looks like we're going to be delayed. I was told there would be roadwork today, but it wasn't supposed to start until this evening. Sorry for the inconvenience."

Ellie heard a siren in the distance getting closer. "It sounds like it may be an accident."

A California highway patrol car drove by on the shoulder of the road, followed by another. Many of the passengers were lifting their butts out of their seats to try to see what was going on.

The driver grabbed the microphone again. "Okay, looks like it's an accident, so we may be here for a bit. We do have free Wi-Fi. The information is in the seat-back pocket. And we'll be serving Jell-o shots and tequila in just a few minutes."

Ellie laughed along with the passengers as many of them began pulling out their laptops and iPads to connect to the Internet. That wasn't even an option for Ellie since her computer was in her suitcase that was stored below. Oh well.

They continued to creep along the freeway. Ellie could have walked faster than the bus. Two agonizing hours later, Ellie saw the scene of the accident. Off the road, to the right, there were at least ten fire trucks, just as many highway patrol cars, and several ambulances. Then Ellie spotted an overturned bus.

"Jesus Christ," said the driver. "That's our other bus."

Police, firemen, and emergency workers were on the scene, treating injured passengers. Ladders were used to extract passengers from the emergency exits of the bus; some were wheeled on stretchers to the ambulances. Two medical helicopters were on the ground, and another just took off, obviously with someone who was more critically injured. Television news reporters were on the scene as well.

This did not look good.

The mood in the bus was somber. Ellie could hear a few people mentioning they knew someone on the other bus. Many of the passengers were on their phones, calling loved ones to let them know they were okay.

But Ellie lost her phone.

"Pickles," she muttered.

She glanced to her left and noticed the woman across from her disconnected a call.

"Excuse me. I lost my phone back at the hotel and was hoping I could borrow yours to let my grandpa know I'm okay. If you don't mind."

"Of course." The woman handed Ellie the phone. "Make as many calls as you need to."

"Thank you so much."

Ellie dialed Grandpa Frank.

"Hello," he answered.

Just the sound of his voice made her want to cry, but she needed to hold it together.

"Hi, Grandpa, it's me."

"Princess! How was the conference?"

"Good, but I only have a minute. There was an accident with one of the buses and …" She felt her eyes starting to burn and took a deep breath. "I'm just calling to let you know I'm okay, just in case they talked about it on the news. I wasn't on the bus that crashed."

"Good heavens, thank God. I had no idea. Where are you?"

"We're still stuck on the freeway in Palo Alto. I think I need to stay with you tonight. I'm a bit shaken up, emotionally, as you can probably imagine."

"Of course. Do you want me to come pick you up?"

"No, no. Once I get home, I'll grab some things and be right over."

"Okay then, see you soon."

Ellie disconnected and called Peggy. She knew she was on vacation and out of cell phone range, but just wanted to leave her a message. She let her know she was okay and to pass the message on to Julio as well.

She handed the phone back to the woman, thanked her, and sent private thoughts of well wishes to the people on that bus.

Even to the two selfish women who were in the front row.

The bus driver glanced over to Ellie. His face said it all.

You could have been on that bus.

Chapter Twenty-Nine

Cedric paced back and forth in his living room. He felt like crap again.

Ellie had texted him earlier in the week, saying he didn't have the balls to talk with her, and she was absolutely right. He was torn and it was killing him. What kind of cruel universe made you choose between your family history and the girl of his dreams? It wasn't fair.

He grabbed the picture frame from the mantel over the fireplace and admired the photo of him with his mom from their Catalina Island cruise. He smiled and kissed the picture, then wiped the smudge marks off the glass with the bottom of his T-shirt.

"What should I do mom? Michael said most likely I'm going to get some sort of a sign from you, so let it rip. I'm waiting."

He stared at the photo and waited.

"Any sign." He listened for noises in the house. Nothing.

He let out a deep breath. "You told me more than a few times you only wanted me to be happy. Well, Ellie makes me happy. So … did you factor that in when you told me nothing would mean more to you than me getting the property back? Speak to me."

"Arf."

"Nice try, Tofu. You stay out of this."

"Arf."

Cedric turned around and eyed Tofu, who had something in his mouth.

"What do you have there?"

Cedric reached down and pulled a bookmark from the dog's mouth. The bookmark Ellie gave him in the library.

Cedric blinked.

He stared at the bookmark for a moment and then looked back down at Tofu.

"Holy crap."

"Arf."

"No, not you. Please don't crap in the house."

He wiped Tofu's slobber from the bookmark.

"Okay, was that the sign I was waiting for?"

Tofu just stared at Cedric and wagged his tail.

"No way, I don't believe it."

Cedric paced again, back and forth, and then stopped and stared at the bookmark again.

"That was just a coincidence, not a sign. Now if I had *another* coincidence, that would be more convincing. Two coincidences in a row would not be a coincidence. I wouldn't be able to ignore that."

Cedric's cell phone rang from the kitchen and he ran to pick up the call, Tofu following so closely he almost tripped over him.

"Hello?"

"Cedric, it's me, Julio."

Cedric didn't reply.

Was this a sign? A second coincidence?

"Cedric?"

"Yeah, I'm here. What's up, Julio."

"I'm going crazy over here, that's what's up. Have you heard from Ellie?"

"No. I—"

"Did you know she went to the librarian conference in San Francisco?"

"No. We haven't—"

"Okay, I need to calm down. Calm down, I'm just going to take a few deep breaths."

Cedric could hear Julio breathing in and out over the phone.

"What's going on, Julio?" asked Cedric, now worried. "Talk to me."

"Ellie took a shuttle bus to the conference and—" Julio let out a loud sigh. "Turn on the television. Channel seven."

"Okay."

Cedric walked to the family room, clicked on the television, and changed it to channel seven. There was a reporter on the scene of an accident. Cedric took a sip of his coffee and watched. "Yeah, it's an accident. And?"

"Turn the volume up."

Cedric turned up the volume to listen to the news report. A graphic appeared on the screen: **Fatal Bus Crash in Palo Alto. Two Dead.**

"That's right," said the television reporter. "Police report the bus veered out of control and overturned at nine-thirty this morning here on the southbound side of Highway 280, near Page Mill Road in Palo Alto. It is confirmed there were sixty-one passengers on board, mostly librarians, returning from a weeklong library conference in San Francisco."

Cedric moved closer to the television. "Holy hell."

The reporter looked down at his notes. "Fifty-nine people were injured, five of those critically, and there are two known fatalities. All of the injured are being transported to Stanford Hospital where—"

Cedric clicked the television off and threw the remote down on the couch. "I'm going to the hospital, Julio. Gotta run."

"If you find out anything, please let me know."

"Of course."

Cedric disconnected and two minutes later was in the car with Tofu, driving toward Stanford Hospital. He called Ellie on her cell phone, but it went straight to voicemail. It took all of his efforts to concentrate on the road. He let off of the gas when he noticed he was going eighty-five miles per hour in a sixty-five zone. The last thing he needed was another accident.

Cedric's thoughts were all over the place. How could this be happening again? It wasn't possible. Not seeing or talking to Ellie over the last few days had been torture enough. Now, the possibility of her being hurt or of losing her completely was almost too much to bear. He gripped the steering wheel so tight, he wondered if it was going to snap off. This was a sign. It had to be a sign.

Calm down. She's okay. Everything's okay. She's an angel.

"My angel," said Cedric. "Ellie, you're an amazing woman. You're going to be okay."

"Arf."

Cedric glanced at Tofu in the rearview mirror. "You agree, buddy?"

"Arf."

"Of course you do. And you know what, Tofu? I love her. God. I fucking love her so much it hurts."

"Arf."

"Of course, I know you love her too. Well, she's going to be okay, buddy. And then you and I are going to spend the rest of our lives with her. You have a problem with that?"

"Arf."

"I didn't think so."

Cedric pulled up to the hospital, left the engine and the air conditioning on for Tofu, and ran inside. The place was a madhouse; people were everywhere, talking, crying, and yelling. Reporters too.

Cedric worked his way through the people to the woman at the reception desk, a woman who looked completely frazzled. "I'm looking for Ellie Fontaine."

"Was she on the bus?" asked the nurse.

"Yes."

The nurse checked her admissions list and seemed to have a hard time finding Ellie's name. She went to the second page. "I don't see her here."

"That doesn't make any sense. She was on the bus. Is that a list of everyone?"

"As far as I know, and it was just updated about thirty minutes ago. Fifty-nine people. The only two names it does not show are those of … the two people who didn't make it."

No. Was she one of the two who died? Cedric's heart couldn't take another death, but he had to know.

"How do I find out the names of the two?"

"They haven't released them yet, so I can't help you there. If you want to check back later …"

Forty minutes later, Cedric was back in Willow Glen and sprinting to the front door of the library. Peggy had to know something. He came to a halt when the automatic door didn't open.

"What the hell."

Cedric looked through the glass. Nobody. He obviously wasn't thinking, it was Sunday. The library was closed Sundays, Mondays, and Tuesdays.

He left another message for Peggy on her cell phone and then drove to Ellie's house. He sat on the front step, waiting with Tofu. Pure torture.

Cedric ended up waiting for over six hours before finally giving up. He was getting tired and obviously Tofu was tired and hungry.

He finally went home and fed Tofu.

He loved so many things about Ellie, the way she grinned after she said something amusing, the feel of her mouth, her flirty nature, her hair, her smarts. He loved that she was a walking Wikipedia.

Cedric's cell phone rang and he jumped. "Hello?"

"Hi, Cedric, it's Peggy. Sorry it took so long to return your phone call, but I was up in the Sierras with no cell phone coverage and I just got—"

"Please tell me Ellie is okay."

"Yes, yes. She's okay. She's perfectly fine. She was on the second bus."

"Thank God." Cedric's eyes tightened and burned, and he let out a deep breath. It was all he wanted to know. Nothing else mattered at the moment. Not even Papa George's old property. She was okay and alive.

It was the best news in the world.

"Cedric?"

"Yeah." He tried to regain his composure. "I'm here. That's … good. Great news. The best."

"I'm so sorry you had to worry like that. I just got off the phone with Julio, who was also worried sick. In fact, he told me to make sure I called you."

Cedric let out another big breath. "Do you know where she's been? I've left so many messages and stopped by her house, I don't know how many times."

"She's been staying with her grandfather. She got spooked after seeing the crash … understandably. And she lost her phone at the conference so nobody was able to get a hold of her."

"That explains that. I left her so many messages."

"Go to the library on Wednesday, I know she'd love to see you."

"I'd love to see her too."

That was an understatement.

"And thanks again for your generous donation, and please tell your friends thank you too."

"Will do." He disconnected and knew there was something he had to do, before anything else.

Cedric drove to the Oak Hill Memorial Park and walked to his mother's tomb. He hadn't visited her site since the service. He kneeled down, pulled a tiny weed that was sprouting up next to the tombstone, set it aside, and smiled.

"Hi, Mom. I've missed you."

He cleared away another tiny weed and set it aside. "I met a girl I know you'd approve of her. Hell, maybe you can even see her. I don't know how this death thing works." He shrugged and continued, "Anyway, I'm not going to buy Papa George's property. This girl is more important to me than the property. She's amazing."

He stood up and brushed off his pants.

"Thank for sending me those signs, they were a wake-up call for me. I love her and she's alive. I love her so much and I'm going to tell her. And I love you too, Mom."

Cedric walked back to the car and pulled out his cell phone and dialed.

"Dominic Cunnings."

"Hi Dominic, it's Cedric Johnson."

"Cedric, we good to go for tomorrow?"

"I've changed my mind."

"What?" he yelled. "You can't do that. Everything is in place. I need to sell that property tomorrow!"

"Well, then you better get that contractor back into the game, it's not going to be me."

"If the offer is back on the table to the contractor, I won't be able to undo it again."

"Count me out." Cedric disconnected and felt like a heavy weight was lifted off his shoulders. He had his priorities and at the top of the list was Ellie.

Sweet Ellie.

His phone rang and he eyed the screen, expecting Dominic to call back. It was Tony instead.

"Hey Tony."

"I want to come with you tomorrow when you buy the property."

"It's not happening."

"What happened?"

"Ellie is alive, that's what happened."

"Of course she is. Why wouldn't she be alive?"

"It's a long story. Anyway, I can't live without her."

"And?"

Cedric stroked Tofu on his back. "Vlad will make the deal fall through on the property if he sees me with Ellie. And Ellie is more important to me than the promise to my mom, so done deal."

"You can have both!"

"No, I can't."

"But—"

"Tony … it's done."

Cedric disconnected and dropped the phone into the center console.

Chapter Thirty

Grandpa Frank kissed Ellie on the cheek and poured himself a cup of coffee. "You doing better this morning?"

Ellie forced a smile for him. "Yeah, thanks. Better. I need to get focused since it's my first day back to work."

"Sure you don't want to take a few days off?"

"I need to get back. I'm excited to jump into things at the library, and it will be a good distraction. Win-win, right?"

Grandpa Frank nodded and kissed her on the cheek. "That's my girl. Call me if you need anything."

"Of course."

Fifteen minutes later, Ellie settled into her desk at the library and organized the new piles of mail and books that weren't there before she'd left for the conference.

Julio bent over to hug Ellie in her chair. "Welcome back. You doing okay?"

"Not really, but I need to catch up on things. Hopefully the work will keep me from thinking about the accident."

Julio nodded and rubbed her back. "That must have been horrible to see that."

"The worst part was the news of the two people who died. When I found out, I almost lost it. That could have been me. I could be dead right now, just like my mom."

That was the ironic part. Ellie's mom died because she was five minutes late, and Ellie was *alive* because she was five minutes late trying to get the front seat in that first bus. Tardiness used to be the worst thing in the world, the reason her mom was no longer alive, but now she had to rethink that logic.

And then there was Cedric. If he hadn't been five minutes late to work that day, she would have never met him on that street corner. Of course, that was over and done with, so no need to travel down that road again. She felt pain in her gut and it traveled to her heart.

She was sure she loved Cedric.

"Have you talked with him?" asked Julio, who was obviously a mind reader.

"I never would have thought in a million years that Cedric was someone who slept around. He didn't seem to have that type of personality."

"I'm a good judge of character and I don't think he sleeps around. Let me see the pictures."

Ellie pulled them from her computer bag and handed them to Julio.

Julio nodded. "They look real alright, but you can do anything in Photoshop these days. I saw a picture of Jennifer Aniston with a penis and I was one hundred percent convinced she had an operation."

Ellie laughed. "Thanks. It feels good to laugh."

"That's what I'm here for."

Ellie's smile disappeared. "That didn't last long. I feel like crap again."

Julio rubbed her back and smiled. "That was quick. Okay, I need to tell you something."

"More bad news?"

"Actually, it's sweet and kind and romantic. And it's love."

"If you are going to brag about Hugo again, now's not a great time."

"Not me. You."

"What are you talking about?"

"Cedric donated the money that got you the promotion."

Ellie blinked rapidly, but didn't speak. Her mouth opened, but words didn't come out.

Julio sat on the edge of her desk. "Actually, I think I may be understating the facts. Cedric donated enough money for you to get the promotion, plus build a new wing on the library, and maybe even re-do the roof."

Ellie's hand flew to her chest. "He—"

"He loves you, that's what I think. The way he looks at you, damn."

"It was a kind gesture, absolutely, and I'm grateful. But money can't buy you love, you know the song. Vlad used to do the same thing, use money to get what he wanted."

"You're comparing Cedric to Vlad?"

Julio was right. That was crazy. There was no comparison between the two.

Ellie stood up. "But the photos don't lie."

"I think they do lie. And just so you know, I called Cedric when I couldn't get a hold of you after the accident and he sounded genuinely worried about you. He even went to the hospital to look for you. No way he was faking that."

Ellie nodded, then noticed the Fed-ex package buried under some papers on her desk. She slid the package out and looked at the return label. Hyatt Regency in San Francisco. "Yes!" Ellie opened the package and pulled her phone out. She plugged it into the charger and powered up the phone. Within a minute, the phone went crazy. Ellie read the screen. "I have fourteen voicemails and ten text messages."

Julio smiled. "Somebody sounds very popular to me. I have a feeling it's sexy Cedric."

"Excuse me," said a female voice behind them.

Ellie and Julio both turned around and froze.

Julio's hand flew to his chest. "Oh my fucking God. You're the woman in the photos."

It was definitely her. The woman who killed Ellie's dreams.

"I—" said Pamela.

"How can I help you?" asked Ellie, her tone cold enough to freeze meat.

Pamela looked toward the floor, unable to meet Ellie's eyes. "It would be good if we talked. May I sit down?"

"Yes." Ellie cleared the books from the other chair, gesturing for Pamela to sit. Julio snuck away as Pamela sat down.

She bit her nails and avoided eye contact with Ellie, moving around in her seat. Ellie didn't understand why she was here or how she had found her.

"I don't know where to start. I'll start with my name. I'm Pamela DeVille." She began to cry.

Ellie handed her a box of Kleenex. "Here."

Pamela grabbed a few out of the box and wiped her eyes. Then she blew her nose.

"Okay," Ellie said, not knowing what was going on. "Is this … library related?"

No way it could have been, but she didn't know what else to say.

Pamela wiped her nose again. "Cedric related. And Vlad related."

Ellie's heartbeat sped up. "Okay."

Pamela sat up in her chair. "Everything you saw in the pictures was a set-up."

Ellie closed her eyes and took a deep breath. "A set-up?"

Pamela nodded. "Vlad told me he loved me and—"

"Wait a minute … you've been seeing Vlad? Oh God, I need a drink …"

"He told me that he wanted to be with me, but he couldn't move forward since he was still heartbroken from you. He asked me to do something I'm ashamed of, to kiss Cedric at the farmers' market while a photographer took pictures. Then he would have closure with you and could be fully with me. I should have listened to my gut, but I was blind. He promised me everything."

She had a sick feeling in her stomach. It didn't look as if Pamela was feeling any better either. Ellie cocked her head to the side and squinted her eyes, thinking, still trying to fully grasp what had happened. "So, why are you here? Why are you telling me this? Shouldn't you be with Vlad, planning the rest of your lives?"

"That's just it. Vlad lied to me. He never wanted me at all and was just using me to get back with *you*. After that day with Cedric, he said he changed his mind about me and asked me to leave. He was so cold, an asshole. Being the fool that I was, I begged him not to leave me. That's when he said he was going to San Francisco for a few days ... to be with you."

Ellie nodded. "It makes sense now."

"I'm so sorry. What I did to you was absolutely horrible and unacceptable. You should be hitting me or throwing things at me, but you're smiling."

Ellie jumped up, ran around to the front of her desk, hugged Pamela and kissed her on her forehead. "Thank you."

Pamela wiped her eyes. "Definitely not the response I expected."

"Before you walked in today, I had no hope. Now I have hope!"

"You think there's still a chance with you and Cedric?"

Ellie eyed her phone. "If any of those voicemails or text messages on my phone are from him, I'd say there's a very good chance."

After Pamela left, Julio approached her desk with a man she didn't recognize. He was dressed like he was ready to play tennis. The only thing that was missing was a racket in his hand.

"Ellie, this is Owen. He says he has something important to tell you regarding Cedric."

Ellie jumped up. "Is he okay?"

"Yes. Well, physically, yes. I'll just get right to the point. I got a call from Cedric's friend, Tony, who alerted me to something very alarming that is going to take place. You need to know about it. It affects you."

Ellie rubbed the silver hummingbird pendant on her neck. "What is it?"

"Cedric has been trying to re-acquire a property in Gilroy that had been in his family for a few generations."

Ellie nodded. "He told me about it."

"But did you know it was being sold by your ex's brother, Dominic?"

"No."

"Vlad blackmailed Cedric and said he wouldn't be able to buy the property unless he stopped seeing you. Cedric made a promise to his mom before she died he would buy the property and that's why he disappeared from your life."

"Oh my God."

"There's more. Cedric changed his mind and decided to pick you over the promise to his mom. That means he's going to lose the property."

Ellie couldn't speak. She covered her face with her hands and tried to maintain her composure. Nobody has ever done something so romantic for her. "What can I do?"

"The property is going to be sold this afternoon to a contractor who has plans to build a strip mall there. The only way we can stop the sale is if we have something on Vlad. Anything at all. Or even his brother, Dominic."

Ellie blinked. She couldn't let Cedric lose the property. She didn't want to be the reason his family history was torn apart.

"I realize this is a lot to take in," continued Owen. "And as I mentioned, we don't have a lot of time. Two hours max or the property will be sold."

"I can handle it. Where's the sale taking place?"

"At the County Supervisor's office."

"I know where it is."

Ellie walked into the County Supervisor's office and the receptionist stood up to greet her. "Ellie! How have you been?"

Ellie hugged the woman. "I've been great, thanks for asking. Is Dominic here yet?"

"Yes, he's in conference room two."

Ellie walked into the conference room and found Dominic sitting at the table with another man.

Dominic stood up. "Ellie, it's great to see you. Do you mind waiting for me in my office?"

"I need to speak to you now."

"Can it wait five minutes? We're just signing a few things and we'll be done in a moment."

"This is an emergency and it involves Vlad."

"Okay. Phil, do you mind waiting just a few minutes outside?"

"Not at all." The man left the conference room and Dominic turned to Ellie. "What's going on? Is Vlad okay?"

"Right now he is. And so are you. But it won't take much for you both to be in jail. That would mess up your plans for re-election, wouldn't it?"

Dominic wiped his forehead. "What did he do this time?"

"Here's the deal, this property you're going to sell needs to be sold to Cedric Johnson."

Dominic threw his palms in the air. "Cedric had an opportunity, but called last night and changed his mind!"

"Vlad blackmailed him and told Cedric if he dated me, you would sell it to someone else."

"I had no idea about that."

"Maybe you didn't. But if you don't sell the property to Cedric, the press and the public are going to receive details about a certain property that Vlad acquired from the county. And since you orchestrated that deal, well, you probably know how it's going to end."

"On paper, I did nothing wrong."

"You will be guilty by association. People will see your name come up during your re-election campaign and think of your brother and the scam he pulled."

"He's such an idiot."

"No argument here."

Dominic paced back and forth behind the conference table. "How do I know this won't come up again in the future and bite me in the ass?"

"You don't. But if Vlad stays out of my life, and Cedric's life, completely, and I mean completely ... I promise you'll never hear from us again. You need to control Vlad, he's getting out of control and he's going to take you down with him."

Dominic nodded. "Consider it done."

Chapter Thirty-One

Ellie stood on the corner next to a group of people and took a drink of her latte, as she waited for the light to change. When the light turned green, she proceeded to step off the curb.

"Don't even think about it," said a male voice behind her.

Cedric.

Ellie spun around and swallowed hard as her eyes began to burn. "That line sounds familiar."

Cedric grinned. "I stole it from an amazing woman."

Ellie smiled.

"I like this corner," Cedric continued. "Must be because it's where we met."

"There isn't a day that goes by I don't think of that when I'm waiting here for the light to change."

Cedric nodded. "We need to talk."

"I gathered that by the fourteen voicemails and ten text messages. And the emails, I can't forget those." She smiled. "I was disappointed you didn't send a telegram, though."

"I contemplated hiring a pilot to fly a plane to write something in the sky, but it's been cloudy lately."

Ellie laughed. "I was going to call you today. I was such a fool. Vlad set up some elaborate plan to make me think you were seeing another woman, and I believed him. I didn't trust you and I'm so, so sorry."

Cedric nodded. "When I heard about the accident, I thought I'd lost you. Then I thought I was such an idiot to not spend every single moment with you. I'd been scared to get involved with someone, but after I heard the news, I would have given anything to spend one more day with you." He moved closer to Ellie. "But I didn't come looking for you today because I found out you were alive. I'm here because I can't live without you and … I love you. Deeply."

"And I wasn't going to call you today because I found out you didn't cheat on me. I was going to call you because I love you too." She grinned. "But my love is much deeper than your love."

"Ha!" Cedric laughed. "Impossible."

"It is!"

Cedric laughed and grabbed the latte from Ellie's hand.

"I'm not done with that."

"I know." He set it on the sidewalk. "I'm just preparing for our kiss."

"You and all of this constant preparation. Just kiss me, would ya?"

"It would be a pleasure." He leaned forward and kissed Ellie, and she fought hard to hold in the tears.

Cedric pulled away. "Dominic left me a message regarding the property. He told me what you did."

Ellie shrugged.

Cedric caressed her cheek and kissed her. "Thank you. It means so much to me. But not as much as you." He checked his watch. "Crap, you need to get going or you'll be late."

"Relax," she said, smiling. "I'd like to hear more about how much I mean to you." She inched up and kissed Cedric on the lips. "I can be five minutes late."

Epilogue

Eighteen months later

Cedric stood with Tony in front of the new garlic museum, smiling and a little misty-eyed.

Tony leaned in to examine Cedric's face. "You going to get all girly on me and cry?"

Cedric turned to Tony. "You're the one who's going to cry."

"Ha! Twenty bucks?"

"You're on. Wimp."

"Pain in the ass."

"Douchebag."

"Dorkwad."

The minister cleared his throat and covered his lapel microphone with the palm of his hand. "FYI ... the microphone is on."

"Shit ... sorry," said Tony.

The minister shot him another look.

"I mean ... darn."

Cedric laughed and looked around at the large gathering and all of the familiar faces. Papa George's old property—now

330

Cedric's property—was the perfect place for a wedding. The garden with the fountain and picnic area next to the museum turned out just as he hoped it would.

After the DJ started the processional, "At Last" by Etta James, Tony reached over and squeezed Cedric's shoulder. "Showtime."

Maria appeared and slowly walked down the aisle toward them with her father.

Cedric got emotional as he thought back to his own wedding day over a year ago, an intimate ceremony and celebration at the Black Stallion Winery in Napa. He winked at Ellie, who was sitting by the aisle in the second row. His gaze dropped to her swollen belly—Jane would be born in a few weeks and he was the happiest man in the world. Love was in full bloom. In fact, everyone seemed to be getting married. A month after the fundraiser, Frank and Peggy got hitched in Lake Tahoe. And Julio and Hugo tied the knot in Las Vegas earlier in the year.

Now it was Tony's turn.

Cedric wiped an eye and Tony held out his palm. "Pay up."

"Must be allergies."

"Yeah, you're allergic to being a pansy. Twenty bucks. Hand it over."

"Later."

"I won't forget."

"I know."

The minister cleared his throat again.

"Shit … sorry." Tony covered his mouth with his hand. "My mouth is like a runaway freight train."

The ceremony was short and sweet, very romantic. Afterward, the guests enjoyed the cocktail hour and a wonderful dinner under the stars.

Cedric raised his glass to everyone at the head table. "To Tony and Maria … love, laughter, and happily ever after."

They clinked glasses and Tony shook his finger at Cedric. "This doesn't get you off the hook. You still have to do the Best Man speech."

"I'm so happy for you, I may do three or four toasts before the night is over."

"Me too!" said Ellie, raising her glass.

Tony pointed to her glass. "That better be apple cider."

Ellie smiled. "It is. You know, back in the fourteenth century, they used to baptize kids with cider, since it was often more sanitary than water."

"That's why I shower in cider everyday," said Cedric.

Ellie pinched Cedric's side.

Cedric laughed and grabbed Ellie's hand, kissing it. Everyone was happy and that was the way it should be. Except for Vlad, of course, who was arrested for tax fraud just last week.

"Friends and family," said the DJ. "Tony and Maria would like you to join them next to the fountain for the cake cutting."

Everyone gathered around as Tony and Maria cut the first slice from the cake and fed each other. The night was perfect. Unless you count the incident later in the evening when the dancing came to a temporary halt after Owen fainted and knocked over Maria's sister, Sara. Ironically, it happened during the song "Crash Into Me" by Dave Matthews.

Owen and Sara started dating three days later.

Dear Reader,

I'm honored that you took the time to read my debut novel, and I truly hope you enjoyed Cedric and Ellie's story. I certainly had fun writing it!

I have a favor to ask! The greatest gift you can give an author after you enjoy their work (besides sharing it on Facebook) is to leave a review online where you bought it. Would you mind doing that? It would mean the world to me. Thank you SO MUCH in advance!

By the way, are you ready for more fun? I hope so! Check out my second novel, *Dog Day Wedding – A Romantic Comedy*. Visit http://www.richamooi.com/dogdaywedding for info.

You can even sign up for my newsletter at http://www.richamooi.com/newsletter and I'll let you know when my new releases are available.

With gratitude,
Rich

Acknowledgements

To my mom. Thank you for making me possible.

Thank you to my editor, Max Dobson, from http://www.polished-pen.com/.

To my very talented cover artist, Sue Traynor, at http://www.suetraynor.com/. Thank you for drawing such a beautiful cover for me!

Special thanks to Romance Author, Deb Julienne (http://www.debjulienne.com), for your help and for swapping countless emails with me.

For your help and feedback, a BIG thanks to Silvi López-Martín, Isabel Anievas, Julita Sofijski, Krasimir Sofijski, Julio Navarrete, Kristi Lassalle, Rachel Daven Skinner, Michelle Josette, B.E. Priest, Libby Hawker, Lee Gaiteri, Shayne Rutherford, Elizabeth Barone, and Jessie Gussman.

And Jean Herriges, Willow Glen Library Branch Manager. Thank you for patiently answering my questions during my research visit.

I would love to hear from you! My email address is rich@richamooi.com

My website and blog are at http://www.richamooi.com

Get social with me!

Facebook: https://www.facebook.com/author.richamooi
Twitter: https://twitter.com/RichAmooi
Goodreads: https://www.goodreads.com/richamooi

16500512R00207

Made in the USA
San Bernardino, CA
06 November 2014